# HAUNT ME

# HAUNT ME

LIZ KESSLER

CANDLEWICK PRESS

Copyright © 2016 by Liz Kessler
Poem on page vii copyright © 2014 by June Crebbin
Poems on pages 30, 96, 125–126, 151, 173, 201–202, 371 copyright © 2016 by Ella Frears

First published in Great Britain by Hodder and Stoughton

First U.S. edition 2017

Library of Congress Catalog Card Number pending
ISBN 978-0-7636-9162-2

17 18 19 20 21 22 BVG 10 9 8 7 6 5 4 3 2 1

Printed in Berryville, VA, U.S.A.

This book was typeset in Berkeley Oldstyle.

Candlewick Press
99 Dover Street
Somerville, Massachusetts 02144

visit us at www.candlewick.com

*This book is dedicated to the Folly Farm crew —*
*especially Elen, Kelly, and June —*
*in gratitude for the sharing of ideas,*
*the inspiration, the fun, and the laughs.*

*If you come to me*
*I will receive you with honor,*
*with respect and gentleness.*

*If you come to me*
*I will dismiss this life*
*of mine and take on yours.*

*If you come to me*
*in the burning sun as it dips*
*behind the tree line,*

*I will know that it's you*
*and keep faith.*
*Come soon. Come now.*

—June Crebbin

# CHAPTER ONE

○———————————○

# JOE

"What the hell?"

A sound like a gunshot pierces my dream, and I'm bolt upright, shaking, wide awake.

I look down my body. I seem to be intact. No blood.

A glance around the room. My bedroom door is closed. Did I shut it last night? Maybe I forgot. That's it, then. The sound, it was just the door slamming shut in the wind. Must have left the window open, too.

I squint at the window. It's closed. The curtains aren't moving. There's no wind, no draft. In fact, as my eyes adjust, I notice there's nothing. I mean, nothing at all. Zip.

I'm lying on the floor.

Where's my bed? Where's my dresser? My desk? My clothes strewn across the carpet, thrown off when I went to bed last night?

I try to remember getting into bed. Can't. I must have been out of it.

My body's aching all over. Not surprising after a night spent sleeping on the floor.

I sit up and stretch. I'm going to kill my brother for this. There's messing around and there's just ridiculous. I mean, stealing my entire bedroom just for a laugh or to make a point? Well, I'm not laughing—and what point was he trying to make, exactly? That I sleep too much?

Dad's always said waking me up is like raising the dead. But even so, it must have been quite a feat, to remove every piece of furniture in my room without my knowing about it.

I drag myself to my feet. My legs feel like weights. My body is like a rag doll. No energy. I can barely stand. I lean against the wall while I try to figure out what's going on.

What's the matter with me? Am I hungover? I try to recall the previous night. Was there a party? Was I with friends? Did I go out and get wasted?

My mind is coming up with nothing but blanks. Blank, blank, blank. There's literally nothing else there.

A cold feeling starts to move around inside me, like a dark storm, swirling in my belly, gathering pace.

*What the hell is going on?*

I stumble to the door and reach for the handle. I can't—can't get hold of it. My hands are shaking. I keep missing the handle, slipping—can't even feel it. The effort is exhausting me.

OK, this is seriously creeping me out now. I can't even get hold of a door handle? I'm in a worse state than I realized. Maybe I'm still drunk.

I need to get out of here. I stand up against the door and call out. "Olly!"

There's no answer.

A beat, and then I try again.

"OLLY! Mum! Dad!"

A soft echo replies. Then nothing. Silence. No one's there. No one's here.

Where are they all? Why aren't I with them? What day is it? Is it the weekend?

Every question brings on another blank and a rising sense of panic, scorching through my body like a flash of forked lightning searing through a night sky.

I force my legs to carry me to the window, where I flop onto the window seat as I recover from the effort of walking those few steps.

I allow myself a moment to close my eyes. As I sit, I have a vague recollection of sitting here before. A vision flickers across my mind: leaning against the side, knees tucked up, ink-stained fingers scrawling poems or songs in well-worn notebooks.

And then it's gone.

The flash of memory doesn't help. If anything, it only increases the confusion that's swirling inside me like a typhoon.

3

I look out the window. Sun's shining. Yard's full of daffodils in full bloom and pink blossoms on the trees.

I see them at last, standing beside the tree. Olly, Mum, Dad. Huddled together, talking.

The sight of them gives me a shot of energy, and I stand up and reach for the window latch. My hands seem almost to be going through it, just like with the door handle. I can't grab it. My fingers won't work.

Why can't I grip the latch? I need to open the window. I need to call to them.

I stare at my brother and my parents, standing together in a tight group. They look completely miserable. What's the matter with them?

"Cheer up, dudes. It's a lovely day, and the sun's shining," I mutter darkly to myself.

Where did that come from?

Another memory: Dad saying it to us—does he say it a lot?

*Dad, what exactly has the weather forecast got to do with my mood?* I find myself thinking in reply. That's it! That's what Olly always says. And Dad always just shrugs and smiles in reply. My dad smiles at everything.

He's not smiling now, though.

Now I'm whispering it to him through murky glass.

"Cheer up, dudes. It's a lovely day and the sun's shining."

I try to bang on the window, try to bash my fists against the glass.

My fists don't make a sound. They barely connect with the window. I can't even feel the glass.

No one looks up.

I slump back down onto the seat, helpless to do anything but watch.

Mum has an arm around Olly. He's leaning into her like he's a kid. It's strange seeing my cool big brother looking so vulnerable. Dad's talking to Mum. She nods.

What are they saying?

Dad leaves the sad little huddle and walks down the driveway to a big van. He opens the back of the van and clambers inside.

My eyes are drawn to the logo on the side, and that's when my stomach tips on its side.

*R & J Movers*

Movers?

My brain is working hard to put the pieces together so that they make sense.

They won't, though. It's as if someone has bought ten different puzzles and mixed all the pieces together. They don't fit. They don't add up to the picture on the box. There *is* no picture on the box.

Olly is breaking away from Mum and Dad. His head still so low his jaw seems to be attached to his chest, he walks up the driveway and into the house.

At last, they're coming to get me! It's all going to be all right. I'd obviously just forgotten that . . .

*Forgotten that we're moving?*

OK, yes, that's quite a big thing to forget. But still—at least they're coming back for me.

A moment later, my bedroom door opens, and there he is. I feel like a man minutes away from dying of thirst being given a jug of water.

"Olly!"

"Joe," Olly says.

"Jeez, mate, you had me worried for a minute there," I begin, getting up from the window seat and smiling as I cross the room. My legs are working better now. "I thought you were all—"

"I guess this is good-bye." Olly cuts across me. His words are like a punch in my gut. They push me backward. I would fall back on my bed if it were still here. Instead, I stand in the middle of my room, my arms limp by my sides, my head swimming with cloudy confusion.

"Olly, what are you talking about? Why would you be saying—?"

"I can't believe it," he says. His voice is like metal. "Any of it. Can't believe what I did. What you did. Can't believe I'm never going to see you again."

My blood is ice.

"Olly." I take a step toward him. "Olly, mate, why are you never going to see—?"

"We had a lot of laughs in this room, though, didn't we?

Before . . ." He stops. His face hardens. I've never seen him look at me like this. Like I don't even exist.

"Yeah. Sure. 'Course we did," I reply. Truth is, I can't remember any of them right now. Aside from snapshot moments that leave as quickly as they arrive, I can't really remember much at all—but I want to agree with him. I want him to meet my eyes. I want to keep him here with me. "Loads of laughs," I agree. "What do you—?"

Olly's face is a closed door. "I just can't believe there won't be any more," he whispers. "I mean, I know we're not going far. We'll still be in the same town. But I'll never come back to this house again. I just can't. None of us can." He's talking right through me again. It's as if he's completely ignoring me. No—it's stronger than that. *It's as if I'm not there.*

"Olly, can you see me?" I ask. "Can you hear me?"

"Olly!" It's Dad, calling from downstairs.

He turns away and calls back. "I'll be there in a sec."

Then, before I have the chance to ask anything else, to move toward him, to do anything, he nods silently, a sad smile on his lips. Then he whispers, "Bye, Joe," and turns to leave.

I cross the room in two seconds. But it's a second too slow. Olly has gone, and he's closed the door behind him. I grab for the handle. I can't reach it. Can't touch it, can't get my fingers to make contact with it.

"No! *No!*"

I try to bang against the door but I still make no impact. No sound. All I hear in response is Olly's footsteps growing fainter on the stairs.

I slump down to the floor in a heap, my body leaning against the door, my head in my hands.

The sound of a revving engine outside brings me back to my feet.

I reach the window in time to see Olly join Mum in the driveway. She puts an arm around him again. He shrugs her off. She's saying something to him. He's shaking his head.

Mum opens the passenger door of the van. I guess Dad is already in the driver's seat. Olly gets in the van. Mum gets in behind him and shuts the door.

The van jerks forward before stuttering to a halt.

Have they remembered that they've left me behind?

Mum's rolling her window down. Leaning out, looking back.

"Mum," I whisper against the glass.

Mum blows a kiss in my direction before rolling the window back up.

The engine starts again. The van moves, more smoothly this time, down the road.

"Please," I whisper. "Please don't leave." My throat is a fire, raging and crackling.

The van signals, turns, and is gone.

# CHAPTER TWO

## Erin

Mum rolls her car window down as we approach the house.

"Listen, girls," she says, turning in her seat and smiling at me and Phoebe, my little sister. "What do you hear?"

I hear a parent trying her hardest to convince me this was what she wanted all along. What we all wanted.

"The sea!" Phoebe yells obligingly. She gets an even bigger Mum-smile for that. Then Mum glances at me. Her eyes say so much: *Please, Erin, try to look happy. We're doing this for you.*

I do my best to ditch my guilt and hide my anxiety. I don't want to dump either of these on my family. Mum's right. Her unspoken words — which I can hear as loudly as if they'd been shouted through a megaphone — are the truth.

This is all because of me. The least I can do is act grateful.

"It's lovely, Mum," I manage.

She nods, half smiles. Our eyes meet. The unspoken words tighten and freeze.

Then Dad breaks the moment. Pulling into the driveway that Phoebe and I haven't even seen and he and Mum have visited once, he switches off the engine and checks the clock.

"Moving van won't be here for a couple of hours yet," he says. "Who wants an ice cream and a paddle in that lovely freezing-cold water, then?"

"Me!" Phoebe yells. She's already undoing her seat belt and clambering out of the car.

Mum glances at me again.

*Stop worrying about me, Mum. I'm fine.*

"How about you take Phoebe down to the beach?" she says to Dad as we get out of the car. "Erin and I will just have a quick look around the house on our own. We'll come and join you."

I know what she's doing. She's trying to make me feel safe. Give me some control over things by showing me the house first. Thing is, she's right. I do want to see where we're going to be living before I have to start jumping around, pretending to be happy on a beach.

Phoebe's already pulling on Dad's sleeve. "Come *on*! I want an ice cream!"

"OK, if you're sure." Dad gives Mum a peck on the cheek and squeezes my shoulder. "See you soon."

Mum takes my hand as we walk up the path. It's a bit overgrown but looks like it was loved once. Cracked paving stones, crazy weeds on either side, a couple of those solar-powered lamps in the ground, leaning over and broken.

Mum jiggles a key in front of my face as we approach the door. "Want to do the honors?"

I take the key and open the door. Mum nudges me forward and we step inside.

First impressions? It's OK. A bit cold. A bit dark. But I don't hate it. It's a big room, painted white, with an archway in the middle. I imagine it used to be two rooms. At one end, a tiny window seat. I go over to it. The window looks out to the front yard. The glass is half obscured by the overgrown weeds. There's a dusty cobweb in the top left corner. But it's cute. Peaceful.

Mum's at the other end of the room. She beckons me to join her. "The kitchen's through here." I follow her in. It's a long narrow room, countertops all down one side. Space for our kitchen table at the end.

"It's nice," I say.

"Look." Mum's unlocking a door that leads to a tiny backyard. A flagged area with a wooden shed in the far corner. There's something about it. About all of it. Kind of—I don't know. Sad. Lost. Neglected.

"I'm going to look upstairs," I say.

The staircase from the living room leads up to a landing of closed doors. When I open the first one, straight ahead of me, I see a small room. *Dad's junk room*, I think instantly. Then I remember. He won't need a junk room anymore. His junk is all going into a shop.

That's how they talked me into this—made me believe that, actually, maybe it *was* what they wanted to do. Dad's given up the office job he hated, Mum's turning her up-cycling hobby into a full-time job, and together they're planning to try and make a living doing up old furniture and selling it for more than it's worth. All in the seaside town where they met and fell in love over twenty years ago.

Sounds nice, doesn't it? Just add one screwed-up older daughter and a younger one who's been ripped away from a life she loves, and your perfect new life is good to go.

I glance at the bathroom as I pass it. Bath. Shower. Toilet. Sink. Nothing special.

On my right is another staircase. I ignore that for now and turn toward the door ahead of me.

I reach for the handle. As I do, I get a shiver. I think of that expression *someone just walked over my grave*. I've always hated it when people say that, but it's the phrase that comes to my mind. There must be a window open some-where. My arms are covered in goose bumps. I rub them, shrug off the shiver, and turn the handle.

There's a moment of resistance as I try to open the door. Is there something on the other side?

I push against it a bit harder, and a second later it swings open so easily that I nearly fall into the room.

I stand in the doorway and look around.

I love it.

I don't even know why, really. It just feels like my room. It *is* my room — it has to be.

I walk around the room, taking it in. Dark wooden floors; simple, clean wallpaper; mostly cream but with tiny thin lines running down it. Every now and then there's a bald patch where it looks as if someone's pulled Blu-Tack from the wall. I wonder what used to be on the walls.

I cross the room. On the far side, there's a walk-in closet. I look into it. It's dark and long, goes back the full length of the staircase above it. Feels like the kind of place you'd set up camp and make a den when you were little. You could fit a mattress in there and have secret midnight feasts.

The front wall across the room has a big bay window in the middle of it. The window has a seat like the one downstairs, only this one's bigger. I can imagine myself sitting there. Curled up with big cushions, scribbling in my notebook, lost in a poem or a story.

I push the flimsy curtains to the side. The room overlooks the front yard, like the one downstairs. Beyond that, it looks across the rows of houses in front, and down to a glimpse of the sea.

I sit on the cold ledge. Yes, it definitely needs some cushions. But even without the comfort of a warm seat, I feel like I've come home.

I look around the room. My bed will go on the wall

opposite this one. Chest of drawers in the corner opposite the walk-in closet. Desk in the other corner. Yeah, I can see it now.

Even with the room empty, I can imagine my life here. It's just a room, but it has—I don't know—a kind of energy to it.

There I go, thinking stupid things as usual. I'm not supposed to be acting that way anymore—I'm supposed to be acting like a normal sixteen-year-old instead of some middle-aged therapist. I guess I've been spending too much time with middle-aged therapists.

For the first time, I can see us starting a new life here. I can imagine it working.

Just as well, really, since it's my fault that we're here.

I check myself. *None of it was my fault.* I can almost hear my therapist's voice saying the words—and I can repeat them so smoothly that most people would be convinced I mean it.

Not always so easy to believe it yourself, though. When your peers spend every minute of their spare time telling you how worthless you are and how much better off everyone would be without you, the words seem to have stronger glue attached to them than anything anyone else says to counter them.

And when the methods you use for coping with their bullying ways are the very things they turn into weapons to use against you, you start to lose faith that anything that feels good can ever be real. The words, the laughter, the hatred—they get stuck fast somewhere deep inside you, and once that happens, it's not easy to know how to tear them off without ripping up your insides.

But I'm not meant to focus on that now. I'm meant to face forward. We agreed. A fresh start for all of us; no what-ifs, no looking back.

"Erin!" Mum's voice breaks into my thoughts. "You ready? We'll need to get going if we want to see the beach before the movers arrive."

"Coming, Mum." I get up and head to the door. I give the bedroom one last look. "See you soon," I whisper. Then I join Mum on the landing, and we look at the last two rooms before going down to the beach to find the others.

Which is pretty easy. It's a cool, windy evening, and Dad and Phoebe are the only people out there. Mum waves, and they amble over to join us.

Phoebe's constant chatter means it's OK that I don't talk much as we wander around the harbor together. I nod and say, "Mmm, yeah, nice," while Mum points out shops and cafés. I link my arm through Dad's and smile as we roam the cobbled streets together, and I let my thoughts drift while we look for the empty shop they're taking over, retracing our steps again and again and getting lost on almost every corner.

And I try not to think about how much I hope that I don't actually get lost myself.

# JOE

I'm awake.

But where am I?

I force my brain to think. When was I last awake? Feels like it was years ago. Or months, at least. I feel as though I've been drifting in and out of sleep forever.

Something's happening. Like a pressure against my back. What is it? Is someone kicking me? I realize I'm slumped against the door. I stumble to my feet, dragging my body up like I'm raising it from the dead. Next thing I know, the door's open and some girl practically comes flying through it.

I step back, partly out of shock, partly to get out of her way before she knocks both of us over.

"Who the hell are you?" I ask. Hearing my own words shocks me. It's almost like hearing a stranger. I don't recognize my deep, gravelly voice.

When did I last speak?

I look her up and down. She's wearing jeans with a rip in one knee and a baggy blue sweater. Her hair is dark and tucked up in a beanie hat. A couple of strands hang over her face, as though she's hiding behind them. Tiny stud in her nose.

"Hey," I say. Clearer this time.

She doesn't reply. Acts like I didn't even speak.

She's walking around my bedroom as if she owns it, touching the walls, looking in my walk-in closet, standing in the middle of the room as though she's surveying her empire.

I pull myself together and follow her across the room. Glancing around, I see that it's empty—and then I have a memory.

My room. I woke up, and there was nothing here. When was that?

There's still nothing. Except now there's a girl.

"You can't just ignore me, you know," I say to the girl as she turns away from my closet.

She ignores me.

"Oi!" I reach out to grab her arm, but she's moved again. She's heading for the window seat. *My* window seat. My special place.

She sits down.

"Hey!" I say, louder, getting pissed off now. Who does she think she is? "That's *my* seat."

She ignores me again, just stares out of the window. I watch her for a moment. There's something about the look on her face as she sits there. It reminds me of something. Or someone. It takes me a moment to work out who she reminds me of. Me.

Another memory. Sitting in the window seat. Taking refuge, escaping from the world.

The connection deflates my anger a little. I still haven't

got a clue what's going on, though. Especially when I follow her gaze. That's when the next bit comes back to me. I remember looking out this window before, but it was different. The garden was coming into bloom then. Pink blossoms, yellow daffodils everywhere. Now it's bare. Wet leaves line the path; straggly dead weeds lie bent double and neglected.

What's happened to the garden? What's happened to *me*? I swallow down the cold feeling that's creeping into my throat and try to remember. Actually, that's a lie. I don't *want* to remember. I don't want to know the truth. In fact, I'd do anything to put it off.

The girl is still sitting in the window. Who the hell is she? Do I know her?

I reach out for her, more gently this time. My hand hovers above her arm—I don't know why. Something stops me. Then I shake myself. *Don't be an idiot.* So I reach for her arm.

My hand slips right through it.

I leap back, as if her skin were on fire, as if she's infected me.

A ghost! I've got a ghost in my bedroom!

Have I, though? Does that make sense?

Does *any* of this make sense?

I'm clutching my hand and staring, just staring. Have I taken drugs? Am I hallucinating? What the *hell* is happening here?

"Erin!"

There's a voice outside. The girl — Erin — calls back. "Coming, Mum." Her voice — it does something to me. The tone of it. Like, soft but hard. Open but protected. Can you get all that from two words?

Erin gets up and crosses the bedroom.

I'm standing in the middle of the room as she pauses by the door. She turns back, her hand on the door handle, and I swear, she stares me straight in the face, right in my eyes, as if she can see all the way inside me, but as if she's looking right through me at the same time. She whispers — to me? — "See you soon."

And then she's gone.

Too late, I follow her to the door. I want to get out. Want to follow her. Want to know more — but she closes the door, and I know even before I try that I won't be able to grip the handle. That much I remember from last time.

A moment later, I hear mumbled voices and two sets of feet going up the stairs to Mum and Dad's bedroom.

*Mum and Dad.*

A picture of my parents blasts into my mind. I can see them both, their faces above me. I can feel my pain as I watch them, feel the tears inside me that won't leave my eyes because they are frozen inside my body.

My dad is crying openly. My mum is kissing my cheek. The vision brings me to my knees as if someone has punched me in the stomach.

As quickly as it arrives, the image is gone. But the memory remains, like a bruise, a dull ache. And with the ache comes the knowledge that I've been avoiding—but I can't ignore any longer.

The house isn't haunted.

At least not by a girl and her mum.

I remember it. Lying in a bed. All of them standing around me, holding my hand, kissing my cheeks, telling me they loved me. I remember the day they said good-bye. The day I died.

This girl isn't a ghost.

I'm the ghost.

# CHAPTER THREE

# Erin

"Come on, girls, we're going to be late," Dad calls up the stairs, and I laugh to myself. We move five hundred miles across the country to start our lives afresh in a brand-new town, and still some things don't change. He's shouted the same thing up the stairs every school day as far back as I can remember.

Something about the familiarity of his words gives me comfort, makes me feel safe. Which is a good thing, since nothing else is making me feel that way this morning.

A memory shoots into my mind. Packing my bag for school. Hopeful. Excited. First day of year seven. My friends from primary school went to three different secondary schools across the city. Just a couple of my best friends and I were going to the same one.

Running down the stairs and across the driveway into the road. The car was going too fast; they all said so. It wasn't my fault.

Broke my leg in three places and shattered my kneecap. But that wasn't the problem.

The problem was the damage that took place under the surface — the parts you couldn't see but that were at least ten times more broken than my leg.

The problem was, afterward I could barely get across a street without having a panic attack.

The problem was, I missed almost half a term — and every opportunity to find my place in the new world of secondary school.

I never found it.

"Sweetheart, you're going to be late." Mum's voice beside me breaks into my thoughts.

I shake the memories away and turn to Mum. She touches my arm. "You OK, darling?"

I nod.

Phoebe's behind me. "Come on, sis," she says, her coat open, shirt hanging out, so casual, so carefree. I push away a pang of envy and follow her out the front door.

Dad parks the car at the end of the road from the school. Phoebe waits in the back as Dad reaches out for me. Touches my chin, turns me toward him. "It's a fresh start, OK?"

I nod. I can't speak at this point. I'm too busy trying to encourage my breaths to get past the thumping in my chest and make it all the way in and out of my mouth.

"It's a small seaside town," he continues. "Everyone's

friendly here. It won't be the same. Just be yourself, and they'll love you." He smiles at me.

My brain tells my mouth to make a smile shape back at Dad.

My mouth obeys, and it seems to satisfy him, since he kisses my cheek and pats my knee. "Good girl. See you tonight."

"We're walking home," I remind him. School is only a mile down the road. Dad wanted to bring us on the first morning, as we've both got loads of new books and stuff to take in with us, but the last thing I want is for people to laugh at me for having to get a ride to school and back from my parents.

"You sure you'll find your way home OK?"

"We'll be fine!" Phoebe insists as she opens her door.

"OK, but make sure you girls wait for each other."

She steps out of the car. "We will. Promise."

Phoebe's classes finish earlier than mine. Now she's starting year seven, and I'm starting year twelve. She's right at the beginning of secondary school, and I'm at the end — starting sixth form, so at least we didn't move in the middle of anything.

I don't think I could do that again.

Phoebe will be fine either way. You could put her in any situation, and she'd make friends straightaway. She's just got that kind of personality. Always smiley, makes everyone feel warm and happy, makes them want to be with her.

Pretty much the opposite of me.

I get out of the car. Dad leans across the passenger seat. "It'll all be OK," he says, and for the first time I realize that he's scared for me, too. Of course he is. He saw the state I got into, even if I never told them what was really going on. He and Mum watched me lose weight, watched me turn more and more inward. They found me the day I . . .

No. I'm not going there. Not now. *It's a fresh start.* I take a deep breath. The deepest breath I can. I do that thing my therapist told me to do, imagining the breath coming all the way from my toes, up through my body—then I breathe it out, getting rid of it.

I do the other thing that always helps me feel like I'm taking control of my situation, too. I make a list in my head.

THREE REASONS NOT TO BE SCARED
1. Nobody knows anything about me here.
2. I never need to see those bullies again.
3. People are nice to strangers in a seaside town.

The third one is a guess, as I don't have any documented evidence, but it feels like it should be true. And the thoughts help me; my breathing calms.

"I know, Dad," I say finally as I shut the door.

"See you later, Dad. Love you," Phoebe says casually, and we make our way up the road together.

"Meet me back here at the end of the day," I tell her as

we pass through the school gates. "I'll be out after you. Just wait for me, OK?"

"I can walk home on my own, you know," she says. "You don't have to walk with me. I know the way."

"No. Wait for me. At least for the first few days. We don't know the roads yet — it's safer to go back together."

Phoebe gives me a look. The kind of look only an eleven-year-old can give you. The kind that says they understand better than you ever will how the world works.

Memories flood in before I can stop them. Walking home alone. Taking the long way across the fields and down the canal towpath so I can avoid crossing any roads. Listening to my favorite tunes on my iPod as I walk. Lost in my music, then suddenly surrounded.

Kaylie, Heather, Darcy. Who else? How many of them were there that first day? Six, seven? More? It was just silly names that time. *Car Crash Katy. Panic Alec.* That first time. They made up fresh names for me every week, each new name drawing me further and further back into my shell. *Silent Movie. Dumb and Dumber. Mute.*

I hold Phoebe's eyes and try to keep my gaze steady. Can she tell? Does she know I need her more than she needs me?

"Yeah, you're right," she says eventually, leaning in to give me a quick squeeze. "Mum'll kill me if anything happens to me on the way home and I didn't wait for you."

I laugh at her logic, and at her generosity. She might be

five years younger than me, but she was there; she knows what I went through, too.

I kiss the top of her head. "See you at the end of the day," I say.

A second later, with a quick swat of her hair to wipe my kiss away, she's gone.

And I'm alone, in a school yard.

I learn two things on that first day. Thing one: school is school, whether you're in a big city or a small seaside town. Either way, it's teachers and homework and groups of kids who all know one another. Thing two: sixth form means that it's not about conjugated French verbs or quadratic equations anymore.

I always knew I was going to study English lit, English language, and history. I'd been stuck on a fourth one. I finally decided on psychology just before moving here. I guess I've become more interested in psychology over the last year or so. It's worth giving it a go. We have to drop one at the end of the first year of sixth form anyway, so I'm doing what Mum always insists on and *keeping my options open.*

I see there's a creative writing lunch club advertised on a notice board. I consider it for about a minute. Half of me really wants to do it—but I'm pretty sure it would mean having to read my work out loud, and there's no way in ten trillion years I'm doing that, so I don't sign up.

I'm assigned a "buddy" named Brooke. She spends half an hour giving me a high-speed tour of the school. "You get lunch here. Best bathrooms for gossip are these ones. Best for putting on makeup are the ones on the second floor. English is down there. Psychology's up that corridor and turn left, and the cafeteria is that way. Any questions?"

I tell her I've got it, and she gives me an *I'm a nice person, but I've done what I was asked to do, and can I go now?* smile, tells me to give her a shout if I need anything, and then leaves me to it. I don't see her again for the rest of the day.

Which is fine by me. I don't want to be a drag on someone else's social life, and I don't want to have to make conversation with a stranger all day just for the sake of it.

After that, the day is mostly spent getting schedules and shuffling along the halls, following others who are doing the same subjects as me. By the end of the day, I think I've pretty much figured it out.

By which I mean I can find my way around. But by which I also mean I think I've sussed out how the pecking order works. I've noticed a group of girls who seem to be the cool gang. The leader is a girl named Zoe, with two or three girls who follow her around and flick their perfect hair in the same way every five minutes.

I know those girls. Girls like them, anyway. Zoe has perfect blond hair, perfect clothes, perfect smile. The kind of smile that makes you either feel warm to be in her presence when it's on you, or want to run fifty miles away when it turns into cold, harsh laughter.

A couple of her followers have blond hair, too. Not quite as perfect as hers, but you can see they style themselves after her. Same mannerisms, same-length skirts. The only one who looks different from the others is a girl with dark hair, dark skin, slightly more genuine-looking smile. If she weren't with them, I'd probably smile back. As it is, I make a very early decision to give the whole group a wide berth.

Then there's the usual sporty group, the nerds, the emos, the misfits. It's the same as anywhere.

And no, I don't suddenly bump into my perfect best friend and become instantly joined at the hip.

And yes, everyone does already know one another, and I can tell that the various social groupings are well established. Which is why I spend break time mostly hiding in the bathroom (the one described by Brooke during our high-speed tour of the school as *good when you need a bit of privacy, if you know what I mean*) and eat my lunch in the library, huddled over a book that I pretend to be absorbed in.

Old habits die hard.

But at least I get through the day without a panic attack. Which means I don't need to breathe into a paper bag at lunchtime.

Which means no one calls me Bag Lady and makes the class laugh so much that the name sticks for the next five years.

So, yeah. Relatively speaking, it's a good day.

Which is what I tell Mum when we get home and she calls, "How was school?" the second we're through the front door.

She can't stop herself from showing how relieved she is when I reply, "It was fine, Mum."

Which shouldn't irritate me but kind of does.

Phoebe saves the moment. "Brilliant!" she exclaims, before raiding the fridge and telling Mum all about her day.

"I'm going upstairs to dump my things," I say, and head up to my room before Mum can grill me any further.

The moment I walk through my bedroom door, I feel better. This room has a weird effect on me. It calms me, makes me feel safe.

I drop my bag on the floor and grab my notebook. There's no way I'd have taken that to school. I made that mistake once. Hearing your innermost thoughts read out to a jeering crowd on a school playground is the kind of mistake you don't allow to happen twice.

The memories of the past swirl around in my mind, merging with my determination about the future.

I grab a pen, snuggle up in my window seat, and start writing.

Am on the floor,
two girls with my notebook
        laughing,
my face hot with tears, head
down against the heavy rain
        of my words.

Am in the bathroom,
        tap running,
watching myself cry
        in the mirror,
red and puffy and
                worthless.

Am opening a can
        of chopped tomatoes
and slicing my finger
        and not knowing
                which red is mine.

Am hearing, *It's not your fault, Erin,*
        staring at the gray carpet
until it blurs,
        *worthless*, numb,
a bottle of pills in my hand.

*Am starting again*
*it's not the same*
*it isn't, it never will be*
*I won't let it*
*they won't beat me.*

# JOE

They've been here two weeks now. Here's how I know.

After I woke up and saw her here that first time, things started to change for me. I don't know if it's because there's someone in my room and that's enough to keep me alert, or because I slept the sleep of the dead for months and I don't need any more sleep for now, or what. All I know is that I've seen the sun go down each night and come back up again in the morning fourteen times since she arrived. And I no longer sleep.

I think I'm getting stronger.

I don't know what that means, either. I'm trying not to hope that it means I'm going to keep on getting stronger and stronger until I come back to life. I couldn't take the crushing disappointment of being wrong if I let that hope in.

But I had a thought the other day. What if I'm in a coma or something? What if I do come back? What if I'm not *actually* dead? Like, say I'm in a kind of halfway house and I have to stay here till, I don't know, I pass a test or something, and if I do, then I get to come back to my life.

I mean, I know it's impossible. But before I died, I'd have said that what's happening now was impossible, too, so who's to say I'm wrong?

No one.

Mainly because there's no one to say anything. Because no one can hear me or see me.

Because I'm dead.

So yeah, I know it's a pipe dream. But it's all I've got, and telling myself stories with happy endings is the only way to get through the days without losing it completely. I guess that's one advantage of having no one to talk to: there's no one to tell me to get a life.

Ha. Get a life. If only.

I've been counting each sunrise, forcing myself to remember the numbers as I add one each morning. My brain is slowly getting used to the task. Each day, I force the fog out of my mind, run through everything I know—which isn't much—and try to add at least one thing.

Usually, it's tiny things like *Today is Sunday.* I learned that yesterday. Her mum stood in the door and said, "Erin, I know it's Sunday, but that doesn't mean you need to sleep for the *entire* day."

I spent the rest of the day trying to recall what all

the other days are called. I got there in the end. Today is Monday. It's the start of the week. I remember what that means. It means school; it means work.

It means everyone leaves the house.

It will be the first day they've all been out of the house. I thought that was what I wanted. To get my room back. But I didn't. Not really.

It was too cold in this room without her.

She's here, now. Sitting in my seat. I don't mind anymore. I like it. I like that she understands what a special place it is. I like that she writes there. I want to tell her it's what I did, too. I wish I could tell her that. I know I can't.

I can watch her, though. Pausing and chewing her pen every now and then. I remember doing that, too.

I want to see what she's writing. I edge forward.

I shouldn't. It feels wrong. I'm not a spy. I'm not a creep. It's her private world. I remember that feeling; I won't invade it.

But then I see something that changes my mind. A drip, falling out of her eyes and onto the page. She's crying. It melts me.

Why's she crying?

I want to know. I argue with myself for a few minutes. In the end, the nosy side wins out. I mean, it's not as if she'll ever know, is it? Not as if I can tell anyone.

I tiptoe toward her and glance at the page.

*staring at the gray carpet*
*until it blurs,*
*worthless, numb*

I pull my eyes away from the words. I feel like a thief, an intruder.

Another drop falls onto the page, and I want to reach out so badly. I want to stroke her hair, console her. She won't feel me, so I know I can't bring her any comfort. But her pain mingles with mine; her tears are like a bridge between us, and I want to cross it more than I have ever wanted anything.

Before I can stop myself, I reach my hand out toward her, even if it's pointless.

I know it's going to freak me out when my hand goes right through her like last time. And I know she won't feel anything, and I'll never be able to make contact with her, however much I might want to.

Which is why I almost faint when I feel the softness of her hair against my palm.

The only reason I don't is because, as far as I know, dead people can't faint.

# CHAPTER FOUR

## Erin

"Yaaarrrrgggghhhh!" I leap off the window seat, dragging my fingers through my hair and yanking my shirt off.

Mum's up the stairs and in my room in a flash. "What's the matter?" she asks, her face flushed, her eyes dark with concern.

I'm bent double, shaking my hair like some old-fashioned headbanger and holding my shirt in my hand. "Spider," I explain. "Huge one, I think."

Mum lets out a breath. "I thought something *awful* had happened," she says.

"Something awful *has* happened! I felt it in my hair; it was as big as a hand, Mum. Help me get it."

Mum comes over and examines my hair, my back, the window, the floor. "There's nothing there," she says. "Where were you?"

"On the window seat."

She points at the curtain. "You probably just brushed against this," she says, wafting it. "There's no spider, I promise."

My breathing has calmed down. "OK. Sorry. Didn't mean to scare you." I feel a bit stupid.

Mum gives me a kiss on my head. "That's what I'm here for," she says. Turning to leave, she adds, "Come and join us when you've done your homework. Dad says we could all go down to the beach for a walk before dinner."

I pull my shirt back over my head. "Mmm," I say non-committally.

Mum leaves me to it without pushing it. She knows better than to do that.

She softly closes the door behind her. After checking the whole of the window frame and the seat, including under the cushion, I sit back down, pick up my notebook, and read through my poem.

But I can't stop thinking about what just happened. How it felt.

The weird thing is, however much I might have screamed and leaped about and acted as if there was a spider in my hair, a part of me doesn't actually think it was a spider at all.

The only trouble is, if I dwell too much on what it *really* felt like, I won't only scream and leap about. I'll go back to the days of wondering if I am in fact going crazy.

See, what it really felt like—what half of me is convinced it was, if I'm honest—was a *hand*. A human hand. Touching my hair.

How sad is that? So desperate for someone to want to reach out to me that I imagine it's happening when it's more likely to have been the curtain brushing against me than anything else.

And you know what's even sadder? I want it to happen again.

## JOE

There's a split second when I can't help myself. I glance at her as she rips her shirt off. Come on. I might be dead, but I'm still a sixteen-year-old boy. Show me any teenage boy who says he wouldn't do the same thing and I'll show you a liar.

Still. It only takes a second for me to feel like some kind of Peeping Tom, so I force myself to turn away. Plus her mum is here too now, and that makes it feel even more wrong to stare at a girl with no shirt on who has no idea I am there.

They're talking to each other like I don't exist, as usual. I'm used to it now. Mostly.

"Come and join us when you've done your homework,"

her mum says. "Dad says we could all go down to the beach for a walk before dinner."

So calm, so casual, like it's the easiest thing in the world to do. Pop down to the beach. Breathe in the salty air. Maybe skim stones at the water's edge.

My body actually hurts with how much I long to do those things.

Her mum's gone and closed the door behind her. I glance around again. Erin's put her shirt back on and is sitting down in the window seat again.

She's still got her notebook out, but she isn't writing. She's running a hand through her hair. Where I touched her.

It feels like an invitation.

Holding my breath, I take a step toward her. She closes her eyes.

I take another step. I'm close enough now that she could probably feel my breath — if I had any.

Her eyes are still closed. I reach my hand out to touch her now. Do I dare? Does she want me to? Something tells me she does — but that's almost certainly wishful thinking on my part. Especially considering she leaped halfway across the room the last time I did.

A moment later, her eyes are open, she's letting out a heavy breath, and the moment's passed.

I sit on the floor, cross my legs, and watch her instead.

She's wearing jeans and a blue T-shirt that looks about three sizes too big. All her clothes are too big, in fact. From the brief flash that I just got, her body is nothing to complain about, so I'm not sure why she's so intent on hiding it under baggy clothes all the time. And hiding her hair under a hat most of the time, too. She's even come into the room with sunglasses on sometimes.

It's as if she's trying to hide herself from the world; as if she's living undercover. I'd like to be able to tell her she doesn't need to do that. I wonder if she'd listen. Maybe you only know how precious it is to be part of the world once your time's up and you no longer get the choice.

She's opened her notebook again.

I sit and watch her until her mum calls again and she sighs, closes her book, and goes off to join her family.

A few minutes later, I hear the sound that has become one of my least favorite things. The front door closing and voices on the path.

I'm alone again.

But something's changed. The door slamming behind them does something to me. Flips a switch inside me. Opens a tap. Lets something out that I've been trying to contain. Something is itching me from the inside, and I don't think I can take it any longer. Not alive, but apparently not dead enough to go off and rest in peace, either. What the hell even *am* I? Will I ever find out? Will I ever make it back?

How long will I have to stay here in this prison? What do I have to do to get out? Was I *so* bad in my life that I have to be punished like this? Held in a hellish waiting room? I can't even remember what I did, who I was—how I died. I can hardly remember any of my life, and the blankness is like being lost in fog. Bits come back to me every now and then. So small. Tiny memories that come in a flash and leave almost as quickly.

I need to remember more. Need to be part of something. Need somewhere for my feelings to go.

It's like a rage, building inside me, threatening to burst out. It's too big for my body.

And then, suddenly, among the maelstrom of emotion . . . a memory.

I've felt this way before. This rage. And I remember something else, too. I remember how I'd get it out of me. Songs. Poems. I used to write, just like she does, and somehow the words would carry the emotion out of me. Out onto the page, where it would dissipate.

I can't do that now. I can't even hold a pen in my hand.

I can't do anything now.

The feeling is mounting inside me. It's like a giant wave out at sea, growing, rising, creeping toward the shore almost in slow motion, until, at last, it picks up the tail end of its energy and crashes against the rocks.

I look around me. I have to be able to touch *something*. I want to smash the place up. I *need* to break something.

I look around me, hungry now, like a tiger on the prowl.

What can I throw?

There's a glass on her nightstand. Perfect. I want to hear the sound of glass smashing against the wall.

I stare at the glass, flex my hands, *will* them to work.

I reach out for the glass. Using every ounce of strength that I have, I try to pick it up.

I can't do it.

The frustration is almost palpable. I can't bear it. With it comes the realization that the stronger my feelings are growing, the more I feel capable of making contact with something.

The more I can't do it, the more I *need* to be able to lift this glass.

I force all my emotion into my hands and reach for the glass again.

And then . . . I can feel it! I've gotten hold of it! I can't lift it, can't throw it against the wall, but my hand is around the glass. I'm holding it!

The glass is shaking in my fingers. The effort is ridiculous, and I have to release my grip.

The glass topples from my hand, falling onto the floor. It misses the rug and smashes on the wooden floorboards. Water spills all around it. The shards of glass break up my rage into a thousand tiny pieces and I stare at the floor, wondering how I could be such an idiot.

I kneel down and try to sweep them up, but my hands slide through the glass. I was right! My ability to physically interact with the world definitely seems to be linked to emotion. Now I don't feel so strongly, I can't touch the glass.

Which is great in that I know a bit more than I did before. And not so great in that Erin is likely to cut her feet to shreds next time she comes in here.

Great move, Joe. Just great.

Exhausted, I sit down on the window seat.

Her notebook is still here. If only I could write her a message:

DEAR ERIN.

SORRY — I DROPPED YOUR GLASS AND IT SHATTERED. PLEASE BE CAREFUL.

LOTS OF LOVE,
JOE,
THE DEAD BOY WHO LIVES IN YOUR BEDROOM

But I can't even touch the book. When I try, my fingers slide through it as if it weren't there. Its pages are like air to me.

So I just sit there. Useless. Powerless. Weak. Miserable.

I flop back against the wall. I guess the silver lining is that the amount of energy it's taken at least means I'm too exhausted to be angry anymore.

# Erin

I hurry upstairs after dinner to do some writing. And to get away.

I'm not saying I don't like being with my family. I do; of course I do. Just, well, sometimes it's exhausting having to put on an act all the time. Pretend I'm happy, pretend I've forgotten everything that happened over the last five years, pretend I think it could never happen again. Pretend to believe that moving and starting again can really extinguish demons when they've set up a permanent camp inside you.

Phoebe's in her room, too, probably chatting online with all the new friends she's made already.

The floor is wet. How did that happen? I look up to see if there's a leak in the ceiling. Nope, nothing. Then I notice shattered glass on the floor next to my nightstand. What the hell?

I pull my door open and stomp out onto the landing. "Phoebe!"

"What?" she calls from inside her bedroom.

"What were you doing in my room?" I call across the landing.

"I haven't been in your room!"

Mum appears at the bottom of the stairs. "Girls! If you've got something to say to each other, can you do it in the same room, please, rather than screaming the house down?"

Phoebe appears in her doorway. "What d'you want?" she asks.

"Come and see," I say.

She drags herself across the landing, and I point out the broken glass all over the floor. "That," I say.

"You knocked your glass over."

"Someone did, but it wasn't me. Phoebe, what were you doing in my bedroom?" I demand. "You are *never* to come in my room without permission, right?"

"I haven't *been* in your room!" Phoebe insists.

"You must have been! What else have you been doing? Have you been snooping around in my nightstand? What do you want with my stuff?" I ask, ignoring her protests.

"Look, I don't care about your stupid nightstand or what's in it. I haven't been in your room, and it's not fair to yell at me when I haven't done anything."

Phoebe's face has turned red. Is it because she's lying or because she's angry? Either way, she's not going to admit it, and there's no point in pushing it. The more I push, the more firmly she's going to dig her heels in.

She *must* have been in my room, though. Who else would it have been? Mum? She hasn't even been upstairs since we got home. Dad?

Phoebe *must* be lying.

Suddenly I can't be bothered. I just want to be alone. "Whatever," I say, waving a hand to dismiss her. I stomp downstairs to fetch a broom and some newspapers. "Just keep out of my room from now on," I mutter as I pass her room on my way back to clean up the mess.

"With pleasure!" Phoebe retorts from inside, and I set to work on the glass in my bedroom.

As I pick up big chunks of glass, sweep up the rest, and dab at the spilled water, I'm hit by an overwhelming heaviness. I'm tired. Tired of everything. Tired of the effort it takes to get through the days. Tired of the effort it takes to be me.

I wrap the glass in the newspaper and put it carefully in the wastebasket. Then I lie down on my bed, close my eyes, and try to shut the world out.

## JOE

This is crazy. She's arguing with her sister now, and it's all my fault. What was I doing, getting so angry like that? That isn't what I'm like.

As far as I can remember.

I'm a good guy. As far as I can remember.

I tiptoe across the room. She's fallen asleep on her bed. I want to cover her up; I want to stroke her hair. I want to lie down behind her and put my arm around her.

I don't know if that sounds creepy, but it's true, and I can't deny it. I am longing for human contact.

I approach her softly, cautiously. I don't want to scare

her. Don't want to make her leap out of her skin. And I don't especially want to be compared to a big hairy spider again, either.

I kneel by the bed and watch her. A strand of her hair has fallen across her face. Her eyelids are dark. Her face is smooth, peaceful. Where is she? Where are her thoughts? I wish I was in them.

My whole body feels as if it's on fire, burning with how much I want to make contact. *So near and yet so far.* Could that ever have been a truer phrase? Literally centimeters apart, and yet separated by a chasm of life and death.

I am falling into that chasm. I can almost feel myself crashing on the rocks.

What harm can it do to lie here?

I carefully position myself behind her and close my eyes. My body burns with longing for her touch. I can always pretend.

So I do. I reach out to put my arm around her, expecting to feel nothing but air.

I'm wrong, though. I don't know if it's the intensity of my longing, the stillness of the night, my imagination, or what, but my arm doesn't go through her. I can feel her.

I tighten my arm around her waist and pull her close. I don't care if I'm imagining it. It's the most real thing I've felt since I died.

If I had any breath in my body, I'd be holding it.

*Please don't be scared, Erin. Don't leap in the air. Please.*

I don't know if, on some crazy level of psychic communication, she hears my pleading words or what, but the most amazing thing happens next.

Two things, actually.

Thing one: she doesn't scream, leap in the air, or shout, "Spider!"

Thing two: she reaches out and closes her hand over mine.

## CHAPTER FIVE

# Erin

When I feel his arm slip around my waist, the thing that surprises me the most is the fact that I'm not surprised.

The other thing that surprises me: I'm not scared.

Probably because I know that I'm dreaming. It's the only explanation. I don't care if it's not real. It's a nice dream.

Trouble is, the moment I start relaxing into it, it begins to fade.

I grip his hand, but it's disappearing, melting away from me, a spirit disappearing into the darkness. I try to grip harder, but there's nothing to hold on to, and I find myself grabbing at my comforter instead.

"No!" I call out. "Stay! Don't go!"

But it's too late. He's gone. It's not just the feel of his arm; it's more than that. His presence has gone. Vanished so completely, I wonder if I imagined the whole thing. I sit up in my bed and look around, but there's no sign of him, or anything. The room feels empty.

Did I imagine it? Am I cracking up? Should I be worried?

Before I get the chance to question myself and my mental health too much, Mum is in the doorway. "Erin, are you OK?" Her eyes are sleepy; she's in her pajamas, has bed hair.

"What time is it?" I ask, looking down at myself. I'm still dressed.

"Nearly one o'clock." Mum comes over and sits on the bed. "We looked in on you earlier. You'd fallen asleep, so we thought it best to leave you."

I nod.

Mum puts a hand on my arm. "Are you all right, darling?" she asks. "I heard you call out."

"I . . ."

I what? *I woke up and felt a boy's arm around me, and then he disappeared, and I didn't want him to.* I can't exactly say that.

"Were you having a nightmare?" Mum asks.

I pause. "Yes. I guess so," I say. "Did I wake you?"

Mum leans forward to kiss my forehead. "It's fine, honey—don't worry. As long as you're OK."

I nod again. I haven't got the words for any of this. I'm happy to let Mum think I was having a nightmare, even though I know that it was nothing of the sort. It was about as far from a nightmare as it could be.

And I don't know what the feeling is, or what just

happened, but I know this. Real or not, those few moments were the most alive I've felt in months.

# Joe

Damn. I panicked. I thought if she touched me, she'd freak out for sure, and I didn't want that. *Could* she feel my hand? *Did* it creep her out? I don't even know what I would feel like to her. Would I be freezing cold? Would it feel like she was touching a corpse?

I mean, she did tell her mum she was having a nightmare, so I guess it was just as well I leaped away, or faded, or whatever it is I've done. All I know is I can't reach her now. The spell's been broken. As far as she's concerned, I've gone.

And no, I didn't want her to freak out. But to be honest, I don't want her thinking she was having a nightmare, either. *Really?* A *nightmare?* Was it *that* awful? Or did she just say that to keep her mum off her back?

I can't help wondering what it means. I could touch her. She felt me.

Does this mean the purgatory is ending? I'm coming back to life?

I don't dare to let myself hope. The disappointment hurts too much.

Her mum's gone and Erin's lying down again. Her eyes are still open — but I'm not going to try again. Not tonight.

Just let her rest. Let her think whatever she wants to think about it.

It's not as if it matters either way. Not like anything could come of it.

Not like there's any point in holding out hope about *anything*.

I sit down on the floor, lean against the wall, and settle down for a long, lonely night.

## Erin

It turns out school really isn't all that bad. Not my favorite thing ever in the world, but not the worst thing ever in the world either—and that is progress.

In five days, I could probably count the number of conversations that go beyond "Please can I have some chips?" or "Is this chair free?" on the fingers of one hand. And yes, OK, I eat my lunch on my own every day with my head down and spend breaks reading a book with my headphones on, so I can't exactly say I'm surprised that I haven't made a bunch of new friends by the end of the week—but at least I've survived. And survival is good enough for me.

Friday afternoon, I'm heading home from school with Phoebe. I try to keep up as she chats away, filling me in on all the things she's done today, who told her what gossip, who she hung out with and what they did, her plans for the weekend with her new friends. I listen to her in a kind of stunned amazement. How does she do it? We've been at that school less than a week and she seems to have maneuvered herself into the center of year seven's social circle.

And what have I done? Given myself ten out of ten for survival.

Is that really all I want to do? Survive? Shouldn't I be setting my sights higher than that?

Listening to Phoebe's easy chatter, I can't help being envious, can't help wishing I had plans this weekend, can't help wishing someone—just one person—had asked me to hang out.

But what do I expect when I hide away and look down and do everything I can to avoid human contact of any kind?

I might as well have been carrying around a billboard that says DO NOT COME NEAR OR TALK TO ME AT ALL!

Sometimes it feels as if I actually *am* carrying that sign around. The only problem is, it's invisible to me and I don't know how to get rid of it.

Phoebe skips up the path and disappears into the house, leaving the front door swinging open for me to follow behind her. I steel myself for Mum's questions about my day. I'm running out of optimistic things to say about my new school.

There wasn't all that much to say in the first place, and there are only so many times I can get away with telling her that lunch was fine and my classes aren't too difficult before she's going to start asking for a bit more detail and wondering why I'm not talking about my new friends yet.

Thankfully, she's busy cooking dinner. And she has other things to badger me about. "Darling, are you going to finish unpacking this weekend?" she asks. "Dad's doing a recycling trip on Sunday. It'd be good to get rid of all the boxes."

I've still got about five boxes of stuff that I haven't emptied yet. I just shoved them in the walk-in closet in my bedroom and haven't bothered to do anything with them since.

"Yeah, I'll do it now," I say, glad of the excuse to spend time alone in my bedroom. I keep hoping he'll be there. Keep wondering if I'll sense his presence again, maybe even see him.

Mum looks up. "Thank you, darling," she says, and the gratitude in her eyes makes me feel guilty. She thinks I'm keen to help out around the house, when really I'm chasing after a—a what? An illusion? A hallucination? An indication that I'm finally going crazy?

"No worries," I say quickly as I hurry up to my room.

## JOE

I jump up as the door opens. She's home. I flatten down my hair and pull my clothes straight. Then I actually laugh out loud at myself.

Dude, you are trying to make yourself look decent when (a) the girl cannot see you anyway, and (b) you are dead, a fact that generally doesn't do wonders for people's appearance at the best of times.

I can't help it, though. It's a reflex. On the off chance she *does* see me, I want to look my best for it. The best that a pale, withered, tired, skinny dead guy can look, anyway.

She normally drops her bag on the bed and sits in the window with her notebook when she comes home from school. I'm used to her routine now. I know she writes poems, but I think mostly it's a diary. Not that I've read it again. Or, well, only a bit, anyway. I'll see her hand whizzing across the page in a rush and it makes me desperate to know what she's saying. But then I read a couple of words and feel bad, so I make myself look away.

I like to watch her write, though. It's as if she has to get the day down in her book before she can move on to the evening. As if the events of the day haven't happened, aren't real, until she's written them down.

I'm just the same. I *was* the same, back when I could do remarkable things like actually hold a pen in my hand.

I've been remembering more and more things. When I'm on my own in the day, I force my brain to think. I see images: Mum, Dad, Olly. Then there are feelings, too. Some of them are hard to put into words—they're like big clouds of emotion, all bunched up and indistinct. Some of it's easier. I can remember how writing made me feel. How it kept me sane. Writing songs and poetry helped me make sense of my life. I remember that.

I can't help thinking that if I could figure out how to grip a pen and drag it across a piece of paper, forming words, maybe I'd stand a chance of making some sort of sense of what's happening to me now.

Then I imagine that if I could write, perhaps I could communicate, and if I could communicate, maybe there's some way I could come back. Back from this blankness. Back to the living.

That's when I know my imagination is working too hard, and I have to stop myself. It only makes the crushing reality of my situation even harder to take.

Yeah, that's another thing. I had thought I was trapped in here because I couldn't grab hold of the door handle. Turns out it's more than that. I've tried to squeeze through the doorway behind her. Even tried to get out on the odd occasion she's left it open. Which she doesn't do very often. But I can't.

It's as if . . . I don't know how to describe it. It's not a feeling I ever had when I was alive, so I don't think alive people have words for it. The nearest I can get is to say it's a bit like the doorway opens into a thick, cold black fog— but a fog that simultaneously scalds and freezes your skin if you make contact with it.

Like I say. It's hard to describe. Hard to make sense of, like all of this.

I don't know why I'm trapped in this room. Don't know why I can't get through the doorway but can sit in the window. Don't know why I can lie on the floor but can't pick up a book. I don't know any of it. Maybe it has something to do with how hard the surface is that I'm making contact with. How porous. Or how old it is. How permanent. I don't know. Maybe if I'd studied more in school, I'd have a few more ideas.

Except I'm not sure which subject would have had Things That a Ghost Can and Cannot Do on its syllabus.

Anyway. I don't care about any of that. Most of my caring is focused on her. I want to know how she feels about what happened between us the other night. Did it freak her out? Did she like it? Does she want it to happen again?

*Will* it happen again?

I settle down to watch her write. But she's not going over to the window today. Instead, she dumps her schoolbag and makes a beeline for the walk-in closet. She left a bunch of boxes in there the day she moved in and hasn't bothered with them since.

She starts dragging the boxes out of the closet. I feel like such a jerk. I want to help. What kind of a guy watches a girl drag heavy boxes around and doesn't even offer to help?

Answer: a dead one.

My feelings of uselessness and despair plummet another notch downward. I want to help her. I want to talk to her. I want *something*. The desire to make contact with her is like a dull thud in my stomach.

I can't watch. Instead, I go to the window seat, lean on my knees, my chin in my hand, and look out the window.

As she lugs boxes across the floor, empties her old life onto the bed, I hug myself as tightly as possible and try not to think about how much I wish it was her hugging me instead.

## Erin

It's at the point where I've dragged all five heavy boxes out of the closet and emptied the contents onto my bed that I suddenly wish I hadn't started the job.

I'm looking at a medium-size mountain of, basically, junk and wondering what on earth made me think I needed all this stuff. Approximately a hundred books, most of which I haven't looked at for years; three pencil cases full of enough pens, pencils, and erasers to write twenty full-length novels; twelve teddy bears with missing ears/eyes/hair that I am slightly embarrassed to still own but for some bizarre reason cannot part with let alone imagine some stranger cuddling; and a pile of clothes that I've mostly grown out of but can't bring myself to throw out, despite the fact that I've worn little other than jeans, T-shirts, hoodies, and beanie hats for the last two years.

Dad bought us all a load of new furniture online and has spent most of the last week putting it together. The stuff that isn't going to the shop to be painted and sprayed in bright colors, that is. I've got a bookshelf, a chest of drawers, and two nightstands waiting to be filled.

It crosses my mind just to shove everything back in the closet and forget about it for now, but that will only put the problem off, not solve it. And I might want to do something with the closet. Maybe I'll put some cushions in there and turn it into a den, where I can hide away from the world whenever I want. I could curl up with a flashlight and read.

Either way, I've got five boxloads of junk to put *somewhere*. I'd better get on with it.

Before I start on the putting away, I decide to hold off another couple of minutes to do one last check of the walk-in closet and make sure I haven't left anything behind.

I flick my phone's flashlight on and have a quick look around. Nope. It's all clear. Just torn carpet, mucky walls, and . . .

Wait. What's that on the wall? I take a few more steps inside it. There's something there.

It looks like writing. I crawl farther into the closet and shine my light on it. Someone must have wallpapered in here a long time ago, because there are bits of paper dotted about, ripped and hanging off the wall. Some of it looks as if it's been pulled off; other bits have rumpled against the wall with age or damp, maybe.

But there's a bit of wall where the paper has definitely been pulled off. In the gap, someone has written something. I lean in, shine the light on the words, and read what it says.

SOMETIMES I WONDER WHO I AM
OR IF I'LL EVER BELONG.
THE LOSER, THE LONER, THE GUY ON HIS OWN,
WASTING HIS TIME ON A SONG.

EVERYONE KNOWS ME YET NOBODY SEES,
THEIR LIVES A CONSTRUCTED PRETENSE.
AND SO I'LL SIT HERE AND BUILD WALLS WITH MY WORDS;
MY PEN IS MY ONLY DEFENSE.

I stare at the words. The poem. The whatever it is. Who wrote it? *When* did they write it?

I feel like an archaeologist discovering evidence of an ancient tribe. Except it's obviously not that ancient if it was written on a wall in a house with a pen. And it's clearly just one person, not a tribe.

But still. It was here before we were, and that makes me want to know more.

I'm leaning forward, looking around on the rest of the wall to see if there's any more, when something glints against the light from my phone. Something at the back, where the closet narrows right down under the stairs.

I crawl farther in, all the way to the shallow far end of

the closet, and shine my light into the corners. It's dark, dusty, musty, and full of stringy cobwebs. I try not to think about how many spiders there might be knocking around in this long-forgotten corner.

Plus I can't see what it was that glinted now. I probably imagined it, anyway. Typical of me. Do everything I can to duck out of real life but get covered in dust and sweat on a wild goose chase that my imagination has conjured up.

I'm about to give up when I see it glint again. What *is* it? It looks like a silver pendant.

I shove spiders and creepy crawlies to the back of my mind and reach out for it.

If I were telling a story about what happened next, I'd probably say it was as if it happened in slow motion. I'd say that deep inside me, a part of me knew something was going to happen. I'd say I saw colors, flashes—maybe my life whizzed before my eyes. But none of those things would be true.

It happens in a split second, with no fanfare and no warning.

I reach out for the pendant, and the second I touch it, a bolt of electricity runs through my arm so ferociously that it throws me backward against the wall. I hit my head—and everything goes dark.

# CHAPTER SIX

## JOE

She's disappeared inside the closet again. What's she doing in there? More boxes? I wait in my bedroom, glancing at the random display of objects scattered across her bed.

I can hear her rustling about. She's gone forever. So long I start to wonder if she's OK.

I approach the entrance. She's sitting inside the closet, shining her flashlight against the wall. What's she doing that for?

Oh no! No! *No!*

It comes back to me in a rush. If I weren't a permanent shade of deathly white, I would probably turn bright red right about now. My poems. Songs.

I remember—I used to write them in there, on the walls.

For a moment, I feel a dart of anger run through my body. She shouldn't be looking at that. It's private. I've tried not to intrude on her writing. Shouldn't she show me the same respect?

A second later, I almost laugh. How can she show respect to someone she doesn't even know exists? Someone who actually *doesn't* exist. Not in the traditional sense of the word, anyway.

I need to think quickly. Maybe I can do something to distract her before she sees too much of my embarrassing, self-indulgent blather.

I bend down and creep into the closet. What can I do? Throw things around? I can barely touch anything, let alone pick it up and throw it. Stand between her and the wall? She can see through me.

I'm out of options. All I can do is watch her read my pathetic words and quietly die of embarrassment. Except I'm already dead, so I can't even do that.

So I turn to leave, and that's when I notice her flashing her light into the back corner of the closet, like she's looking for something.

What's she looking for?

I turn back and creep alongside her. I follow the light from her phone — and then I see it.

The surfboard. I remember it.

Must have been four or five years ago. Olly won the local under-fourteen surf contest. Dad bought it for him to say well done. A silver surfboard pendant on a leather strap. Olly didn't take it off. Not once. The leather had worn quite a lot and the surfboard had faded, but he wore it day in, day out, for years, like a badge of honor. Then one day, he wasn't wearing it anymore.

What the hell is it doing in here?

The sensation of a huge wave builds inside me again. It feels like the swell of the entire ocean is moving through me, threatening to crash over my head and drown me.

I move toward the pendant.

As I do, I can feel the boundaries between my current so-called existence and my old life melt away. I'm in some kind of no-man's-land, linked to it by a leather strap and a silver surfboard. I'm reaching out for it. I want to feel it. I *need* to touch it.

And then—

My hand outstretched.

The silver pendant glinting against the light from the phone.

I touch it and—

"*Arrrrgggghhhhhhhh!*"

I'm flung backward. It feels as though I've been electrocuted.

I have a sudden memory of being about seven. I'd got my bread stuck in the toaster and reached inside with my knife to get it. The buzz I got through my arm was so intense, it threw me across the kitchen. I saw bright white zigzags across my eyes for an hour afterward. I never did it again. Never felt anything like it again, either.

Till now.

What on earth *was* that?

I pick myself up and rub my hand where I touched the surfboard. My fingers are still buzzing, as if there's a thin thread of electricity running through them. But it's fine—doesn't hurt.

I look around, still dazed, and that's when I see Erin, lying in the corner, her hands curled around the leather strap of the necklace. She's lying in a weird position, her head half propped up against the wall. Why would she . . . ?

Then I realize. She's unconscious. Did the pendant shock her, too?

My mind is full of questions—but more than that, it's full of panic. I need to help her. I need to get someone.

But *how*? I can't get out of my bedroom. Can't call out—no one will hear me. What can I do?

The panic is turning into a boulder inside my chest. What if she's . . . what if . . . ? No, I'm not going to do that. Not going to think about what-ifs and maybes. I just need to be here for her.

I bend down, crouch beside her, whisper her name.

"Erin."

Nothing. She doesn't hear me. Of course she doesn't. Even if she hadn't just cracked her head against a wall and knocked herself unconscious, she still wouldn't hear me. Anger mixes with the panic. Impotent, useless, pointless anger turning to fury inside me. Building to a peak. A mountain of rage.

A strand of hair has fallen across her face. I want to put it behind her ear. I reach out, knowing I won't be able to.

But as I reach toward her, my fingers make contact. I feel her hair.

Holding my breath, I place the strand gently behind her ear. My fingers still in her hair, I'm staring at her face, gasping and unbelieving, and begging for the moment to last. I don't know if it's really happening. Maybe I bashed my head when I fell. Maybe I'm having some weird kind of ghost dream. I don't care what it is. It's the most alive I've felt since I died, and I'm happy to indulge myself in a fantasy that it's real.

And then she opens her eyes.

# Erin

I hold his eyes with mine.

His face is pale, almost gray. His eyes—I think they're green or maybe hazel. In the dim light, they look dark, almost black. His hair, short, messy. A bit of it flopping over his forehead, almost into his eyes. The rest pulled back, as though he's run his hands through it many times, and possibly not washed it for a while.

Like maybe he's got more important things to think about than obsessing over his appearance.

Stubble covering his face. Bags under his eyes. He's looking at me in a way I don't think I've ever been looked at before. As if he's not just seeing my face, my eyes — anything on the outside. It's as if his eyes are seeing through all of that, dispensing with it as irrelevant and, instead, looking all the way inside me. Actually seeing *me,* not just the parts I project to the world to hide behind.

It's making me want to run. It's making me want to stay forever.

It's making me remember that I just hit my head and knocked myself out, and now I'm probably asleep and dreaming. Thing is, I don't remember ever having had a dream that felt so real before.

*Is* it a dream?

Our eyes are like a tightrope between us. I want to cross it.

I reach out a hand toward his face, letting the necklace fall from my fingers as I do. I urge my hand to feel the touch of him. I silently beg for this to be real.

Please, please don't be a dream.

As I reach out, he tilts his face toward mine. My palm makes contact with his skin. Yes, he's a bit cold; yes, his face is as rough to the touch as it looks — but it's real. He's real.

He lifts his hand, closing his fingers around mine.

And then he smiles, and the rest of the world—everything that exists outside of this room, this closet, this moment—melts away.

## JOE

Her eyes are blurry and unfocused. She glances around, confused. And then they find mine. She's looking right at me. Does she see me? *Does she?*

Half of me wants to turn away. It's too much. Her eyes feel like a laser, burning into my soul. But I force myself to keep looking at her, to keep my hand in her hair, to stop this contact from breaking. I'm not giving up this moment for anything.

Her eyes locked with mine, she reaches a hand out toward my face. The necklace falls from her hand as she does. She doesn't seem to care, nor do I.

I tilt my head toward her hand. If I had a breath in me, the feel of her fingers on my face would take it away. I reach out and close my own hand around hers.

I'm dreaming. I know I am. I must be.

I don't care. I don't want the dream to end.

I try to speak. My mouth is full of sawdust. Clearing my throat, I smile at her.

"Hi," I say.

Then I want to kick myself. *Really?* That's the best I can do? *Hi?*

She smiles back, and I realize it's the first time I've seen her smile.

Her face is transformed. It's like — how can I describe it? It's like one of those time-lapse videos of a beautiful rose opening up. You knew it was there inside all along, but it was covered with leaves. Then it blooms, opens, fills the screen with color. That's what her smile is like.

"Hi," she says back, so softly that the word is little more than a whisper on a breeze.

I shake my head. I don't know what to say. Where have my words gone? What else can I say? Have I forgotten all the words except *hi*?

"I'm Erin," she says while I'm still trying to figure out my next line.

"I know," I say before I can stop myself. No! She'll think I'm some kind of stalker now.

*Seriously?* I'm worried about what she'll think of me? I'm crouched inside a walk-in closet, dead, holding hands with a girl who has literally just seen a ghost, and I think I need to add something else to worry about into the mix? I think there's enough in there already.

Still. Her face clouds. She pulls her hand away, backs off a little.

"I'm not a stalker," I add quickly. Jesus. Am I really determined to make myself look like more and more of a total loser with every word I utter? "I mean. I . . ." I look down and try to compose myself.

I don't know how to do this. I have a sudden recollection that I wasn't much good at it when I was alive. I've got even less going for me now.

I want to walk away. The fact that I have nowhere to go makes me feel claustrophobic. When is this situation going to *end*? Why am I trapped here? What do I have to do to release myself from it?

"What's your name?"

Her voice is like oxygen, breathing life into me, banishing my self-indulgent spiral of thoughts.

"Joe," I say. "I . . . I don't know how this is happening."

"What *is* happening? What are you doing here? How did you get in? Are you *real*?"

I open my mouth. Then shake my head. "I . . . I don't know," I confess.

She laughs. "You don't know what's happening, or you don't know if you're real?" She sits up, then clutches her head and closes her eyes.

"Are you OK?" I ask.

There's a beat before she answers. "You mean apart from having a lump the size of a golf ball on the side of my head and possible concussion, plus the fact that I'm sitting in a walk-in closet, talking to a guy who isn't sure if he actually exists or not?" she asks with another soft smile.

Her voice is so beautiful. "Yeah, apart from that," I say.

The smile fades for a second. "Are you . . . ?"

"What?"

She shakes her head. "I feel stupid even asking it."

"Ask," I insist.

She laughs, as if she's making a joke, although her eyes don't look like she's joking. "Are you a ghost?" she asks eventually.

Should I be honest with her? Is there anything else I could be? I mean, is there a better explanation for why I'm sitting in a closet in her bedroom?

I shrug. "I think so," I reply.

She exhales heavily. "Wow," she says after a moment.

I'm in the process of wondering if this stuttering exchange is going to go down in history as one of the great romantic conversations of our time when she says, "I'm better at doing words on paper."

"Me too!"

She nods. She's thinking about the lines on the wall. I still don't know exactly what she saw. If I'm honest, I can't remember what I wrote in here. My life still feels like a jigsaw puzzle, with random pieces popping up in front of me only when something jogs my memory enough to put them there.

Either way, I know I'm embarrassed that she's seen something I wrote. Even if I can't remember exactly what it was, the fact that I scribbled it on a wall in a dark closet where no one except me ever went seems to indicate that the words weren't intended for sharing.

"Are you a poet — or a songwriter?" she asks, just like that.

There's a split second when it occurs to me that I could tell her anything. I could make up a whole persona. I could be a famous pop star, killed in an accident while driving my Porsche. I could be a celebrated poet, deeply mourned by academics around the country. I could be anything. I could tell her anything.

Except, when I look in her pale-blue eyes, I know that I can only tell her the truth.

"Bit of both, I guess. And a total failure on both counts."

She laughs. "I know what you mean," she says. "I'd hold my hand up for a high five, but maybe that'd be, y'know, weird."

"Like this isn't?" I ask.

She holds my eyes for — what — a split second? Eternity? One or the other, anyway, and my insides feel like they've been zapped with the same bolt of electricity that burned my hand earlier.

Then in a really soft voice that's almost a whisper, she says, "Yeah, that's the weirdest thing. It's not weird at all."

And I know exactly what she means.

# Erin

He's looking back at me with a loopy grin on his face, and it's as if he sees right inside me. The defenses I've spent years building, honing, strengthening—he leaps across them as though they're flimsy sticks on the ground.

If I stopped to think about it, I might find it creepy or scary. In fact, if I *really* stopped to think about it, the only sensible thing to do would be to completely freak out and run screaming in the opposite direction. Or maybe phone up my therapist from back home and demand an emergency session.

But I don't want to stop and think about it. And I don't want to run away. And I don't want to phone anyone. I just want to stay here, sitting in a walk-in closet, talking to a pale, scruffy but kind of hot guy who is almost definitely a ghost.

What the hell does that say about me?

"You look lost in thought," he says softly.

I smile at him. "I'm just contemplating how to break the news to my parents that I've finally cracked. They'll cart me off to the funny farm once and for all."

He laughs. I like that. I like the way he throws his head back. I like the way it makes his hair flop to the side. I like the way he runs his fingers through it to put it back in place. I even like the fact that he doesn't do it with enough commitment that the hair actually goes back into place.

I guess what I'm saying is I like him.

"Erin! Phoebe! Dinner!"

My mum's voice breaks into the moment, and it is so out of place for a moment that I can't even remember where I am, what I'm doing.

I tear my eyes away from him for two seconds. "Down in a minute!" I call to Mum.

Then I turn back to him. The boy in my closet. He's still there. I'd half expected him to have disappeared in a puff of smoke.

Joe.

I like his name.

He meets my eyes. Holds them for a moment. His gaze is like an anchor. Keeping me here with him. Making me feel safe. I don't think I could leave right now even if I tried.

"So, now what?" I ask, more to break the silence than anything else. It was starting to feel too intense to bear.

"Now what, what?" he asks.

"I mean, do we, how do we . . . ?" My voice trails away, and I can feel my face burning with embarrassment. Is this really where I've come to in my life? My family moves halfway across the country so I can sit in a closet, stuttering and blushing as I barely stop short of asking a ghost out on a date?

"I'd like to see you again, if that's what you mean," he says. "If I can. If it's possible. If you want to."

"I . . ."

It occurs to me for a millisecond that maybe I should play hard to get. I mean, isn't that what girls are meant to do? Isn't that what the cool girls at my old school—Kaylie and Heather and Darcy—would do? They would never show their real feelings about anything, other than expressing laughter and pleasure at making someone else's life a misery.

But then, I spent five years trying to be like them, trying to get them to like me. And how did that work out for me?

Maybe it's time to believe what Mum and Dad have been telling me. That this really is a new beginning. I can start again. I don't need to be the same person I was. Don't need to be afraid to be myself.

Maybe the starting again starts here.

I take a breath, then kind of nod, making an agreement with myself. "Yeah," I say. "I'd like to see you again. That's exactly what I mean."

As a reward, Joe smiles so broadly that it fills his whole face, fills everything. It's as if he's switched on a light in the closet. It's like the sun coming up. His smile is like warmth, like color. It's like a doorway, drawing me into an unfamiliar place that I want to explore, even though it makes me nervous as anything.

"*Erin!*" Mum's voice again.

"I've got to go," I say.

He picks something up from the floor and holds it out to me. "Here, take this," he says.

I look at the leather strap in his hand—the pendant I'd been reaching for before I'd been knocked unconscious. I can see a little silver surfboard dangling from the cord.

"It brought us together," he says by way of an explanation. "It might help us to do it again."

I reach out for it. "Thank you," I whisper.

"See you soon," he says as I take the surfboard necklace from him.

"I hope so," I reply shyly, and turn to leave.

I finally drag myself away and go downstairs to eat dinner and make small talk with my family. But all I'm doing in my head is replaying our conversation, over and over, and hoping I really *will* see him again.

# CHAPTER SEVEN

## Erin

"Favorite season and why."

I think for a moment. "Hmm. Autumn, because: best colors, and it's the only time of year when walking along with your hands in your pockets and scuffing your feet along the ground means you get to kick piles of crunchy leaves in the air. You?"

"Mine is winter, because everyone's tans have worn off, so it's not quite so obvious that I'm the only one who doesn't spend all day worshipping the sun and burning their skin raw."

I laugh. "OK, my turn. Favorite movie and why."

Joe and I are sitting in the window seat, playing our favorite game of Getting to Know You. We've done this pretty much every day for the last couple of weeks. It's become the thing my day revolves around. Go to school, get through the day, hurry home, and sit with Joe for as long as I can before Mum and Dad tell me to stop being a recluse.

"*Memento.* 'Cause it's dark, creepy, and completely blows your mind from start to finish."

"Mine has to be *It's a Wonderful Life,*" I say, then I stop.

"And why?" Joe asks.

I hesitate. Then in a quiet voice, I add, "Because it reminds me that even when you think your life doesn't feel worth living, it matters to someone else."

Joe nods. I reach out for his hand—but I can't take hold of it. We haven't managed to make contact again since that first time. Mostly I don't bother trying. Every now and then I do, but nothing happens.

There's a question preying on my mind. It's about Joe. About him being dead. I've been thinking about it every day, but I don't know how to ask. It's not the kind of thing you can slip into conversation. "Hey, so, favorite color, and oh, by the way, do you happen to know exactly how you died?"

But I think it. A lot. Couple of times I've wondered about going online, doing a bit of investigating to see what I can find out. But it feels wrong and disloyal, looking up personal stuff about him without him knowing. I can't do it.

"Joe, do you ever wonder . . . ?" I begin.

"Wonder what?"

"Why you're . . . how you . . . what happened . . . ?"

"How I died, you mean?"

I laugh. I can't help it. After all my worrying, he just comes out with it. "Yeah," I admit. "That."

Joe shakes his head. "I don't want to know," he says. "I mean, I kind of do. Sometimes. But if I ever think about it, I get this . . . I don't know how to describe it. Like a dark feeling inside me. A blackness. I don't like it. I don't think I want to go there."

"Do you want *me* to? Like, see if I can find anything out?"

He thinks for a moment. "No. I don't think so. What if you look it up and find out something so terrible happened to me that you can't bear to be with me again? Or you can't tell me 'cause it'll upset me, and then you're stuck on your own with knowledge you'd rather not have."

"When you put it like that . . ."

"And what if it breaks the contact?" Joe goes on. "This — whatever it is that's making us able to be with each other — what if as soon as you have the real, concrete facts, it breaks the spell or something?"

That's decided it. "No," I agree. "I'm not taking the risk. I couldn't bear any of those things to happen."

"I don't want to know," Joe says again. "I don't need to know."

"Me neither. I'm happy with what we've got. I don't want anything to change it."

Joe smiles, his face relaxing as he does.

"Plus . . ." he begins, but doesn't carry on.

"Plus what?"

He shakes his head and sighs. "I dunno. I guess if you look it up and read the facts in black and white, there's no going back."

"And if I don't, we can tell ourselves that maybe this isn't as impossible as it feels, and one day we can hang out like any normal boy and girl?"

Joe smiles. "Exactly."

I smile back. I love that I get him, that he gets me. And yeah, I love that he feels the same way I do, holds out a hope that perhaps one day we can figure out a way to be together for real—even if I was too shy to actually put it like that out loud.

"Erin! Dinner!" Mum's voice bursts incongruously into the room from downstairs.

I get up from the window seat. "I'd better go."

"See you later," Joe says. "I'm not going anywhere."

I head downstairs to join the others, only half with them. The other half is playing my conversation with Joe over and over on a loop in my head.

"Someone's a bit happier." Dad nudges me.

I look up. "What?"

"Leave her alone," Mum urges gently.

"I'm just saying—it's nice. It's good to see you smiling a bit more often, that's all."

I look at them both, and at Phoebe wolfing her dinner down. The content little family unit. I can't help wondering if they'd be quite so welcoming of my happy state if they knew what was causing it.

No point wondering, since they're never going to find out.

"Thanks, Dad," I say as I get back to my dinner and do my best to join in the casual chat while, on the inside, all I'm really doing is counting the minutes till I can be with Joe again.

# Joe

"OK, are you ready for this one?" I ask.

Erin laughs. "How do I know if I'm ready till I know what it is?"

She's right. She can't know. And she probably *isn't* ready. But we've been talking like this for over two weeks now, and I want to get deeper. I want to know what it is that's behind her eyes—the darkness I know I've glimpsed but that is always hidden by a veil she won't lift.

"Try me," she says.

"OK." I hesitate for a second, then jump in. "Worst memory."

Erin stops laughing. She stares at me.

"Sorry," I say quickly. "You don't have to. I was just—"

"No," she stops me. "I want to."

She looks at her hands in her lap for a minute or two,

then raises her head and nods at me. "It's hard to pick one specific thing," she begins. "A precise moment that I can point to and say, 'Yes, that was it. That was the worst bit.' It would be like watching a landslide and having to choose which rock was responsible. You know?"

"Yeah, I do."

"I had an accident when I was eleven, and I missed the first half term of secondary school," she goes on. She's looking away from me. Her voice has changed; it's as if she's describing a distant scene that is nothing to do with her. "I wasn't there when everyone was forming their groups of friends. That all happened without me."

"That must have been tough."

"Yeah. But not as tough as the five years that followed. I never found my footing, and it threw me so badly. I got really anxious. I stopped going out or talking to people or anything."

Her words hit a nerve for me. I've always found it hard to make friends, too. Growing up in the shadow of a big brother who has everything—looks, talent, physique, surfing medals—it's easy to feel you're not worth anything much.

"Go on," I say.

"I was hit by a car—got knocked over and busted my leg pretty badly. It took weeks to heal. By the time I started secondary school, there were no openings for best friend still available."

"Harsh."

"Yeah. But it wasn't just that. The accident did more damage than just to my leg."

"How d'you mean?"

She hesitates, looks away. Then she quickly nods, as if making up her mind to tell me. "It started off as a fear of streets. I couldn't cross a street on my own. Then it was sidewalks. Then, basically, anywhere that people were walking or cars moving. I just got anxious the whole time. Within a few months, it had completely taken over. I'd never felt anxiety before—but after the accident, I felt it more and more. It was more crippling than my shattered kneecap."

"Erin, that sounds awful."

She goes on, talking quickly, breathlessly. "Afterward I had to go to the hospital a lot for checkups. One of the nurses was lovely. I could talk to her, you know?"

I nod.

"I told her how sometimes I would get so anxious that I found it hard to catch my breath. My chest would pound so hard and so fast, I actually thought I was having a heart attack. She told me it was a panic attack. She showed me a technique that worked."

"Paper bag?" I ask.

Erin looks at me, her jaw open.

I shrug. "I've done it, too. Every time Olly had his mates over—especially when there were girls there."

Erin half smiles and carries on. "There was a gang of girls who liked picking on anyone who showed weakness. Made them feel cool."

"Oh, I know the type."

"They could see what I was like. Shy. Quiet. Nervous. I tried to hide it, but my anxiety got so bad, I sometimes found it hard to speak. Coupled with the fact that I didn't really have proper friends to hang out with, I ended up not even trying most of the time. So they started with the names."

"God, why are kids so cruel?" I ask.

She shakes her head, looking down at her lap. "I wish I knew. It was just stupid names at first. 'Car Crash Katy' was one. Then when they saw how upset I got, it was 'Panic Alec.' And when I wouldn't respond, they started calling me 'Silent Movie.' Then one of them hit on 'Silent But Deadly.' They liked that one. It lasted a good few months. Then one day, I was going into school, and they were walking along behind me, humming a tune. I didn't know what it was at first, then I realized. It was 'The Sound of Silence,' and I just wanted to crawl away and hide."

She looks up at me. "Does this all sound really stupid?"

"No. It doesn't sound stupid at all. It sounds awful. I hate the fact that this happened to you."

"It sounds stupid to me. They were such small things, silly things, and yet it was as if they were like sticking little pins into me, needling me, getting under my skin. So subtle you could hardly say anything. It was the power of their actions, I think. They had this control over me. I had none."

"I get it. I know what you mean."

"Then one day, they found me in the bathroom, breathing into a paper bag. They took it off me. It wasn't too bad at first; they just laughed at me. Then one of them hit on a name. 'Bag Lady.' It stuck. From that point on, all the way through school, that was my name."

"Oh God, that's awful." I want to reach out to her, I want to touch her hand so badly. I know I can't, so I just look into her sad eyes and listen as she continues.

"They ratcheted it up, bit by bit. First it was the name. Then they made up songs and phrases. 'Bag Lady Gaga,' 'The Bag Lady and the Tramp.' The more ridiculous, the better, since it gave them more opportunities to laugh at me. I came to dread their laughter. I heard it in my sleep. It was the sound track to my anxiety."

She pauses, and I wait for her to go on. Then she takes a deep breath, lets it out slowly, and continues. "Eventually, they got bored of just words and songs, and they moved on to coming up with creative ideas for what I could do with the bag. Every day, there was a new suggestion. Then one day, one of them, Kaylie, started waving a plastic bag around. 'Here's a new bag for you, Bag Lady,' she said. I can see her now, waving the bag in the air, laughing—I can still *hear* the laughter."

I feel as though I know what she's about to say. I pray I'm wrong.

"Then another one, Heather, suggested that I put it on my head and tie it tight."

No! I can't bear it. The thought of them saying that to her. "They knew what they were saying?" I ask.

"Oh, yes. And in case *I* didn't, they spelled it out more and more clearly every day. In the end, they were practically telling me to off myself. Telling me no one cared about me."

"Did you tell anyone? Your parents?"

Erin shakes her head. "I was ashamed. And scared, I suppose. Mum had lost her job when I was recovering from the accident because she took so much time off to look after me. I'd already done enough to ruin their lives. I didn't want to bother them. I kept telling myself that it was my fault for being so weak and that if I could just learn to shrug them off, they'd go away and stop bothering me."

"But you *couldn't* shrug them off."

"No. And they didn't leave me alone. I walked into class one day, opened my desk, and inside was a plastic bag with a piece of string and a note. In capital letters, it said: 'SPECIAL DELIVERY FOR ERIN MATTHEWS. PLACE HEAD INSIDE BAG. ATTACH STRING. TIGHTEN. DO US ALL A FAVOR.' I looked at it for a second. Then I shut my desk and looked around the room. I thought—I should tell the teacher. I should show it to her now. Right now. I could put my hand up, call her over, tell her."

"And did you?"

Erin shakes her head. "I couldn't. I didn't dare. We all know that if you tell the teachers on a bully, you get bullied even more. They just go underground for a bit, and then come back harder and harsher. But more than that, it was the shame of it. What if they were right? What if everyone *did* want me to do it? It was the words at the end that hit me the hardest. *Do us all a favor.* They spun around and around in my head for days. I couldn't stop thinking about them. The more I thought about them, the more sense they made."

My hands are in front of my face. As if I can hide from what's coming. As if I can shield myself from what I know she's about to say.

"And so I did it. I tried. Not with a bag. That seemed too complicated. I took the coward's way. I used to get quite bad pains with my leg. Still do sometimes. The hospital prescribed strong painkillers, which I barely ever took — so I had a load of them at home. One evening, no one else was at home, and I stood looking at the bottle for about an hour. It felt like an escape. I wanted to be gone." Her words gulp out through a sob.

"I emptied the contents of the bottle into my hand and took them in one go," she says quietly. "Didn't even count them. I didn't want to hesitate long enough to do that. I just wanted it over."

I think my heart is going to break. Without stopping to

question whether it'll work or not, I reach out to stroke her arm. My fingers make contact! I can feel her skin.

Erin looks up at me. "Joe, I can feel you," she whispers.

I hold her eyes. "Never let anyone do that to you again, you hear me?" My voice is choked. I can barely get the words out.

"I won't," she replies softly.

She closes a hand over mine. For a moment, the touch of her warm fingers makes me forget the reality of our situation. I don't care about any of it. I just care about her.

"You promise?" I ask.

She nods. "I promise."

We sit there together, skin against skin, eyes locked on eyes, until the contact finally fades and, once again, my hands reach out for nothing but air.


# Erin

Everything has changed. And everyone has noticed. Dad comments on the number of times I'm smiling. Mum stops giving me those sympathetic/sad little sideways looks that she thinks I don't notice. Phoebe doesn't make me want to scream with frustration at her constant chatter about all her new friends.

Even school is different. OK, maybe it's not different. The teachers are still teaching; the other students still don't take all that much notice of me. Thing is, I don't care so much. Or at all. I don't care about any of it.

Because it's not that everything around me has changed; it's that *I've* changed. He's changed me. This—whatever it is—this *thing* going on between us, it turns everything else into a blurry backdrop that I barely notice.

Meeting up with Joe, talking to him, sharing thoughts, ideas, jokes, stories—that's what's real. The rest is just what I have to put up with in between the times we're together.

It's a couple of days after we had that big conversation, and I'm hurrying home and heading straight for my room as usual.

"Nice day, darling?" Mum calls after me.

"Yep, great, thanks," I reply over my shoulder as I make my way up the stairs.

Joe is waiting for me in the window seat. Every time I see him, my tummy does a little skip out of relief that he's still here. I'm wearing the necklace he gave me under my clothes so no one can see it. Only Joe and I know it's there. I still don't know if it's got anything to do with why I can see him, but I'm not going to take it off just in case. I'm not willing to take the risk.

"Good day?" I ask, squeezing onto the opposite end of the window seat and pulling my knees up. We're like bookends.

"Busy," he replies.

I raise an eyebrow. "Oh, yes?"

Joe puts on a serious face. "Yup. I had a hectic morning of sitting around not doing very much. Then this afternoon I did a bit of mooching around, squeezed in a spot of loafing around, achieving exactly zilch, and topped it off with an hour or two of pacing the floor, waiting for you to come home."

He looks me right in the eye when he says the last bit, and my heart does that thing where it throws in a couple of extra beats.

"Sounds hectic," I reply. "You must be due a rest about now."

Joe pretends to look at a watch on his wrist. "Hmm, you're right. I'd better get going. Can't sit around doing nothing all day now, can I?"

I know he's joking, but I can't help thinking how awful it must be for him. Not only that he's stuck here with nothing to do, but that he's on his own for most of the time, too. Not to mention the worst part of it all: the fact that he's dead. He still can't remember anything about how he died, or much about his life, either.

Every day feels like borrowed time, and every conversation could be our last. And while I know that there's nothing I can do to change it, I can't help hoping that maybe there's something we've missed. That perhaps he isn't completely dead. I have this fantasy where the "real" Joe is lying in a bed in a hospital somewhere in a coma. Everyone thinks he's dead; the doctors are about to turn off the machines, but something to do with this, with us—stops them. That maybe the way he feels about me, the times we spend together, they—I don't know—wake him up or something. And then he comes back to life properly, comes and finds me, and we can be together in real life.

All of which is another good reason not to go looking things up online. The last thing I want to see is confirmation that my fantasy has absolutely zero chance of ever coming true.

"Any more come back to you today?" I ask instead.

"Actually, yes," he says, getting up from the window seat. "I've been thinking about something I used to do. Thought I might share it with you."

He reaches for my hand. I try to take hold of his. We haven't really figured out how to make contact every time. Sometimes it works; other times it's as impossible as trying to get hold of a puff of smoke. Sometimes, I go right through his skin, and it burns him and scares the life out of me.

I have a theory: it seems that the higher the stakes are emotionally, the more physical Joe becomes. If things are really intense between us, or if one of us is feeling really strongly about something, that's when he seems to get more real. Like the other day when I was really upset, we managed to touch, but in the middle of an average conversation, it won't happen.

We give up after a few attempts. I try not to show him how disappointed I am as I jump down from the window seat and join him.

"I want to show you something," he says, heading for the closet and indicating for me to join him. "Bring a flashlight," he adds as an afterthought.

I grab my phone from my bag, flick the flashlight app on, and follow Joe into the closet.

We crawl to the far end together, and Joe kneels down. I sit cross-legged in front of him.

"We've shared a lot over this last couple of weeks, haven't we?" he begins.

"Uh-huh."

"But there's one thing we haven't mentioned. We haven't talked about what you saw in here."

"The necklace?" I ask.

He pauses. "The other thing."

He means the poem. He's right. I hadn't mentioned it since I didn't know if he realized I'd actually read the words. And I didn't want to embarrass him. I mean, before meeting him, it was just random words on a wall. Now that I know him, it feels as if I've been reading his diary — and I know how crappy it feels when someone reads your diary.

So I didn't want to tell him I'd seen it. But at the same time, I've been feeling just as uncomfortable keeping it from him.

"It's fine," he says, reading my mind.

"You saw me?"

"Yup," he says, and my heart melts for him.

"I didn't mean to pry, I just—"

"It's cool. Really." He reaches out with his hand, places a finger on my lips. This time, his finger makes contact with my skin. Makes my face buzz and burn. Makes my body heat up. A second later the moment has passed, and I can't feel him at all.

*Did I imagine it?*

I ask myself that question about fifty times a day. Am I making up the whole thing? I'm still not totally convinced all this isn't a figment of my imagination. A great way of avoiding the outside world. And that thought scares me. What if I'm growing more and more detached from reality? What if I actually am going properly insane?

"There are more." Joe breaks into my thoughts, thank goodness. I didn't like where they were heading.

I shine the light and look around. I can't see any more writing. "More poetry? Where? I can't see it."

"See, that's what I remembered. I used to write all the time. But I had to be on my own. Mostly, I'd write in my room, sitting in our window seat."

I can't help a small smile at that. He called it *our* window seat. I've never had somewhere that's been "our place" with someone before.

"Sometimes, when I *really* had to get away from everyone, I'd go to this place out along the coast path," Joe goes on. "There are some rocks and a little shelter. I remember it. I used to sit in there and write. I called it my poetry cave."

"Why are you bringing me back in here, then?" I ask.

"This was my other writing cave. The one when I didn't feel like scrambling along a coast path and down slippery rocks. This closet was my stay-at-home writing cave."

I laugh.

"I remember what I used to do. I'd write on the walls, then cover it up, in case anyone else came in."

He crawls farther inside the closet. "Shine your light there."

I shine the light right into the back part of the closet, where the stairs above make ledges in the ceiling. He's right. There's a sheet of wallpaper stuck down at the top, but the bottom half of it is unattached.

"It's under that," Joe says. "I can't remember what I wrote, but I remember writing something."

"How come you haven't looked while I was at school?" I ask, then mentally kick myself. I'm guessing he wouldn't have been able to take hold of the paper.

"Believe me, I've tried."

"Sorry," I mumble.

"Hey. It's OK. Honestly."

He turns back to me, a twinkle in his eye. He's trying to look calm about it, but he must be nervous, too. I would be. Showing me something he's written when he can't even remember what it is? I'm hoping that means he trusts me.

"So," he says. "Want to see what I wrote, back when I was alive?"

I look at him, realizing that not only is it a chance for me to find out more about him, but it's his chance to as well. "If you're sure," I say carefully.

He grins. "Not remotely. But let's do it."

## JOE

It's a bit of a gamble, this. A catch-22, or whatever you call it. Is it ironic? Maybe.

On the one hand, now that I've remembered I used to write poems in here and how I used to hide them, I'm desperate to see what's in here. I feel like it holds some kind of key for me. A key to myself, even. I mean, all this time, I've been completely lost. The first thing I remember at all was the daffodils and blossoms, so I figure I must have died early in the year. It's October now. And I've been in here the whole time. Stuck in this room, which is mine and not mine. Held prisoner in the house that is like an outer skin to me, but lost and cut off from everything else I ever knew.

And mostly lost from myself. I don't know who I am.

I've been avoiding thinking about the past, but maybe it's time. I need to find out who I was, and maybe what got me here. And this may give me a clue. Which is a good thing, even if it's also a bit terrifying.

Plus, the only way I can get to see it is with Erin's help, since I still haven't figured out how to do incredibly hard and sophisticated things like lift up a sheet of paper whenever I want to. But I've got to say, I'm hesitant about letting her see the inner workings of my mind. Not when I don't even know what's in there myself.

"OK, I'm all set with the flashlight," Erin's saying. "You ready?"

I don't even answer her question. I don't know how to. Of course I'm not ready. But I need to do it. "Shine the light on the first ledge," I say.

Erin shines her light onto the lowest ledge. There's a flimsy piece of wallpaper hanging from the top of it, flapping down, unattached at the bottom. My insides flip over. Last chance to duck out.

I need to see it. Need to know who I was.

"That's it," I say, pointing at the wallpaper. "Under there."

Erin lifts the flap, shines her light on the ledge below it, and exposes my words to the light, to me, to her. I hold my breath.

SOMETIMES I FEEL I'M IN A FILM,
WEAR A FIXED SMILE WALKING HOME.
I SWALLOW EACH DAY LIKE A PILL
UNTIL I CAN BE ON MY OWN.

YESTERDAY I RAN TO THE CLIFFS,
STARED INTO THE ROARING DEPTHS,
BEGGED FOR SOMEONE TO LISTEN—
THE WIND THREW MY TEARS OFF THE EDGE.

I JUST WANT SOMEONE TO SEE ME.
THE GIRLS, THEY DON'T WANT TO KNOW.
I OPEN, I CLOSE, THE SAME PHRASE REPEATS:
YOU'RE JUST LIKE A BROTHER TO ME, JOE.

SOMETIMES I THINK I'M DOING OK,
THEN A VOICE DEEP INSIDE ME SAYS,
DUDE, WHY EVEN BOTHER WRITING THESE LINES?
WHO THE HELL ARE YOU TRYING TO IMPRESS?

## Erin

He's waiting for me to say something. Problem is, right now my mouth is as dry as the last undiscovered desert, with the added complication of having a tongue stuck to the inside of it.

His poem doesn't just make me want to cry till my eyes are empty. His poem is me. His words feel like the other half to mine.

How do I tell him all that without freaking him out?

I tear my eyes away from his words and look at his face.

"You hate it, don't you?" he says nervously.

I can't stop myself from bursting out laughing. He couldn't have said anything that was further from the truth. He flinches as if he's been stung in his face.

"Don't laugh at me, Erin," he says softly. "Please."

I stare at him. "Joe," I whisper. "How could you think I would laugh at you?" I point at his poem. "At this?"

"I—I don't . . ." His voice trails off.

"Joe, it's amazing," I say, wishing my words weren't so insignificant. "It's everything I feel, everything I've always felt. I want more of it."

*I want more of you,* I add silently.

Joe's face transforms. His eyes glimmer as if a light is shining out through them. "Really?"

I laugh again—more confidently this time. "Really," I assure him. "I love it."

As I say the word *love,* something flips inside me. I keep wanting to use the word, whenever I'm with him. "I *love* being with you." "I *love* the poem." "I *love* the time we spend together." It's as if the word is waiting in the wings of the stage where we're together—looking for any chance to step in and show itself. An actor trying to steal the limelight and take over the show.

But it's too soon. It's *way* too soon. And too crazy, and too . . .

It's just not possible. However much I might wish otherwise.

Plus, he's looking at me now with a strange expression on his face. Just staring. Not saying anything. I shouldn't have used that word. So obvious. So over the top. Typical girl, getting overemotional about a guy she's known a matter of weeks. A dead guy she's known a matter of weeks.

What a loser.

Can he see inside my mind? Does he read my thoughts? How much access to my life does he have?

His stare is making me feel too exposed, and I turn away.

Joe reaches out for my arm. This time, he makes contact.

I look down at his hand on my arm and don't move a muscle in case the contact breaks.

"Don't go," he says. His voice is husky and dark. Rough like the stubble on his face, like his messy hair, like all of him. The rawness of it makes me want to smooth everything down, soothe him, take his pain away.

I turn to face him. His hand still on my arm, his eyes locked on mine, he reaches out with his other hand. Touches my face softly with the palm of his hand. I tilt my face to meet his skin. My cheek against his palm.

I think I'm going to pass out. I have never been touched like this.

I've held hands in the back row at the movies with Timothy Bolton, the one boy who gave me the time of day. And I only did that so I could have something to say to the girls who bragged about how far their boyfriends wanted to go with them and how they were making them wait. The girls never asked me, anyway. Even if they had, I only wanted to talk about it to prove I was likable, fanciable, attractive to someone. To kid myself that I could fit in.

But this. This isn't the same. This is something I have never known. This is about a moment when time has stopped. When my heart has stopped. When the whole world has stopped moving and, instead, has been sucked into the moment, here, now, when nothing else matters or exists.

I am falling.

And in that moment, it's as if the truth of this whole situation is suddenly revealed. This isn't a relationship. It isn't real. It isn't *life*.

It's dangerous. It's like the top of a ride—those rides I always hated but went on anyway. Always trying to be part of the gang, show how I could do it, too. But I couldn't, not without putting myself through all that fear.

The fear, that's the thing I can't deal with. The anxiety, the nights it took me over, threatened to engulf me, drown me, tear me apart. And then it nearly did.

I told myself I would never care again. Never need anyone, want anything from anyone. I ran away from needing
people. Ran away from pain. Ran from all of them, from
everything. From their words, their gossip, their laughter.
The laughter followed me all the way to the edge of a cliff.

I'm not going there again. I refuse to let someone in if
it means opening myself up to need, to fear and anxiety. I
won't. I can't.

And that's when I realize the horrible truth, the truth I
wish I didn't have to face but I know I can't escape.

I can't go back there. I can't be here. I can't do this. I
can't afford to show my hand. Can't go to the edge of the
cliff.

How can I let myself fall when there is no feasible way
that Joe could ever catch me?

# CHAPTER EIGHT

## JOE

I don't know how long the moment lasts.

I don't know much nowadays. I've woken from a deep sleep only to watch my family move out of my house. I've called out to my brother as he looked through me and said good-bye to an empty room. I've watched a new family move in. I've fought to release myself from the trap of these four walls. And I've made contact with a girl who moved into my room and into my heart in equal measure.

But this—this throws me more than any of those things. The look in her eyes. The feel of her skin, her soft, warm skin, on my hand. The electrifying bridge of unspoken words between us.

Where can we go from here? Only closer together, surely.

The wanting makes me hope. *Can* we get closer? Can we overcome this gulf? Does it *have* to be like this? I ask myself every day: Am I definitely gone for good, or could she literally bring me back from the dead? I'm sure I'm just making up stories to get through the day. Myths. Fables. Crazy dreams.

But everything else about this situation is crazy, so why not? *Why not?*

I'm watching her mouth. Her lips are moving. She's speaking. The need in my chest is so intense, it's reached my ears and is blocking out sound.

Her lips. I want to kiss them.

I lean forward, just a tiny bit. Imperceptible.

In that moment, sound gets through. She's speaking.

"I have to go," she says.

I jump back as if she had struck me.

"I — sorry," I say. "I thought — I — sorry."

I pull my hands away. They fall by my sides, limp and stupid. Like me.

"No. It's not you," she says.

I laugh drily. "It's not you, it's me?" I ask bitterly.

Another unwanted memory crashes into my mind. Or memories, I should say. The girls at school. The ones I liked, the ones who saw me as their safe best friend. Liked me as a brother. Or liked me *for* my brother, I should say. Wormed their way into my life, thinking it was a shortcut to Olly's inner circle. How many times did I fall for it? And then, when I was getting close to them, getting to like them, maybe trying to kiss them, that was the moment I found out the truth. It was Olly they were after. It was always Olly.

*"It's not you, Joe. You're perfect. It's me. You'll make someone a wonderful boyfriend one day. I wish I felt differently so it could be me."*

The feeling is so familiar, it's like an old bruise.

Erin takes my hand. Her hand, warm in mine. Her touch is like a first sight of land to a drowning man. I am drowning. But is she my lifesaving shoreline or the mirage that just makes my dying hopes even more painful?

"I'm sorry," she's saying, answering my question. It was a mirage after all. "I just—I don't know if I can do this."

As my hopes crash and burn, her touch disappears. I can't feel her hand anymore. My skin is ice. My heart is, too.

"It's fine," I say coldly.

"Joe, it's really not your fault." Her voice is like a thin wire slicing through me. "It's—"

"Please, Erin, just go."

I turn away from her. I don't want her to see my pain. And I haven't got it in me to put on a brave face while she tells me I'm like a brother to her, or a best friend. I got it wrong again. More wrong than I've ever gotten anything.

I don't turn back around. I need something to focus on. Numbers. I'll count them. Just keep counting in my head. Feels like an old childhood game of hide-and-seek. How many times did I hide in this closet?

*One, two, three . . .*

Run. Go.

*Eight, nine, ten . . .*

I hear her move away. Her footsteps, one by one, walking away from me.

*Seventeen, eighteen, nineteen . . .*

I hear her walk across her bedroom. I hear her sniff. I close myself off to the sound of her. I hear her open the door. Close it. Leave me here. On my own again. Safe, alone, just how I like it.

*Twenty. Coming, ready or not.*

She's gone.

I turn to face my demons, my prison, the room that feels empty for the first time in weeks.

# Erin

I barely even know what just happened there. One minute, we were the closest we've ever been. Then I freaked out. I mean, I know it was me. But still, a tiny part of me wanted him to save me. Instead he sent me away. I guess that proves I was right. He *can't* save me. No one can. I've only got myself.

I feel as if he's taken away my oxygen. How can it feel like this? I've known him less than a month. How can he have wormed his way into my—my what? My heart? How *can* he? And then send me away when I need him the most?

Fury courses through me as I pace the landing. Not just at him—at everything, at *them* for making me live my life under the cloud of what they did to me. Fury at myself for thinking I could move on without looking back. You can't do that. It's not possible. It's like constructing a skyscraper and taking away each floor as you build the one above it. Not possible. The whole thing would collapse. Implode. Like I'm doing now.

I can't go back in there, not for him to look at me with steel in his eyes and tell me to leave. I don't want to see that again.

So instead, I do the thing my old therapist told me and try to settle my breathing. Deep breaths into my stomach. Count to ten. Feel my heart rate settle.

Then I go and join my parents downstairs.

"Hey there, sweet pea," Dad says. He's sitting on one of the sofas, with Phoebe at the other end. She's got her legs curled up under her and is staring at her phone. Texting one of her new friends, as usual. "Are you gracing us with your company for once?"

I ignore both the childish greeting and the sarcasm.

Mum gives Dad a *Don't!* look and puts her arm out for me. "Come and join me. I'm lonely over here," she says. "I'll get dinner on in a minute."

I plonk myself down on the sofa next to Mum and

snuggle into her arm, my head on her shoulder. Then I spend the next couple of hours eating dinner and staring blankly at the television with the rest of them, trying to make my thoughts equally blank.

Sometime later, I realize I'm drifting off, but I don't want to go to bed. Don't want to go back in my bedroom at all. Phoebe went up ages ago, and Dad's in the bath. It's just me and Mum down here now. It's nearly eleven o'clock, and I need to go to bed. School night and all that.

Mum gets up from the sofa and switches the TV off. She catches my eye as she turns away from the television. She comes back to the sofa and sits next to me. "You haven't said much this evening."

I shrug.

"You've been a lot happier lately. But you seem a little low tonight. Are you OK, love?"

It's not her usual "Nice day?" that she asks every day in the middle of doing five other things. It's a proper question. I guess it deserves a proper answer.

But what can I say? I can't say *anything*. To her or anyone. After everything I put them through, after being in such a state that they packed up our lives and moved the whole family five hundred miles away to start a new life, the last thing I can land on Mum is the truth. How would I even begin?

*Well, I've just had my first argument with the dead guy who lives in my bedroom. But don't worry—I'll be fine.*

I'll never be able to talk to anyone about him.

The thought slams into my mind so hard it's like a car crash. But then I've never felt able to really share things before, so why should this be different?

"Honey?" Mum is still looking at me.

"Sorry, Mum," I say eventually. "I'm just tired." I pull myself up from the sofa.

She gets up, too. "Come here," she says, pulling me in for a hug.

I let her hold me. Let myself take at least a bit of comfort from her. When she pulls away, she holds my arms. "You can always talk to me, you know," she says. "About anything."

I force myself not to laugh in her face. For one thing, I don't want to hurt her feelings. For another, I think the laughter would turn to tears in about a millisecond. Instead I settle for a mumbled "I know, Mum, thanks" and go off upstairs.

My heart speeds up as I push my bedroom door open. I look around. He's not here. Has he gone, or is he just invisible to me, like when I first moved in? Will I ever see him again?

I don't know the answers to any of the questions that swirl through my mind as I get ready for bed.

But in the moment before I fall asleep, or maybe it's in

my dream—I don't know, and at that point I don't *want* to know—I hear a voice. Soft, barely audible, yet so close it feels like it is being whispered against my ear.

*I'm sorry.*

A moment later, I have drifted into a deep, troubled sleep.

# JOE

They say a night is like a lifetime when you're dead.

Actually, they don't. No one says that. But only because they don't know how true it is. I do, though.

I'm not going to wake her. I don't even know if I could. When she came back to her room last night, she couldn't see me. We've gotten used to an awkward routine where I turn around whenever she's getting changed, and where we put up with all the things we can and can't do. But this— I don't know. Is it deliberate? Maybe she's turned herself against me so much that she won't see me again. Switched something off. Broken the contact.

The thought is unbearable.

Did she hear me apologize before she fell asleep? Will I ever speak to her again? Will she see me again?

I sit by her bed all night, asking myself the same questions, over and over again.

The deepening, darkening night offers no reply.

Eventually, I curl up on the floor and drift into a troubled, stuttering kind of rest myself. A light, unsatisfying slumber that only the dead can sleep.


# Erin


Thursday morning. Mum is at the door. "Darling, did you hear me?"

I drag my head from my pillow. "Whuh?" I ask.

"I've called you three times now. You're going to be late for school."

I glance at my alarm clock. She's right. I've got twenty minutes to get myself up, showered, breakfasted, and out the door. Yikes.

"OK, I'm getting up," I say, sitting up in bed. "I'll be down in a minute."

Mum's still in the doorway.

"What?" I ask.

She's looking at me with this expression on her face. Like she wants to tell me off but she's forcing herself not to. She never does, not anymore. Sometimes I wish she would. It's funny. Most girls my age would give anything for parents who never tell them off.

But then I guess most girls my age haven't sunk to such dark places in their lives that their parents are terrified of doing anything to tip them over the edge.

Their refusal to treat me like any other irresponsible teenager just reminds me of everything I've gone through. The heartache, the pain, the fear, the anxiety—the extremes that I've been to.

I don't want to be reminded. I want to forget. I don't want special treatment; I want my mum to treat me like a normal sixteen-year-old girl. I want to *be* a normal sixteen-year-old girl.

Fat chance of that when I spend every waking minute I can talking to a ghost.

Or did, anyway.

My irritation with Mum mingles with my regret about what happened last night with Joe, and for a moment all I want to do is lie back down and pull the comforter over my head. I feel numb. I want to sleep the day away. Maybe if I decide not to deal with today, I can wake up tomorrow instead and it will all be different.

"Come on, love," Mum says softly. "I'll get you some breakfast."

"Thanks," I mumble as I pull the comforter off and swing my legs out of bed.

"Dad'll run you both to school. That'll give you an extra ten minutes."

"OK. Thanks."

Eventually, Mum closes the door and leaves me alone. And I *am* alone. I still can't see Joe. Have I blocked him out, or has he left?

I sit on the side of the bed for a minute, gathering my thoughts. The main one that keeps circling is that no matter how much I might not want to do it, I have to break out of this thing and get on with my life. Whatever's been going on here is crazy—and I can't afford to do crazy.

As I get ready for school, I'm filled with a new sense of determination. I owe it to my family, if nothing else. They gave up their lives to move here, too. It's time I made an effort to get this fresh start under way.

By the time Dad drops us off at the school gates, I have convinced myself I can do it. I'm filled with optimism. "Today is the first day of the rest of your life," and all those other clichés that grace Mum's dish towels and fridge magnets.

But it's true. It is. I'm ready to leave behind *everything* that's held me back and start moving forward at last.

My new optimism lasts approximately thirty seconds— and half the length of the school yard—before something happens that wipes out thoughts of a fresh start so thoroughly, they might as well have been specks of dust blown into nothingness by a sudden breeze.

When I say *something happens,* what I mean more precisely is that for a moment, I forget everything I have taught myself about surviving school and shout the most ridiculous thing across the yard, so loud that everyone in the yard turns around to stare at me.

Then I completely freeze—cannot speak, cannot move,

have no idea what to do next, and wish more than anything in the entire world that it actually was possible for the ground to open up and swallow me whole.

This was not exactly what I had in mind by fresh start.

## *Olly*

Tod throws the tennis ball to me as we cross the school yard. I bounce it a couple of times before throwing it back to him. We carry on like this as we cross the yard. *Throw, catch, bounce, bounce, throw, catch, bounce.*

I'm not even thinking about it. Just throwing, catching, bouncing as I make my way into school with a brain that feels as empty as the inside of the ball. Autopilot. My usual state.

Maybe that's why it catches me off guard. I don't know. Whatever. We're crossing the yard and I'm half looking ahead of me and half looking out for the ball to my right when I hear it.

"*Joe!*"

It's weird. I sort of feel my body freeze, and my brain go with it. Freeze right over inside my head. Like each brain cell goes cold and switches off, one by one. *Dunk, dunk, dunk,* frozen. Dead.

Then the ball hits my shoulder and breaks the spell.

"Sorry, dude," Tod calls over.

I barely notice the feeling in my shoulder where the ball's hit me. I don't really notice anything much except that word. That name. No one has said his name out loud for months, let alone yelled it across the school yard. They've all been so careful. Funny, really; we moved to get away from all the sadness and pain, but you can't really get away from it. It's still there at school. It's still there everywhere.

I wave a *Don't worry about it* hand at Tod and turn in the direction of the voice.

A girl I've never noticed before is staring at me as if . . .

Yeah, yeah, OK. Sounds pathetic, I know. Clichéd and all that. But still, it's true, and I can't find a better way of putting it right now.

She's looking at me as if she's seen a ghost.

Her face is pale, but it looks like it's probably that way anyway. She doesn't look like the kind of girl who spends time in the sun, getting the perfect tan. She's wearing jeans with holes in the knees and a big, baggy blue sweater that my grandma might wear. A cream beanie hat pulling her hair back.

I register all this in the two seconds before anyone speaks. In the third second, I remember that I used to look at girls a lot. They looked at me, too. Then I remember that the fourth second would usually involve a smile, maybe some cheesy line from me, and a blush from her. By the tenth or eleventh second, we'd already know if we were likely to go on a date.

That was a long time ago. Back in the life I used to have. Back when I had a life.

Now we're about ten seconds in, and still neither of us has moved or spoken.

As our eyes lock, her expression changes. Goes from—I don't know—maybe excitement or hope or something like that to what I could only describe as complete and utter panic.

For a moment, it's as if there is only the girl and me in the yard. Like everything else melts or blurs or fades to gray, leaving just her and me, frozen and staring at each other.

"Oh, my God, I'm . . ." she begins. Then she claps a hand over her mouth.

I just keep staring at her. It's like—it's like I've got this wall inside me. Like I've spent a while building it. Six months. Since the worst thing happened. Since I did the worst thing.

And then she's come along in a speeding car and driven right into the wall.

"I'm so sorry," the girl is saying. "I thought you were someone else. Sorry."

I have no idea what to say. I used to be able to talk to girls so easily. Some said *too* easily. I have no words now.

The girl is turning, hurrying away, apologizing again as she goes.

Tod is by my side. "Did you hear me?" he asks with a goofy smile.

I shake myself out of whatever state the girl has gotten me into. I don't turn to Tod, though. I'm watching her back as she runs into school. "Sorry, no," I reply to Tod without looking at him. "What?"

Tod gives me a knowing nudge. "Just that she doesn't look like your type," he says.

The girl has gone inside. I turn to Tod. "What d'you mean?"

He nods his head toward the door into school. "Come on, I know you're out of practice, but she's not exactly in your league, mate," he says.

If it wasn't for the fact that I can barely believe I heard him right, I'd go mental at him for saying something like that.

I settle for giving him a death stare.

"What?" Tod looks genuinely bemused, and it occurs to me that that's probably how we normally talk about girls. Or used to. Did we?

It's only then that I realize I have come so far from myself that I no longer know who I am.

I start walking away without replying.

Tod's at my heels. "Dude, what is it?"

"Just leave me alone, Tod," I say through gritted teeth. I shove my hands in my pockets, fists tight and cold.

Tod hangs back as I march toward the same door the girl used into school.

It takes every bit of self-control I have to stop myself from kicking the door open so hard that the glass splinters into a thousand pieces.

## Erin

It's as if none of it happened. We never moved. I never started a new life. Never met someone who made me feel I was worth something.

One word. That's all it took. One stupid word.

*Joe.*

It's the word in my head all the time. The person in my head all the time. Anything I do, it's him I want to talk to about it. All the little things that happen in my day — they don't add up to anything until I share them with him and watch him smile and laugh as I tell him the most inane anecdotes from my day.

And look where it's led me. First, I freak out, he disappears, and I don't know if I'll ever see him again. Then I shout his name across the school yard to some random guy I've never met before, and everyone turns to look at me. The thing I have been so careful to avoid happening since I got here.

What on earth made me think that guy was Joe? Something about the way he walked? Where was my *brain*? What was I *doing*?

I'm right back where I started, and it's all going to happen again. The stares, then the laughs. Next they'll be whispering behind their hands, calling me names, making up songs about me, leaving hateful notes in my desk. I can't go through that again. I can't. I won't.

I sit through homeroom with my head down, pretending to get things out of my bag until everyone starts filing out of the room. Then I get up and mingle into the crowd as I slink to my English class.

I don't dare to look up. I don't want to see the faces turn away from me, the hands covering the mouths as they pass my shame from person to person.

Which is why I pretty much walk straight into him.

"Whoops, sorr—" I begin automatically. Then I look up. And that's when I see it. The resemblance. His face is set and stony. It looks like Joe's when he's trying to hold my hand and can't do anything but grip the air. The expression is the same—but everything else is different.

But then he meets my eyes and something softens.

"I'm sorry about before," I say before he can tell me what an idiot I am. He doesn't have to; I know.

He nods curtly. "Don't worry about it," he says in a cold voice. His eyes are locked on mine like a laser, as if he's challenging me—is he questioning me?

I need to explain. "I just—I thought you were someone else," I say.

The boy's face darkens. "Yeah," he says. "I know you

did. Like I said, don't worry about it. Didn't you hear me the first time?"

And with that, he shoves past me and storms away down the corridor.

It's no more than I deserve.

It crosses my mind to get my coat, head for the door, and cut class for the rest of the day. But before I get the chance to do anything, someone's beside me.

"That's Olly. Don't worry about him. He's like that with everyone."

I turn to see who's speaking. It's a girl named Nia. She's in my English class. We haven't really spoken to each other before now. She's part of the cool gang I noticed on my first day — the tight group of girls who rarely talk to anyone outside their clique. But to be fair, she has smiled at me a couple of times. She might even have tried to talk to me before now if I didn't run away and hide every time someone so much as looks at me.

I don't really know how to reply, so I just nod and keep walking.

Nia falls into step beside me. She's still talking. "It's really tragic, actually," she says.

Something about the word *tragic* gets my attention. Maybe I'm addicted to drama and intense emotions. Maybe it feels too familiar to me right now. I don't know. Whichever it is, I glance at her as we walk. "Tragic?" I ask.

Nia's mouth tightens in that way that happens when people want to say something but they're not sure if they should. As if the words might just burst out in a mad rush if she opens her mouth.

"I won't tell anyone," I add. Which nearly makes me laugh. I mean, who am I likely to tell? I wonder if she has any idea that this is in fact already the longest conversation I've had with a fellow student since I got here.

"It's not that," she says, lowering her voice. "I just don't want to be a gossip."

I shrug and keep walking. To be honest, I'm not even that interested. *Tragic* to a guy like that probably means that he forgot to put his hair gel on that morning, or he didn't get picked to be captain of the soccer team. I know his sort. I've met way too many of them before now.

My lack of interest clearly wasn't the response Nia wanted. "I mean, I feel a bit bad about saying it out loud," she says. Which I interpret as *I know I shouldn't, but actually I really, really want to tell you, and I will probably spill the beans completely if you ask me one more time.*

I relent. "Tell me. What's the big tragedy?" I say, stopping just before we get to English class.

Nia bites her lip. Her eyes actually moisten, and I realize I might have sounded too sarcastic.

"I mean — if you want to tell me, if you think it's OK." She pauses, then says, "He lost his brother."

I stare at her. My mouth has gone dry. "Lost?" I ask, just to make sure I've got it right.

Nia nods. "His brother died earlier this year."

"What was his name?" I croak, the words struggling to get past the crumbling dry rubble of my throat. As if I don't know what she's going to say.

Nia takes a breath, glances down the corridor, then looks back at me.

"Joe," she replies, and the floor tilts away from me.

# CHAPTER NINE

## Erin

"Are you OK?"

Nia is looking at me, her brows frowning with concern. Why is she asking if I'm OK? Is it obvious? Can she tell?

I realize I'm gripping the door handle. There's a group of students behind us, waiting to go in. I look at my hand, wrapped around the handle so tightly that my skin is almost translucent. If I let go, I think I'll probably fall. But if I keep standing here like this, then I might as well make myself a sign that says I AM AN UTTER FOOL AND A CRAZY PERSON. PLEASE AVOID ME AT ALL COSTS.

I slowly unclasp my hand from the handle, force my breath to go in and out of my mouth, and finally put every bit of mental energy I've got into telling the corners of my mouth to point upward. I hope I look as though I'm smiling, although I think I probably look more like I'm eating the sourest lemon in the world while also being punched in the stomach.

That gives me an idea.

"Sorry," I say. "Stomach cramps." I give her a knowing look, one that will hopefully bring our conversation to a close. "You know. Time of the month. I get it really bad."

Nia's face is sympathy and relief all rolled into one. "Oh, me too!" she says. "I get terrible cramps. Poor you."

I manage another smile. "Thanks. I'm sure I'll be OK in a minute."

As we head into English, I try not to think about the fact that I just got cold-shouldered by Joe's brother in front of a corridor full of students, or the fact that Nia and I now seem to have bonded over our periods.

I fall back on my tried and trusted defense: I bury my head in my work, and except when absolutely necessary, I don't look up from my books, my bag, or my desk for the rest of the day.

## JOE

She's home. The day has been like an eternity. Well, my whole existence is one big fat eternity going nowhere, but today has been like a mini-eternity lost somewhere in the midst of that whole other, bigger eternity.

Either way, it's over now. She's home, and right now I'd

swap everything I can think of for her being able to see me again. She's literally all I've got; I can't lose her.

I watch her walk up the driveway. She looks different. I've gotten used to seeing her hurry home and come straight up to see me. Today she's dragging her heels. Her head is down. *Just please come straight upstairs. Please be able to see me again. I need to talk to you. I need to explain.*

I count to twenty, then fifty, then a hundred.

And then she's here.

"Erin!" I'm standing by the window. I don't want to crowd her out. *Please see me, please!*

She looks across the room. Looks into my eyes. And smiles.

I smile back and whisper my thanks. Who to, exactly, I'm not sure. I haven't had some kind of spiritual awakening since I died. If anything, it's the opposite. I'm not sure there are any religions that describe the afterlife like this.

Either way, I feel like I can relax at last.

"You're back," she says simply.

"I never went anywhere," I say. I take a step closer to her. I know what I want to say to her. I've been rehearsing it all day. Except now she's here, the words don't come quite as smoothly as they did when I only had myself to practice them on.

"And I don't plan to go anywhere, either," I mumble. "Look, I know it's impossible, stupid. I know I can't offer you much . . . but I want to be with you. Simple as that. I'm not going to push you or pressure you. I know it's a lot to ask of you, and if you don't feel the same way, then just say, and I will leave you alone. But if you want to be with me, I want to be with you, too, and I'll do everything I can to figure out some way to make it work."

She keeps looking at me, her face dark, like a door hiding her thoughts. Damn, I've done it again. Come on too strong. I've probably freaked her out and scared her off again. I'm trying to figure out a way of clawing back everything I've just said, when something changes in her face. A slow hint of a smile touches her eyes. And then . . .

"I want to be with you, too," she says.

The relief is like an explosion inside me. She wants to be with me, too! I want to run around the house, whooping and yelling, I want to jump onto the roof, shout it out for all the world to hear.

As I don't really have the option of doing any of those things, I settle for the only thing I can give her.

"I remembered where there's another one," I say.

She tilts her head in a question.

"Another poem." I beckon her back toward the window and point to the wall that I used to lean against, out of view unless you were sitting just where I used to sit, where she sits.

"It was there," I say, feeling suddenly like a fool. I'm pointing to a sheet of wallpaper. But I can't help thinking there might be some remnant of it somewhere. I can't remember the words, but I remember the experience: sitting on the seat, hunched over as I scribbled my words on the wall.

Erin follows me to the window and looks at the wall. The seam of paper runs along the edge of the window frame. She fiddles with the bottom of it, picking at it till there is a loose edge. Then she stops and looks at me. "Shall I . . . ?" she asks.

I nod.

So, very carefully, gently, and achingly slowly, she pulls at the wallpaper, lifting it bit by bit from the wall, until it exposes what is below it. Exposes me.

We read it together.

WHILE I BUMP SHOULDERS, TRY TO SPEAK UP AND STUTTER,
HE CUTS THROUGH A CROWD LIKE A HOT KNIFE THROUGH BUTTER.

WHILE I'M LOST, IN THE WAY, HER HAIR GRAZES HER CHEEK,
HE'S ALREADY MADE A DATE FOR NEXT WEEK.

I SPEND HOURS WRITING SONGS WHERE NO ONE WILL FIND THEM;
HE HATES ALL THAT STUFF, KEEPS HIS FEELINGS INSIDE HIM.

I'M FUMBLING AND AWKWARD; MY VOICE DOESN'T FIT ME.
HE SHRUGS WHEN HE LAUGHS; HIS SMILE'S WARM AND EASY.

SOCCER BALL IN ONE HAND, HIS PHONE IN THE OTHER —
THAT'S LIFE FOR MY EASY-COME, EASY-GO BROTHER.

HE STRUTS AROUND SCHOOL LIKE A HOMECOMING KING —
AND YET STILL HE'S THE ONE I CAN TELL ANYTHING.

DAD TELLS ME TO CHEER UP. I WISH HE UNDERSTOOD:
IF I COULD SWAP BODIES AND BE OLLY — I WOULD.

I stare at the words. My face is hot.

If I'd known it was going to reveal to Erin what a completely inadequate loser I was, I'm not quite so sure I'd have shown her the poem. Actually, that's not true. I'd have shown it to her anyway. I don't want to put on an act for her, and I don't want to be someone I'm not. Erin gets me — and seems to like me — for who I am, not who I think I need to pretend to be.

She's looking intensely at me. "I love it," she says, and I know she means it.

I make a face. "You don't think I'm just a pathetic loser, then?"

She shakes her head. "No. I get it. Reminds me of me and Phoebe in a way. I mean, it's completely different — but that thing about how easy life feels for them, and how it's such a struggle for us."

"Yeah. And it's even harder when you're dead," I say with half a smile.

Erin claps a hand over her mouth. "Oh, God, I'm sorry. I didn't mean—"

"It's fine," I interrupt her. "I was joking. Kind of. 'Cause in a way, it isn't harder. It's almost easier, in fact. Some of it is, anyway. Like this, us. I've never found *anyone* as easy to talk to and be with as you, never mind any girl. So actually, whatever this is, whatever I am right now—you make all of it better, and I wouldn't swap it for anything."

I watch her face transform as a smile spreads slowly across it. A smile just for me. I can't help smiling back at her, and as I do, I reach a hand out for her. She does the same.

Our hands meet. More strongly than ever before. It's hard to explain how it's different. It's as if I've touched only the outside of her skin before now. This time I feel as if we're connecting on a deeper level. A more solid meeting place.

I know she can feel it, too, because she holds my hand more firmly and takes a step closer to me.

Every corny thing I've ever heard in my life, every oversentimental poem I've written, every song I've composed about wanting to find love . . . all of them, they're in here with us, right now, in this moment. We're wrapped in them.

I'm lost, and there's nothing I want more than to stay here with her and never be found.

I take her other hand and move even closer. There are millimeters between us now. Her face is so close I could . . .

I could kiss her.

Is that the ultimate act of madness? Or is it just plain selfish? I'm dead. She's got a whole life to live. Look at what happened the first time we touched. The electricity was so powerful, it threw her across the room. What if kissing is like that, only worse?

But then, what if a kiss is all it would take to make this more real? What if a kiss would make *me* more real? And yeah, I know I'm telling myself a fairy tale—but what if it's true? What if kissing her could bring me back to life?

I'm debating all of this in my head in fast motion. I don't want the moment to pass. I might miss the opportunity and never get another one. But I don't want to freak her out. I need to be so careful.

Her eyes meet mine. Her lips are slightly parted. Does she feel the same way? Have I got this right?

I move a tiny bit closer, tilt my head toward her. Her eyes start to close.

And . . .

"Erin!"

Her mum, from downstairs.

I step back. Erin pulls me closer. "Ignore her," she whispers.

I think that's good advice. Try again. Move in. Try to be smooth. Try to act like the cool guy that this beautiful girl seems to think I am, rather than the clumsy, ink-stained, head-in-the-clouds loser I really am.

Really *was*, that is.

This is it. I'm going to do it. I'm—*"Erin!"*

Her mum again—only she's closer now. Sounds like she's on the landing.

Erin turns her head toward the door. "I'm busy, Mum!" she calls. Then she turns back to me and smiles. "Where were we?" she asks softly.

I'm about to answer—and not with words—when there's a knock on the door.

"Erin, I need to speak to you!"

A moment later, the door is open, her mum's head is poking around it—and the magical, wondrous moment has well and truly passed.

I jump back. I don't want to, but I can't do this. Standing here holding Erin's hand, about to kiss her, with her mum right there in the doorway!

I try to let go of Erin's hand, but she won't let me. She grips my hand even more firmly.

"Mum!" Erin's voice is sharp. I haven't heard her speak like that before. "You can't just barge in here like this!"

Her mum looks around the room. Her eyes skim past my face without her even realizing it. She looks right through me as if I'm not there, as if I'm not important, as if I don't exist. Something about it flips a switch inside me, mingling with everything else I'm feeling. It feels like a cauldron is starting to bubble in my gut. I can't deal with this semi-existence anymore.

"I didn't just barge in," she says. "I called you twice."

"What is it?" Erin asks.

"I just wondered if you wanted to come with us. We're going for a walk around the harbor once your dad's finished watching the match."

"I'm busy," Erin says quickly.

Her mum laughs.

*Don't laugh at me. Don't laugh at us!*

Something's starting to overflow inside me. My feelings for Erin, how near to me she was standing a moment ago, so close I felt her breath on my cheek. How close I was to kissing her. All of it. It's building like a storm, like a tornado spinning around and around inside me, more and more fiercely.

"Busy doing what?" Erin's mum is asking, somewhere outside the cloudy fog of my swirling emotions. "Come on, Erin. It'll be nice. It's not right, you cooping yourself up in your room all the time."

"I'm not cooping myself up," Erin replies tightly. She takes a breath, smiles a forced smile at her mum. I run my thumb over the back of her hand.

*I'm here for you. Don't worry. Don't worry—we'll be together when she's gone.*

Can she hear my thoughts? Can she feel them?

Erin speaks more gently. "I'm fine, Mum, really. You go."

*Yes. Go. Leave us to it. Please!*

Her mum is still in the doorway. She looks as though she's considering something. As though she's trying to find the words. She's biting the edge of a fingernail. Erin does that, too, when she's thinking.

I look at Erin's lips now. I'm overwhelmed by how much I want to kiss them. I can't bear it.

Somewhere in the distance, her mum is speaking again. "I'm worried about you, Erin. I don't want you locking yourself away from the world. I thought we'd left all of that in the past. These last few weeks, you've been so much happier. I don't want to see you going backward again."

She comes farther into the room.

Erin sighs. "Mum, honestly, I'm fine. Please leave me alone."

Her mum is beside her now. "I only want to look after you," she says.

"I know, Mum, but I can look after myself." Erin smiles. "Honestly. I'm OK. *I just want to be on my own.*"

Her words roll around, repeating in my head. She wants to be on her own.

I know she's talking to her mum. I *know* she wants to be with me. But she says it so pointedly, and suddenly I doubt everything. After what happened last night, is she not sure about us? As sure as I am? I've got nothing to lose being with her. I've literally got nothing except her. But she's got a whole life that I'm stopping her from living by pulling her back to be with me all the time.

How selfish. How unfair. What should I do?

Her mum is coming closer.

Erin's holding my hand.

My mind is . . . my thoughts . . . they're breaking up. I can't seem to hold on to my thinking, my beliefs. It's all a mess. It's too much for me.

The ground doesn't feel firm under my feet anymore. I need to sit down.

Where . . . ?

What's . . . ?

I feel like I'm going to faint. Erin must sense it, because she grips my hand harder. I focus on her face, on the obstinate strand of hair that always falls in front of her eyes—reach out automatically to smooth it back—and at the same moment, her mum reaches out to do the same. I see her hand—I swear I see it in slow motion—rising into the air, edging forward, both of us reaching out, touching her hair and—

*"AARRRRGGGGHHHH!"*

Erin screams as her mum is thrown backward. She trips, falls against the bed. Luckily, the mattress saves her from a nasty fall.

Erin drops my hand and runs to her mum. "Mum, are you OK?"

Her mum's face has turned so white that for a moment I think we've somehow sucked all the blood out of her body.

Nothing is making sense right now. I don't know what's going on. "Erin, is she . . . ? What's—?"

"What — what was that?" Erin's mum asks at the same moment. Her voice is shaking.

How is Erin going to answer?

She turns to me, her eyes pleading, confused, questioning.

Suddenly I am all panic. Nothing else. Panic at being found out, panic at being lost, at losing Erin, at Erin being taken away from me. Am I slipping away? Is this it? It's all been a halfway house up to now, and this is death for real?

I'm not ready.

The emotion is out of control. It's like a firework going off inside a bottle. Something has to blow.

And then it does.

Big-time.

# Erin

Mum is getting up from the bed. Her face is deadly pale. I'm reaching out for her. I don't know exactly what happened to her, but I felt it, too. It was like that first time when Joe and I reached for the necklace at the same moment.

Does this mean *she* can see him now?

She's not looking at him. She's looking at me. Her eyes are wide, scared.

"What — what was that?" she asks.

I've never heard my mum sound like this before. Even in

the middle of my crisis, when I dragged her and Dad to hell and back—even as she sat by my hospital bed, holding a glass up to my face so I could take tiny sips of water through a straw after they'd pumped my stomach out and brought me back from the dead—even then, she never lost control. She was my anchor. She was the person who kept me sane. She never raised her voice, never showed she was upset by what was going on, never panicked. She was just there for me.

"What—what the—? What is happening?" she asks. I see she's pointing at the window now, and, if it's possible, her face has drained of even more color.

I look where she's pointing.

The curtain is flapping. I'm about to tell her it must be a breeze from outside, when I remember the window is still painted closed. I've been meaning to get Dad to fix that, but I haven't gotten around to it. So there's no breeze, no draft. The air is completely still. So still and tight, in fact, that it feels as if the air in the room is running out.

Then the window starts to rattle.

Mum is staring at the window. "Erin," she says in a hoarse whisper. "What the hell is happening?"

That's another thing I've never seen my mum do. Swear. At all. Even use the word *hell*.

I don't know how to answer her.

"I thought—" she begins, then she shakes her head and stops.

"You thought what, Mum?" I ask.

"Look, don't be angry," she begins. "I came in here the other day, just to see if you had any clothes that needed washing. And, well, there was something odd then."

"Odd? Odd how?" I ask. I can feel my body stiffen. I don't like the idea of Mum rooting through my things, but that might be the least of my worries right now.

"I don't know. I can't explain it. Like it was colder than the rest of the house. It made me shiver. It was weird."

I turn to Joe.

"Tell her it's the wind coming through the cracks," he says. "That's why they're rattling. That's why it was cold."

"What cracks?"

"What?" Mum asks.

"I . . . I was just talking to myself," I say stupidly. "Thinking aloud."

"Yes. And that," Mum says. "I've heard a voice up here. I've assumed you've been talking on the phone to your friends, but once or twice, I noticed your phone was downstairs. I thought maybe you were talking to yourself. I didn't want to say anything, make you feel bad about it or anything, but . . ."

"Tell her it's just a drafty room. Tell her you were doing your homework out loud," Joe insists. "Tell her anything — but say something. It's getting worse. I can't control it." His face has turned gray, and he's shaking. He looks as though he's about to throw up or faint or something.

"Are you OK?" I ask before I can stop myself. "You're not going to —"

"Of course I'm not OK," Mum cuts in. "Your windows are rattling, the room is about ten degrees colder than the rest of the house, *something* just electrocuted me, and I'm worried about my daughter talking to an empty room. How can you even ask if I'm OK?"

"I wasn't—" I begin, then stop myself.

"And that's another thing," Mum goes on. "The bumps."

"Bumps?" I don't even want her to go on. I just want her out of here, want Joe to be OK, want to get back to where we were before Mum came in.

"I've been hearing them for weeks when I'm in the living room. I put it down to the water pipes or something, but . . ."

Mum's voice trails off.

"Erin, get her out of here. *Please,*" Joe begs. "The more I'm freaking out, the worse it's all getting. I can feel it. It's going to start going berserk, and I don't want your mum to see it."

Joe's right. I have to distract her, have to get her out of my room, before things get even worse. I need to tell her *something.* It's not just the window rattling now. Joe slumps down onto the bed; two seconds later, it starts to shake as well.

Mum claps a hand over her mouth as she watches the bed. "Erin," she says through her fingers. She reaches out to me with her other hand. "The—the bed. It's moving."

"Mum, it's . . ." I can't finish my sentence. There is absolutely nothing I can say to explain away what she's seeing with her own eyes.

"Erin, come with me. Come on. We need to get out of here."

I don't move. I'm not leaving Joe, not in the state he's in. But I can't stay here with him. I can't exactly tell Mum I'd rather stay in a room where the furniture is shaking and the windows are rattling than go with her.

I take Mum's hand. She starts to turn. "Come on," she whispers.

"Why are you whispering?" I ask.

"I don't want—*it*—to hear me."

"Mum!" I drop her hand.

"*What?* What is the *matter* with you, Erin? We need to get *out of here!*"

How can I tell her what's really the matter with me? How can I explain how much it hurts me to hear her refer to Joe as *it* while he's actually sitting there on the bed, terrified and shaking?

I need to give him some sort of signal, to check if he's OK, but I can't speak to him again without Mum thinking I'm losing it.

"Mum, what do you mean by 'it'?" I ask, partly to buy myself some time before she drags me out of the room, and partly, yes, because I don't like it.

"*What?*" she hisses. "Can't you see what's going on here? The place is—I can't even say it." She puts her hand out for me again. "Please, Erin. Just come with me. We're not safe. There's something evil here. A poltergeist or something."

"For God's sake, Mum!" I can't help it. I *know* I should stop myself, but I can't. She's insulting my—well, I guess, my boyfriend. He's the nearest thing I've ever had to a proper boyfriend, anyway. And she's calling him evil while he's in the room. He's right here, listening to every word! *She* might not know it, but I do.

"Erin, will you *please* stop arguing with me and come out of this room? It is clearly *haunted,* and I do not want to be in here a moment longer!" Mum is talking in a way that I've never heard before. All clipped and staccato and breathless. I know she's not deliberately insulting Joe. She's not purposely being mean to me. She's scared.

I risk another glance at Joe. "Just go with her," he says. "Please. Go. I'll be fine. It'll stop. Don't make things bad with your mum. Please, Erin."

I let out a heavy breath and shake my head. It's not fair.

"OK," I say eventually.

"Good," Mum and Joe say in unison. Ironic that they are in complete agreement on this.

As Mum turns to leave, I look at Joe.

"I'll be fine," he whispers, but his eyes are dark and terrified. His hands are clutching the bed. He's making himself look as OK as he can, for me, to make me feel better.

I've never had a boy care enough about me to do that before.

"I'll come back as soon as I can," I whisper. And with that, I reluctantly follow Mum out of the room.

# CHAPTER TEN

## JOE

The door closes behind them. The second they leave, it gets worse. It was bad enough when they were here, but I was doing my best to hold it back. Rein it in.

Now that they've gone, there's no reason to hold anything back, and the dam breaks.

I'm freezing cold, boiling hot. I'm sweating, shaking, ready to drop with exhaustion and wired like a live electric cable — I don't know what I am. Everything and nothing.

I try to get up from the bed. I don't even know where I'm trying to get to. Maybe the window seat. I struggle to my feet, but my legs won't hold me, and I collapse on the floor.

Is this it? Is *this* the actual end? Have I been in some kind of semi-dead waiting room up to now, and a place has finally opened up for me on the other side? Is this the point where I disappear forever?

For a moment, the thought terrifies me.

Then it strengthens me.

No. I'm not going to let it happen. I'll fight it. I'm not ready to go. Not now. Not yet.

I've got a reason to stay here. I need to see Erin again. Need to be close to her, to hold her. I need to kiss her. We came so close. I want to feel her breath, hot against my cheek. I want to see her smile again.

The wanting is stronger than everything else.

I focus on thoughts of Erin, being with her again. Her smile. Her lips. The things she says to me.

She is like a life preserver, drawing me back to safety. I drag myself to the window seat. Our seat. Pull myself up. Collapse on the seat and close my eyes.

I don't know how long I sit there. Eternity? Minutes?

Eventually, the furniture stops shaking. It's OK. I'm still here. The worst is over.

# Erin

Mum marches downstairs and through the living room, passing Dad without saying anything. He's watching sports on the telly and doesn't look up. I don't think he even notices us come through, let alone picks up on the mood Mum is in.

I follow her into the kitchen. She grabs her laptop from

next to the fridge, puts it on the kitchen table, and powers it up.

"What are you doing?" I ask.

"Dealing with it," she answers in a clipped voice.

I watch her in silence as she logs in and waits for her laptop to connect to the Internet.

A moment later, Dad shouts from the lounge. "Erin!"

I call back. "Yes?"

He gets off the sofa and lumbers into the kitchen. "Oh! You're in here. I didn't see you come down. Are you OK?"

"Yes. Why?" I reply, too quickly.

Dad points back through to the living room. "I heard a loud bump. Thought someone had fallen over upstairs."

"Not me," I reply.

Dad shrugs. "Must've been Phoebe."

He starts to walk away.

Mum looks at me, then says to his back, "Phoebe isn't here. She's at a sleepover, remember?"

Dad turns around again. "Oh. Well, *someone's* up there."

He says it so calmly, so casually, so sure that there's nothing particularly weird about hearing noises in the room directly above the living room. My bedroom. So unquestioning of why there might be a loud thump coming from a bedroom that we've just pointed out is empty.

Mum and I both know that there's nothing calm or casual about it at all.

What did Dad hear? What's happened to Joe? I want to go to him. I need an excuse to leave the room.

I start to edge away, but Mum puts a hand on my arm. "Erin, please stay away."

"Stay away from what?" Dad asks.

Mum takes a breath. How's she going to explain this?

"We've got a poltergeist," she says.

Dad stops for a second. A split second before he bursts out laughing. "We've what?" he asks. "Thought you said we've got a poltergeist for a moment there."

"That *is* what I said," Mum replies.

Dad's still laughing. Then I see him clock Mum's face, then mine, then think about what he heard upstairs. I can almost see the cogs in his brain turning, one by one, as he processes each piece of information. Puts it all together. Realizes what it adds up to.

"What are you talking about?" He laughs again, but it doesn't sound quite so natural this time. "You're messing around, right?"

"Do I look as if I'm messing around?" Mum asks. "There's been something funny going on for weeks."

"Something funny?" Dad asks. "What kind of funny?"

Mum shakes her head. "Noises. Voices. Just . . . just a feeling. I tried to brush it off. Told myself I was being ridiculous." She glances at me, then back to Dad. "But if you'd seen what we've just seen," she says in a whisper. She shakes her head again. "There's no room for doubting it anymore."

Dad steps toward us. "What do you mean?" he asks, his voice lower now. "Is this for real?"

Mum nods. Then she tells him what happened while we were up there.

I try not to take it personally as I listen to her describing what happened, but I wince each time she says *poltergeist* or *evil* or *ghost*. I try not to butt in.

It's hard, though, because all the time she's talking, I want to jump in and say, "It's not like that." But how can I? I can't tell her it's not the way she's describing it without telling her exactly how it *is*. And that means telling her about Joe and me. And I can't do that. After everything I put them through, there is simply no way in this world that I can tell them that the evil spirit she is describing in hushed tones is actually my boyfriend and that he's the only thing keeping me sane right now.

Because what if I'm wrong? What if he *isn't* keeping me sane? What if he is the thing that will send me over the edge? How can I be choosing a ghost over holding my family together?

I can't answer any of the questions lining up in my head. And I can't say anything to Mum. Ever. I know that.

Instead, I watch her typing words into her computer while she talks. She's looking up "how to get rid of a poltergeist" on Google.

"Mum, *really*?" I ask.

She looks up from her laptop. "Really, what?"

"I—I don't know. It just seems a bit . . . extreme."

"Your bed is shaking; the windows are rattling. Wouldn't you say *that* is the extreme thing?" Mum asks.

"Yes—I mean—no. I mean, look, nothing like this has happened before," I flounder. "Maybe there's some kind of explanation."

"I've already told you," Mum says, her voice set. "It *has* happened before. I've wondered a few times what's going on up there. I wasn't going to say anything to you because I didn't want to worry you. And yes, when it was just a bit of a draft and a couple of bumps, I told myself that maybe there *was* an explanation."

She holds my eyes.

"But this," she insists. "Come on, Erin. You know there is no explanation for what just happened there. No *other* explanation."

She's right. There's nothing I could say that could convince her that what just happened up there was normal. Normal to her. Normal to normal people. I turn away.

"Where are you going?" Mum asks instantly.

"I'm just going to get my stuff. I've still got homework to do."

"You're not going up there." It's Dad this time. He's gone from disbeliever to big protector in two minutes. I decide against pointing this out. I don't want to cause trouble, don't want to make waves.

I just want to be with Joe.

"Dad, I'll be fine. Please. I'm just going to get my school-bag. So I can do my homework." If I play the homework card, perhaps they'll let me go.

Dad glances at Mum.

"Mum, I'll be fine," I insist.

Dad squares his shoulders. "I'll come with you," he says.

I sigh. "Dad, you really don't have to come—"

"You're not going up there on your own," Mum interrupts.

Dad's opening kitchen drawers, scrambling around. He grabs something and shoves it in his pocket. I don't notice what it is. Then he opens the tall cupboard at the end of the room, rummages around a bit, and pulls out a tennis racket.

"Ideally, I'd have preferred a bat, but this'll have to do," he says.

I stare at him. "Do for what?"

"Just in case," he says.

If my mind wasn't filled with images of Joe sitting on the edge of the bed, shaking, white and terrified, I would find this funny. My dad is going to protect me from my dead boyfriend with a tennis racket.

I mean, is there any situation, any scenario—any universe—in which anyone might ever have imagined a scene like this being an actual thing?

"Dad. Seriously. We'll be fine."

Dad tucks the racket under his arm and goes ahead of me. "Come on," he says.

He leads the way up the stairs and gingerly nudges my door open a crack. "Hello?" he calls.

This time I do stifle a laugh. I have to stifle it. If I don't, I'm in danger of getting hysterical.

There's no reply. Obviously.

Dad pushes the door fully open, and we go inside.

Joe is curled up on the window seat. He looks calmer now but still shaken. All I want is to go to him. The effort of stopping myself makes my chest ache. His eyes meet mine and I can see he feels the same way.

"You OK?" he asks.

"Seems all right to me," Dad says, looking around.

"Yeah, fine," I answer—hoping it will do for them both.

"Well, you're not sleeping in here tonight, are you? Get your things. You can sleep in Phoebe's room till we figure out what to do next."

"Dad! Really, it's fine!"

"It's not *fine* at all," Dad replies.

Joe gets down from the window seat. "Erin, just go along with it. I'll be OK," he says.

"Are you sure?" I ask.

Joe nods.

"'Course I'm sure," Dad says. "No question of it. I'm not having you sleep in a haunted room. Come on. Get your stuff. I'll stay here."

"Really, Dad, I don't need you to wait for me."

"I'm not going anywhere." Dad folds his arms. "Sweetheart, in all we've been through as a family, have I ever let you down before?"

He's playing the *after everything we've done for you* card, but so subtly I don't think even *he* realizes that's what he's doing. Which means I can't be annoyed with him. And I can't think of any way around this. I'm beaten.

He waits, arms folded, tennis racket tucked under his arm, standing like a prison officer guarding the room, studying it intently as I pick up clothes, books, and whatever else I might need till I can sneak back in.

At one point, I hold out my hand toward Joe. I do it really carefully so Dad will think I'm just reaching out for some books.

My hand is on his arm. Joe closes his hand around mine. For two seconds, I can breathe, and the world rights itself.

"It'll be OK," I say to Joe before I can stop myself.

"'Course it will," Dad replies. "I told you, we're in this together, sweetheart. We're not going to let anything happen to you. We'll figure it out."

Joe smiles. "We'll figure it out," he echoes. I smile back. Then I let go and join Dad in the doorway.

"You got everything, sweets?" Dad asks as I pull my schoolbag onto my shoulder.

I nod.

He unfolds his arms, slings an arm around my shoulder.

"Come on, then," he says. "Hey, don't look so worried. We'll get rid of it, whatever it is. And until we do, you don't need to come back in here again."

As we leave the bedroom, he puts his hand in his pocket. Gets something out.

No! That was what he was getting out of the kitchen drawer! A key! I didn't even know my bedroom *had* a key!

He pulls my bedroom door closed behind us and puts the key in the lock. "Whatever's in there, it isn't coming out now," he says as he turns the key.

"Dad! You can't do that!"

He looks at me, genuinely puzzled. "Why not?"

"I—because—you—"

*Because you don't need a key to keep him out. He's confined to that room. And because you're stopping me from getting to the one thing, the one person, I want.*

"Because what, sweetheart?"

"It's my bedroom," I say weakly.

Dad joins me on the landing, stands in front of me, and lifts my chin. "Not for now, it isn't, darling. I've told you, it's my job to protect you. And no, if there really is an evil poltergeist in there, then I guess a locked door probably isn't going to protect us from it, but—who knows?—I'd feel happier with the door locked."

He says this last bit with a smile, Dad the Affable Defender, not absolutely one hundred percent convinced it's real, but erring on the side of caution and looking after his little girl. I'm stumped. I can't even reply.

"Plus it'll stop you from accidentally going back in there without thinking about it. I'm not having *anything* bad happen to you," he adds. "We're going to deal with whatever is in there," he goes on, utterly oblivious to how all of this is making me feel. "And once we've done that, we'll redecorate, make it lovely, paint it any color you like. We'll make it really special for you, OK?"

I've got nothing to counter his argument with. I've got nothing.

From where he's standing, it makes total sense. He doesn't know that each lick of paint will wipe out a line of Joe's beautiful words. He doesn't know that when he says he'll *deal with whatever is in there,* he might as well be stabbing me with a knife. He doesn't know that the only thing I want is the very thing he thinks he's protecting me from.

He doesn't know any of it. And unless I want him to think I'm losing my mind and need dragging back to hospitals and therapists, that's the way it'll have to stay.

I reach up and give him a hug. "Thank you, Dad," I say. "Thanks for everything."

He hugs me back. "We'll look after you," he whispers into my hair. "I promise."

I grit my teeth and force myself not to show my real feelings. I'm good at that. I've done it enough times before.

I just have to be nice to him and Mum, show them how grateful I am. Play along. I can do that. And in the meantime, all I'll really be doing is trying my hardest to figure out a way to get the key and be reunited with Joe.

# JOE

If I thought this existence had been like a prison before now, I was kidding myself. Hearing someone turn a key in a lock and walk away is pretty much the moment you *know* you're in a prison.

A prison where you are invisible to everyone.

Where the last you saw of your family was when you watched them drive down the road in a moving van.

Where the only person who can see you has been banned from coming near you.

Where all of these things are about keeping everyone else safe, and there is no one to worry about keeping *you* safe.

That's when you start understanding words like *prison*.

I need to write. My songs are the only way I have of picking the lock on my cell.

I can't even hold a pen in my hand.

I have an idea. The floor. I can feel the floor. Maybe . . .

There's a big rug covering most of it, but it doesn't go all the way to the walls. I stumble to the corner near the walk-in closet and scratch my fingernail along the wood. It works! It marks a line in the wood.

What if they hear me?

I nearly laugh. I don't care about that anymore. I need to get these words out.

I manage to lift one tiny corner of the rug. Then, keeping my hand tight, my letters small, I scratch out my words with my fingernail.

I'M LOCKED IN A PLACE THAT YOU CAN'T EVEN SEE,
A PLACE IN MY MIND WHERE IT'S HARD TO BE ME.
YOU DON'T EVEN KNOW WHAT IT MEANS TO BE FREE.
JUST GO. LEAVE ME HERE. SHUT THE DOOR. TURN THE KEY.

I've managed one verse. How long has that taken me? Best part of an hour? Longer? I don't even know. It's getting dark out, though, and I'm exhausted from the effort. I drag the corner of the rug back over my words.

It's helped. A bit.

Body and mind utterly drained, I heave myself onto the bed, curl into a ball, close my eyes, and settle in for what I know is going to be the longest, loneliest night yet.

# CHAPTER ELEVEN

## Erin

Dad won't let me in my room on Friday morning. I feel like I'm being punished. I want to tell him I haven't done anything wrong, but what's the point? He and Mum are so intent on this idea that they're protecting me, if I so much as suggest anything different, they won't even hear it.

I spend most of the day going through the motions at school while trying to figure out ways of getting my bedroom key back and being reunited with Joe. I *have* to see him — even just for a few minutes. I need to know he's OK.

What if he's gone? What if he's in pain? Can he feel pain?

I'm riddled with questions I have no way of answering, and in the meantime, I have to get through the day as if I'm happy, as if there's no problem, as if they aren't taking away from me the only thing in my life that I want.

By the time I get home, I've hatched a plan. I'll get Mum to accompany me to my room. I'll tell her I need to get some stuff for the weekend. Then while we're in there, I'll get Phoebe to call her downstairs, tell her there's an emergency in the kitchen or something, and she'll have to leave me alone for a few minutes while she checks it out.

It's not the most sophisticated plan ever, and it relies way too heavily on an eleven-year-old who has nothing to gain from it and whose social life will probably get in the way of it anyway—but it's all I've got.

Except, when I get home, it turns out Mum has other ideas.

Phoebe runs into the house ahead of me.

"Hi, Mum," she calls before disappearing up to her room to change.

I follow her inside and close the door behind me. Mum is in the living room, sitting on the sofa with some woman I've never seen before.

She jumps up as soon as she sees me. "This is Erin," she says to the woman. "Erin, darling, this is Rose."

I look at Rose. She's small with a round face, short gray hair, and brown-flecked eyes shining out from behind thick black-rimmed glasses. "Hi, Rose," I say slowly, aware that my words sound like a question.

"Rose has come to help," Mum says. She looks as embarrassed as I must look bewildered.

Rose takes a sip of her tea. Mum's put out the best china for her. *Why?*

"Help with what?" I ask.

A tiny bit of me knows what she's going to say before she says it. The rest of me doesn't want to listen.

"She's going to see if she can get rid of the . . ." Mum's voice trails away.

*No!*

"You're going to do an exorcism!"

Rose looks at me. "We don't really use that word nowadays," she says seriously. "We prefer to call it an expulsion." Her eyes lock on to mine as if she can see inside me. Does she know what's in there?

I turn to Mum. "But that's what you're going to do. Get rid of him?"

"Or her," Rose says, a smile in her eyes, like we're all on the same side, like we're all friends, comrades. "Let's not be sexist, now."

I stare at her.

"Rose is going to see if she can help us to get rid of it, yes," Mum says calmly.

*It.*

"What if I don't want you to?" I ask. I can't stop myself. I can't believe they're doing this to me.

Mum takes a couple of steps toward me. "Erin, are you all right, darling?" she asks. "You look —"

"I'm fine. I just don't see why we have to leap into doing something so drastic over a few odd noises in the house. I mean, it could have been the pipes or — or — or anything," I say, faltering. "Who says it's a ghost? I mean, why rush into doing something so extreme?"

"Erin, you *know* it's more than a few odd noises," Mum says.

Rose puts down her cup, gets a hankie out of her pocket, and dabs at her mouth. "It's honestly nothing to worry about," she says. "You don't need to be scared."

"I'm *not* scared."

"Well, whatever you are, don't worry — it'll be fine. Nothing to be nervous about," Rose carries on, oblivious of the fact that I want to scream at the top of my lungs and tell her to get the hell out of our house and leave me and Joe alone. "It's perfectly safe. Very low-key." She turns to Mum and smiles. "And look, I don't want to brag, but I have a very high success rate."

*Success rate?* Where is this woman even *from*?

"Rose came into the shop with her leaflets this morning," Mum says, as if she heard my thoughts. Did I accidentally say them out loud? "She's been doing this for a long time. She knows what she's doing, Erin. It feels like it was meant to be."

At this, Rose rummages in her bag and pulls out a leaflet. She holds it out to me. Grudgingly, I step forward and take the leaflet.

# *Rose Simmons*

CLAIRVOYANT. MEDIUM. PSYCHIC.
READINGS, CONNECTIONS, EXPULSIONS.
A SUPPORTIVE SHOULDER AND A FRIENDLY EAR.

I think I'm going to be sick.

Mum reaches out for my hand. I pull away. I don't want her gentle reassurance; I just want them to stop talking about getting rid of Joe as if they're discussing throwing out the trash. And I definitely don't want to hear about high success rates.

"You don't need to be involved," Mum says softly, ignoring my rejection.

"Involved? What d'you mean? What exactly are you going to do?"

Rose gets up from the sofa. "We're going to see if we can get rid of it. No time like the present."

"Rose is willing to give it a go," Mum adds. "She's not going to charge us or anything. Said she wants to help us settle into the community. Which is nice of her, isn't it?"

"*Nice* of her?" My words come out like nails.

"I often find that a few stern words and burning some white sage is all that's needed." Rose reaches into her bag. "Sometimes it takes a couple of sessions. I won't know till I get started."

I shake my head, as if it'll make her words fall into place in my brain in a way that I can make sense of. This woman has come into our house with a bag of white sage and wants to have "a few stern words" with Joe. She thinks that'll get rid of him?

I'm torn between derision and fury. But actually, right now mostly I feel relief. For a minute there, I'd seen fire and brimstone and preachers denouncing Satan and things like that. Instead, we have a round-faced middle-aged lady who wants to shake some herbs around the house.

"The spirit usually resides in a place that has the strongest physical or emotional connection for them," Rose is saying. "The stronger the emotion, the stronger the link. Such a link can keep a spirit tied to a place. Break the connection and we're halfway there."

"Well, I don't know about any of that," Mum says. "But it seems to be happening in Erin's bedroom, so I suppose that must be the place with the . . . connection."

"And then what?" I ask. "Supposing you do get rid of him—it. Then what?"

"It's hard to tell. If a spirit has unfinished business, I've found that it can linger a bit."

"Linger where?"

"It can often move to a place that holds the next strongest emotional connection. I've seen a spirit disappear from a house only to reappear in a church, for example."

"Evil spirits haunting a church?" Mum says with a shudder.

"Oh, no," Rose says. "It's not about evil. And what we're

doing isn't about punishment. It's about helping them to move on to where they need to go. I'm not here to stand in judgment. I merely help to untangle the lines and keep everyone where they're meant to be."

She makes it sound so simple, so benign.

"So, are you . . . ? Can you . . ." Mum falters.

"Can I sense something in your house?" Rose asks with a smile.

Mum nods. "Can you?"

Rose holds her hands up and closes her eyes. "I can, yes," she says, her voice a shade deeper. "I don't think it's a bad spirit." She opens her eyes and looks at me. "But it is troubled. And it needs to go."

I can't speak. Her words have clogged up my throat.

"Come on, then," she says, handing Mum a piece of what I guess is the white sage. "Let's get started."

Speechless and numb, I watch them make their way up to my room. What else can I do?

## JOE

I'm asleep on the bed when it begins. Maybe that's why it gets me. The unexpectedness of it.

It starts as a tingle. A bit like having pins and needles. Wakes me up. My first thought is that I've been asleep on my arm, so I shake it out. But the pins and needles aren't just in my arm. They're in my hands, my fingers, my toes, legs—they're in my neck, my face.

They're everywhere.

I jump up from the bed and blink a few times as I adjust to the light.

I can hear mumbling outside the room.

Rubbing my arms and legs to try and relieve them of the weird feeling, I stumble over to the door. I don't even try to open it. I gave up trying to do that ages ago—even before Erin's dad locked me in. If I could have spoken to him, I'd have told him not to bother. I'd have told him I'm already locked in here, without his help.

I press my ear against the door and listen to the voices outside on the landing. They're coming closer.

"What do I do with this?" That's Erin's mum's voice.

"Here, let me light it. . . . Good, now just hold it in all the corners. Wave it a little, and shake it, to release its aroma and potency."

I don't know the second voice. It's a woman. Sounds quite well spoken. The kind of person my mum would have had over for tea, maybe.

"Even out here on the landing?" Erin's mum again.

"Look, like this," the other voice replies. "I surround myself with the white light of protection. I fill this house with the white light of protection. I welcome the white light of protection."

*What the hell?*

The tingling in my body is getting stronger. It feels like tiny knives are stabbing and poking me. And there's a cold feeling snaking around my body, wrapping itself around me, working its way toward my neck.

A key turning. Then the door opens.

"This is the main place it's happened," Erin's mum is saying. "Actually, it's the only room where any of us have seen anything."

"What did you see?" The other woman is behind Erin's mum. Small, slight. Thick-rimmed glasses. She looks harmless enough.

I guess looks can be deceptive.

She holds out a bunch of something that could be cooking herbs and lights the tip of it.

My neck constricts a bit more; the snake wraps itself tighter around me.

Is *she* doing this to me?

Erin's mum purses her lips. "Things moving. The curtains were flapping. The — the bed was shaking."

*I'm sorry. I didn't mean to scare you.*

The other woman nods. "Poltergeist," she says smugly. As if she's seen it all before. As if she knows all about it, all about me. As if she knows *anything*.

This woman is not pleasant. I don't like her.

She shuffles over to a corner of the room, starts waving her herbs around. There's smoke coming from them. She's muttering; same kind of stuff she was saying out on the landing. Then she breaks off, turns back to Erin's mum. Gives her some of the herbs. It looks like a bunch of lavender or something.

"Here. Take some more of the sage. Light the top of it and repeat after me," she says.

Erin's mum takes the sage and a box of matches. She lights the sage and holds it awkwardly in front of her. To be fair, she looks like she feels a bit stupid doing it. Good.

"Are you sure it's OK to do this?" she's asking. "There won't be any . . . retaliation?"

The other woman shakes her head. "Like I said, we're not punishing it." *Like hell you're not.* "We're just helping it to move on."

She goes back to her sage. "I surround myself with the white light of protection," she mutters. Then looks at Erin's mum and nods to her.

"I—um—I surround myself with the white light of protection," Erin's mum mumbles.

A pain stabs at my side. *Youch.* "I cleanse this room with the white light of protection," the woman says, waving the sage around.

Erin's mum gives her sage a shake. "I cleanse this room with the white light of protection," she repeats awkwardly.

The pain stabs me again. Harder this time. I clutch my stomach. Really? A handful of herbs can do *this* to me?

The woman moves around the room. Her eyes are glazed over, like she's in a state of ecstasy or something. She indicates for Erin's mum to follow her.

Together they keep going on about white light and protection. Every word is a sharper and sharper knife, stabbing harder and deeper into my skin. I'm doubled over, pain jabbing at my body, my insides on fire.

I want to scream. I *need* to scream. I can barely think, never mind utter any sound. It's as if they are surrounding me, as if there's an army of them. Jabbing me with knives and arrows and spears, poking me. Prodding me. Shoving me backward, edging me to the wall. Knocking me down.

"I cleanse this room with the white light of protection."

Needles pierce my arms.

"I clothe myself in the white light of protection."

Knives slash at my legs.

"I ask that the white light of protection release the spirit from this house."

A kick in the gut.

"Set it free."

Another kick.

"Release it."

A punch in my stomach.

I'm doubled over, lying on the floor behind the bed, when the door opens.

"What the hell are you doing?" It's Erin.

I don't want her to see me like this, curled up and writhing in agony. I pray she can't see me.

"Erin, go back downstairs. We're dealing with it," her mum says. She turns to the woman. "Is anything happening, Rose?"

Rose nods. "Yes, it is. It's leaving. I can feel its power dissipating. We need to keep it up."

Erin's eyes scan the room. She hasn't seen me. Yet.

"Erin should stay," the woman says calmly. How can someone who looks so benign be capable of so much damage? "She could be useful," the woman goes on. "If this is her room, she'll have the strongest connection. Her presence might even help us to get rid of it."

"I don't want to help," Erin says firmly.

The others turn to look at her. But she's not looking at them. Her eyes are still scanning the room.

"Are you sure?" her mum is asking. "I know you don't want to, but it might be good for you to be part of dealing with this."

And that is the point when Erin walks around the bed and her eyes finally land on me. Writhing on the floor. Weak, pathetic, in pain. If I had any doubts about whether she'd be able to see me or not, the look in her eyes gives me my answer.

"Please. Erin. Go. I don't want you to see me like this."

"I — I can't," she stammers.

"Why not?" her mum asks.

Erin takes a step toward me.

"No!" I shuffle away from her.

"I can't bear to see you like this," Erin whispers.

"I know," her mum replies. "I can't quite believe I'm doing it, either. It definitely feels a bit odd to begin with. But if you just repeat what Rose says, you'll get the hang of it."

"We need to get back to it," Rose says. "We're getting somewhere. We can't afford to lose the connection now. Erin, just join in when you feel ready." She reaches into her pocket and pulls out some of that evil herb stuff. Holds it out to Erin. "Here. Take some of this. Get the matches from your mother and take it into the corner over there."

Erin doesn't take her eyes off me. "No," she says. "I'm not going to help."

Rose holds the sage out for a moment longer. Then Erin's mum shakes her head, and Rose puts it back in her pocket.

An old memory bursts into my brain. Goofing around with Olly. I must have been about eight or nine, I guess. I was a weedy runt back then. He was always the cool older brother. Summer holidays down on the beach. We were playing at the water's edge. Running into the sea, farther and farther. Swimming across the bay.

We swam farther out than usual that day, messing around as always. Olly kept grabbing my head and shoving me under the water. He was just playing — trying to get me to grow up. I remember his words. "Come on, big man. Take a breath." He'd give me half a second each time, then dunk me again.

It was fun and games. To him, it was. I never told him how scared it made me feel. The dunking. The gasping for breath.

The memory slips away as the chanting begins again. They dunk me under the water. Again and again. Barely any time to take a breath in between.

I'm drowning.

I do all I can to focus on Erin. Her face, her eyes. She's fading.

I reach out to her.

She's crying.

"No. Please. Please don't cry," I urge her. My voice is hoarse. Can she even hear me? I don't know. I don't know anything. Who I am. Where I am. What's happening.

All I know is that I want this pain to end.

## Erin

Rose and Mum keep going on about white light. Waving that horrible stuff around the room. It stinks.

"It's working!" Rose exclaims joyfully. The furniture's shaking; the bed looks like it's about to collapse in on itself. Drawers are opening. Curtains are flying around. Even by the standards I've grown used to over these last few weeks, this is weird. And yes, it's terrifying.

Joe's on the floor, writhing in agony. I kneel by his side.

"Are you OK?" I ask. Ridiculously. Of course he's not OK.

I want to scream at them: *Look what you're doing to Joe!*

I settle for "Please stop."

"We can't stop now," Rose snaps. She's transformed from nice lady coming over for tea into some kind of crazed preacher, wreaking havoc all around her. "This is it. It's happening! Open the window!" she barks.

Mum crosses the room and starts battling to open the window. "Give me a hand," she calls to me over her shoulder.

"It won't open. It's painted shut," I reply.

"It's coming loose. Help me!" Mum urges.

I ignore her. Instead, I take advantage of both her and Rose facing away from me and reach out to Joe.

My hand goes through him.

"Joe," I whisper. Tears are blocking my throat.

He doesn't reply. His eyes are closed. He's veering in and out of my vision.

Mum's still battling with the window. "Erin! Do you want this to go on all day?"

Joe's eyes flicker open. "Don't forget me," he croaks. His voice is like gravel.

"Of course not."

"So give me a hand, then," Mum calls over her shoulder, still thinking I'm talking to her. Still oblivious of the fact that she's destroying my life.

I can't keep on ignoring her. "Mum, I don't know if we —"

"Got it!" Mum gasps as the window finally slides open.

Rose is in the middle of the room now. She's almost standing on Joe. Not that she knows it. Not that he knows it. Joe is fading faster and faster. I can barely see him.

Rose's hands are outstretched, her eyes closed. That bag of stupid herbs in her hand. Right now she is possibly the most terrifying thing I've ever witnessed.

"CLEANSE THIS PLACE. CLEANSE THE ROOM. LET THE WHITE LIGHT TAKE THIS SPIRIT AWAY NOW!"

She's shouting, lost in her chanting. The room is shaking, and Joe is screaming, curled up in a ball.

And then—

# JOE

The white light comes.

The scary woman is shouting, lost in her chanting. The room is shaking, and I'm screaming, curled up in a ball. All of my senses are alive. Too alive. The floor is digging into my bones, warping my flesh, scalding me. The air is clogging up my nostrils; it's too thick, too stagnant.

The sound of their chanting is filling my ears so much, it feels as if every sound in the world—every sound that has ever been uttered—is being screamed through this room. The taste in my mouth is the bitterness and salty grief of my tears.

But it's the sight that takes everything away.

All the rest of it fades away, dissolving into nothingness. In its place, there is only light. Bright. White. It's coming for me, like an escalator I cannot run from. It is filling the room, searching, spreading, spilling into every gap.

I don't want it. Don't want to go to it—and yet I can't resist, and soon there is nowhere else to go. The white light is here for me, and I know it won't leave without me.

*Erin. Erin. Please. Save me. Keep me here.*

I'm clutching, grabbing at anything.

*Don't let it get me.*

The voices are instructing it. I can hear them through the thickness of the mist and the fog of my brain.

*Let the white light remove this spirit from the house. Let the white light protect us from this spirit. Let the white light let the white light letthewhitelight letthewhitelightletthewhitelightletthewhitelightletthewhitelight . . .*

There is nothing but the white light.

Eventually, I stop fighting. I know, more surely than I have ever known anything, that I am not strong enough to resist any longer. I have nothing left to fight it. It has me beaten.

I hold my hands out. I stop curling up. Stop scrabbling around, running from the light like an insect under the glare of a boy with a magnifying glass.

*Did we do that? I think I remember.*

Was that me? Or Olly? I want to apologize. *I'm sorry, insect.*

I'm losing my mind.

I'm losing myself.

The light is taking me. Taking me from here. From this. From my home. From Erin.

"Let the white light take it away, remove it from our presence, leave this house, and be gone forevermore."

My mind is closing down.

*You win. You have me. It's over.*

# CHAPTER TWELVE

## Erin

I realize it before either Mum or Rose does.

One minute, he was there, writhing on the floor. I've never seen anything or anyone that looked like such a picture of agony. So bad that, for just a moment, even I wished it would work. Anything to release him from his pain.

And then, fading, fading, until, finally, I couldn't see him at all.

He's gone.

Everything stops. The curtains waving, the furniture shaking, the floor vibrating.

Stops dead.

Rose is still mumbling. "May the white light of protection cleanse this house and this room and keep it safe from now and forever."

Mum is looking at me. It's not till she comes over to me, kneels beside me on the floor, puts an arm over my shoulders and pulls me close that I realize I'm crying.

And once I realize it, I can't stop. Tears are running down my face like rivers, dropping off the end of my chin onto my chest, my legs, the floor.

Sobs rack my body. A tiny bit of me can hear the sound of a wounded animal and wants it to stop. The rest knows it won't, knows it's coming from me.

I'm not just crying for myself. I'm crying for Joe. For his loss, for mine. For his past, for mine.

"Shhhh, darling, it's all OK. It's gone now. You're safe."

Mum's words, whispered into my cheek as she strokes my hair, only make everything worse. They remind me how alone I am now. How I can never share this grief with anyone.

But they do something else for me, too. They stop my tears. Something hardens inside me.

Rose has finally stopped mumbling into the walls of my bedroom. She turns to me and nods slowly. "I think we're done," she says. "It's gone. I can sense it. You're free."

*Free.*

I swallow hard. I try to gulp down my rage and my grief. I want to scream. I straighten my back, shaking Mum off my shoulders as I do. "Get out," I say as calmly as I can. The words feel like a low rumble of thunder burning through my throat. It's all I can do—literally *all* I can manage—to add "please."

Rose opens her mouth to speak. She glances at Mum, who shakes her head.

Rose tightens her lips, decides against saying anything, and turns to leave. Mum leans forward and gives me a kiss on the cheek. "I'm sorry, darling. I know that was all a bit traumatic, but it's done now," she says. "It's all OK. I won't let anything bad happen to you, I promise."

I nod. I'm not giving her any more than that. "Please go, Mum," I say carefully.

With that, Mum gives me one last sad smile before getting up. She straightens the covers on my bed — the comforter came half off while everything was going crazy — then holds the door open for Rose.

"Come down in a bit, OK?" she says at the door.

I nod tightly.

I get up to close the door behind them. And then I lean against the door and wonder where the hell to go from here. My bedroom seems to be echoing with silence and emptiness.

I turn back around to face the room, walk around it. I stroke the window seat we shared, look down at my bed and remember feeling his arm around me that first time. I stand in the doorway of the walk-in closet and think of the first time we spoke. The memory is a physical pain.

I reach down to straighten the rug. It got crumpled in the corners while Joe was writhing around on the floor.

As I straighten it, I notice something on the floor. It looks like writing.

I kneel down and scan the lines. It's Joe's words; there's no doubt. The writing is scratchy and shaky, but I can just about make out what it says.

I'M LOCKED IN A PLACE THAT YOU CAN'T EVEN SEE,
A PLACE IN MY MIND WHERE IT'S HARD TO BE ME.
YOU DON'T EVEN KNOW WHAT IT MEANS TO BE FREE.
JUST GO. LEAVE ME HERE. SHUT THE DOOR. TURN THE KEY.

When did he write this? It's different from his other poems. Was it when he was alive? Or since I've known him?

I guess I'll never know—but finding it now makes me feel close to him. And I know how to feel even closer.

I grab a pen out of my bag. Then I lift the corner of the rug again. Kneeling down, and scratching carefully into the wood, I lay my verse beside his.

This room, your face, these walls, I'm trapped.
My thoughts never freed me; your words did that.
Now I'm stuck with my life and the life skills I lack.
Can't bear being left here alone—
                              please come back.

# Olly

Monday afternoon, I'm heading out to play soccer with the lads after school. I'm late, so running to catch up. I'm texting as I run to let them know I'll be there soon. That's why I don't see her till I almost run slap-bang into the back of her in the middle of the school yard.

"Whoops, sorry!"

The girl barely flinches.

I turn to glance at her, semi-running backward as I do. She looks familiar. I think she does, anyway. Something about her—do I know her?

She's barely acknowledged I'm even here, never mind the fact that I almost knocked her over. She's walking with her head down, earphones on, beanie hat pulled right down, hair flopping over what bit of face is showing, baggy coat. Shuffling along like she's in a different world from the rest of us.

"I said I'm sorry," I repeat, a bit louder. Don't know why I'm bothering. It's obvious she doesn't care either way.

I'm about to shrug and move on when the girl glances up from under her hat. Pulls her bangs aside and looks at me. Her eyes are light blue, like an early spring morning full of promise.

*What?* Did I just think that? Jesus.

She pulls out an earphone. "Sorry, did you say something?" she asks.

Then her face changes. Her pale cheeks heat up a bit. That's when I recognize her.

"Oh, it's you!" We say it in unison.

I'm expecting us both to say *jinx* at the same time, or something.

Neither of us says anything.

She looks back down and keeps on walking before I've even said a word. I'm standing there with my mouth hanging open.

I try to remember the guy I used to be. I talked to anyone and everyone. No cares. No worries. Now who am I?

I actually have no idea.

There's something about her, though. Something that makes me want to try to clamber over the wall I've built around myself. I don't know why. Pride? Ego? I don't like the idea of being rejected? Or is it something else?

Whatever it is, I find myself kind of jogging alongside her, half forward, half backward, trying to engage her in conversation.

"Hey. Look, I'm sorry."

She nods briefly as she carries on walking. "It's fine," she says. "No biggie."

*No biggie?* I envy her ability to say something so casual. When was I last as carefree as that?

I know exactly when.

Although there's something about her that tells me she's not really feeling as casual as she's trying to make out.

Which might be why, despite my better judgment, I find myself saying, "No, look. I was way out of line the other day. I need to apologize properly. And introduce myself—my name is Olly, by the way. Let me take you out for a coffee."

It's the first time I've asked a girl out since Joe died.

# Erin

Well, *that* was unexpected.

His words stop me in my tracks. For a second, anyway. It doesn't take all that long to figure out what's going on, though. I mean, come on. A guy like him doesn't ask a girl like me out on a date.

Here is the process of my thoughts.

The first second: complete shock.

The next millionth of a second: a hint of flattery.

The rest of time after that: the realization that I am almost certainly being set up. I've got to be.

I almost glance over my shoulder to see if there's a crowd of onlookers waiting to high-five each other and fall over laughing when I accept the offer and he tells me he didn't mean it and was only doing it on a bet.

I've known guys like that before. It's happened to me before. Which is why I reply, "Sorry, I can't. Thanks, anyway, though," and keep on walking across the yard.

The only thing tugging at me, slightly making me regret the speed of my reply, is the fact that he's Joe's brother. The fact that there's a small chance that he could be the one person in the world who might be able to help me.

Only as soon as I have that thought, it's swiftly followed by another.

How the hell do I think he would be able to help me, unless as well as being a relative of Joe's, he also happens to be a medium?

And that's followed by the thought that's been there all along. What if *I'm* the medium? Like that woman. What if that's why I can see him? What if I'm the one who brought Joe into being? Caused him all that anguish? What if *all* of it is my fault? I can't bear the thought of it. It's worse, even, than the thought that I'm losing my mind—and that one is never far from the surface.

It's been three days and he hasn't been back.

The pain of his absence is like a dark hole inside me, growing bigger each day. After everything I went through at my old school, even when I look back on the worst days, not one of them ever felt as sad or as lonely as this.

A couple of times I've thought of trying to escape the loneliness at home by looking things up online. Looking him up. I've come close, but I always stop myself. I'm scared of what I might see. And anyway, what good would it do? How would it make anything better? It wouldn't. It could only make me feel worse, so I haven't done it.

Meanwhile, back in the real world, Olly shrugs. "Suit yourself," he says as he turns around, running off with a soccer ball under one arm and his phone in the other.

There's something about the gesture that reminds me of something.

What is it? Where have I seen it before?

Then I remember. I haven't *seen* the gesture—I've *read* about it. It was in Joe's description of Olly in the poem he showed me. What was it?

SOCCER BALL IN ONE HAND, HIS PHONE IN THE OTHER —
THAT'S LIFE FOR MY EASY-COME, EASY-GO BROTHER.

It's exactly right. Exactly what he's doing now. The thought of it makes me feel odd—Joe describing his brother in such an accurate way, exactly as I'm seeing him in front of me right now.

I try to remember the rest of the poem. See how much of it matches up. Something about how Joe wished he could swap bodies with him.

There was more. What was that line? Didn't it say something about how Olly was the only person he could tell everything to? I know almost all of the poem. I've read and reread it countless times over the weekend. What was it again?

HE STRUTS AROUND SCHOOL LIKE A HOMECOMING KING —
AND YET STILL HE'S THE ONE I CAN TELL ANYTHING.

It's so true. He does strut. In fact, he's exactly the kind of boy I've always kept my distance from. The kind that never notices me anyway, so it's not hard. The kind where there's a mutually agreed invisible fence separating us, keeping us out of each other's space, each other's lives—each other's awareness, even.

But not now. For whatever reason, Olly seems to want to know me. Even if it is only out of guilt for acting like such an idiot with me when we last met. And even though the feeling isn't remotely reciprocated, I realize now that I was too quick to dismiss him.

He's walking away, and I can't let him. Rose's words come back to me. She said that there's a chance Joe might have been banished to the next-most significant place. If Joe told Olly everything, then perhaps he's my only chance of finding out where that place might be.

I must be desperate. Well, I *know* I'm desperate. But I'd have to be, because there is no way on this earth that I would ever have imagined I would do what I do next. Quiet little mouse me, the one who does everything she can not to be noticed, to melt into the background, to avoid causing a fuss or creating a drama. Or attracting the attention of one of the most popular boys in the school.

For the next couple of seconds, I forget that's the person I'm meant to be, and I force myself to be someone completely different.

# Olly

"Hey!"

Someone's shouting across the yard.

"Hey. Olly."

I turn around and point at my chest. "You talking to me?" I ask.

The girl blushes, and I feel bad. "Or the other Olly?" I ask, trying to make a joke. I'm a bit rusty at that kind of thing, though, and it falls flat.

"Oh, is there another one?" she asks. "I—"

"Relax," I say. "I'm pulling your leg." I fall into step with her and we walk together.

"Look, if you really want to apologize, I'll let you take me for a coffee," she says in a voice that's so flat and miserable, it sounds like she's agreeing to let me put her dog down.

Bizarrely, I quite like it. Sure, it's not how things used to work. But that was then; this is now. I don't deserve anything better. Maybe what I really need is exactly this: a reality check. Someone who can see that everything is pointless and stupid, instead of the girls I used to date, the ones who spent longer pouting at themselves into their camera phones than actually indulging in conversation with me. Not that it bothered me. I was no different.

But I am now.

Which is why I can't help smiling at her again.

She scowls. "What?"

I shake my head. "Nothing," I say. My voice comes out more softly than I've heard it for a while. "Good. I'm glad. How about tomorrow after school? There's a place in town, Charabungas."

"I know it, yeah," she says. "Spotted the crazy name when my dad forced us all to go out and have ice cream over the weekend."

I laugh. I like her.

"OK, how about meeting there at five tomorrow?"

She nods. "Cool."

"Cool," I echo. Tongue-tied. Seriously? When have I ever been tongue-tied?

She keeps on walking. I keep on accompanying her. Feeling like a fool walking alongside her. "Right. I'll . . . er, I'd better get going," I say after a few more paces, pointing at my soccer ball. "Lads'll be waiting for me."

"OK," she says.

"See you tomorrow, then." I start jogging again. Couple of steps later, I turn around, jogging backward. "I look forward to it," I add.

"Sure," she replies.

What is it with her? Why am I drawn to a miserable emo girl who doesn't even seem to like me? What the hell am I even doing making this arrangement, never mind looking forward to it? Because it's true. I *am* looking forward to seeing her. There's something about her. She's different from all the girls I know. Different from all the girls I've ever bothered with. So, why? *Why* am I bothering with her?

There's a thought at the back of my mind. An answer to my question.

I'm trying my hardest to push it away, but it's like a boulder, gathering pace as it comes toward me, and I'm not sure I can avoid it. It keeps rolling as I jog away to join my mates on the soccer field.

Then, with a thud that plows into my chest so hard it doubles me over and I can barely breathe for a moment, let alone run, it hits me.

*She's the kind of girl Joe would have gone for.*

# CHAPTER THIRTEEN

# Erin

As I continue walking home, something's niggling at me. For once, I wish I had Phoebe with me but she's staying for volleyball club. Shame. Her incessant chatter would distract me enough to take my mind off whatever it is.

No such luck. My mind isn't prepared to let me off that easily. Doesn't take long to figure out what the feeling is.

*Guilt.* I can feel the anxiety levels rise as I pinpoint the word. I need to calm it down.

A list.

### FIVE REASONS I DO NOT NEED TO FEEL GUILTY

1. It's only a coffee.

2. I'm only doing it in case it can help me find out more about Joe. Maybe even find

that he still exists somewhere else. However unlikely that might be.

3. Joe is gone.

4. I don't even like this guy. He's rude and bad-tempered.

5. Like I said, it's only a coffee.

By the time I get home, I've managed to quash the feelings down enough to put them to one side. Which is good timing, because once I'm home, I need to be ready to put on my happy smiley face, and play happy smiley family, and do everything I can to avoid my parents even remotely suspecting that I might be grieving for my boyfriend who is not only a ghost but who they have exorcised from the house and thus broken my heart.

Because there really isn't any way I will ever be able to explain that one to them. Not without a return trip to the therapist's chair. And believe me, I had enough fun there last time to keep me going for a good while yet.

I skillfully negotiate the "Nice day, darling?" greetings from Mum and Dad. I give them a few answers that will keep them reassured that all is well at school. Give them a few smiles that will keep them happy that all is well with me.

And then I head up to my room.

I try to ignore the banging in my chest as I open the door. Try to stop the little voice inside me from asking, "What if he's there? What if he's come back?" as I slope into my bedroom.

Because, as usual, the answer is "He isn't and he hasn't."

These evenings are getting longer and lonelier and harder to wade through.

And the fact that I've got a date with Joe's brother tomorrow only makes everything feel even worse.


# Olly


Tuesday, ten to five. I'm waiting outside the café. Bit early. I lift my phone to my face, pretend I'm studying a message really closely, when what I'm really doing is switching the camera to selfie mode and checking that my hair looks all right.

It's not like me to care what a girl thinks of me. Especially not lately — my own opinion of myself is so low, it doesn't usually matter what someone else thinks of me. Still.

"Hi."

She's by my side. I shove my phone in my pocket and pull my bangs out of my eyes. "Hi," I say, like an awkward kid. The thought makes me laugh.

The girl looks at me with a question in her eyes.

That's when I suddenly realize—I don't even know her name. That makes me laugh again. Nervously.

The question in her eyes turns to an awkward grimace. "Is something funny?" she asks defensively.

"No. Sorry. It's not you, it's—"

Now it's her turn to laugh. "It's not you, it's me? We're at that point already? And we've hardly even exchanged names."

I stare at her. "Yeah, that's kind of what I was laughing at," I mumble. "Look. Shall we start again?"

"Might not be a bad idea," she agrees.

"OK, I'm Olly."

I hold out my hand. She stares at it. "We're shaking hands?" she asks. "That's what we're doing?"

I pull my hand away. Move toward her to kiss her cheek instead. She flinches as if I were about to throw a cockroach down her top.

"Maybe let's go with a handshake after all," she says, holding her hand out to me. "Hi, Olly. I'm Erin."

We shake hands. It's awkward. Odd. Different.

But maybe awkward, odd, and different is exactly what I need in my life. It would certainly fit with how I feel about most things nowadays. "Nice to meet you, Erin," I say. Then I take a step back and hold the café door open for her. "Shall we . . . ?"

# Erin

Three things that happen in the café that afternoon that completely throw me off balance.

Thing one: time passes really quickly.

Thing two: we seem to laugh quite a lot. I don't even know what we laugh about. Stupid things, like showing each other our favorite YouTube videos (his: the one with a guy falling off a playground ride; mine: the one with a ferret falling off a cupboard) and then laughing about trying to figure out why falling over is so funny.

Thing three: I feel really comfortable with him. We talk so easily. Not even *about* anything. It's not like with Joe, where everything we talk about feels important and intense. In fact, it's probably the opposite. We chat about the bad weather and stupid school rules and TV and—I don't know. I can't explain it. It's just easy.

All of which adds up to a fourth thing: a helping of guilt so heavy it actually feels like a weight settling on my shoulders. And in my heart.

I can't be doing this.

But then, what am I doing that's so bad? It's only a coffee.

I check my watch. It's nearly six thirty.

"Sorry, am I boring you?" Olly asks, with that slow smile that only the confident can smile. So different from Joe's. It seems to come so easily. Joe's is a hard-won prize.

"Actually, no, I was just thinking how fast the time has passed." I bite my lip immediately. Did that sound like I was flirting? I can't flirt with him.

"Me, too," Olly says, smiling again. "We should do it again."

That has me stumped. I mean, really. Why? Why is he interested in me? Am I just a challenge because I'm not fawning all over him? Is he just the type who wants what he can't have?

Either way, it's time I did something about getting the information I came for. I spent last night rereading Joe's poems, looking for clues, looking for answers. I didn't find any—but I did at least find some questions. Some of them jumped out at me like big signposts. The line in his poem about Olly:

AND YET STILL HE'S THE ONE I CAN TELL ANYTHING.

What did he tell Olly? What might Olly know that could lead me to him?

And then there was this verse:

YESTERDAY I RAN TO THE CLIFFS,
STARED INTO THE ROARING DEPTHS,
BEGGED FOR SOMEONE TO LISTEN—
THE WIND THREW MY TEARS OFF THE EDGE.

Which cliffs did he run to? I remember when we talked, he told me there was a place he used to go to when he wanted to get away from everything. He said he sat there for hours on end, writing poems, looking out at the sea. He had a poetry cave there or something.

Where was that place? Why did I never ask him? I guess I never realized how significant it could be. And it probably isn't. I know I have to face up to the fact that he's gone, but I can't stop thinking about what Rose said: that if he's got unfinished business, he might be somewhere else with an emotional connection. Well, surely he's got unfinished business. Me.

And if anyone has a chance of helping me find the place, it's the boy sitting across the table from me now.

Which is what gives me the nerve to smile at him and say, "I'd love to do it again. How about tomorrow? Maybe we could go for a walk or something?"

And I only feel a tiny bit bad about it.

## Olly

We've arranged to meet outside the huts at the end of the beach. Like yesterday, I'm here first. This time I keep my phone in my pocket. I don't want to get caught again. Plus, I've figured out by now that she's not the kind of girl who's obsessed with how someone looks. I had never realized I'd gotten so used to being with a girl who took constant selfies of us together, who wore so much makeup you're not sure if they're real at all. How had I ever thought that was what I wanted?

This girl — Erin — is like a breath of fresh sea air next to my ex Zoe's thickly painted facade.

And you don't question fresh air, do you? You just open up and let it wash over you. You let it make you feel revived and cleansed and alive.

She's coming toward me. Head down against the wind, sunglasses on against the brightness, hat covering up most of her hair, hands thrust in her pockets. Watching her walking toward me before she's noticed me, I get the chance to look at her properly. I can't do it when she's with me — any time I look at her for longer than a second, she always turns away or hides her face under her hair or something.

It's as if everything about her is closed off. What is she protecting herself from? What is she hiding from?

And why do I have the urge to tell her I'll keep her safe?

"Hi!" I amble over to join her.

She looks up. "Hey."

I'm not going to offer her a handshake this time. And I don't really want to make her flinch from me either, so we settle for an awkward wave/nod/smile.

"Where d'you fancy walking, then?" I ask.

She pauses, looks uncomfortable for a moment. Like

I've asked her a really difficult question and she has to think hard to figure out how to answer it. I'm pretty sure all I asked was where she'd like to go for a walk.

She answers slowly. Carefully.

"It would be nice to walk somewhere special," she says. "Maybe somewhere a bit different. I've seen the touristy side of the town. I'd love to see somewhere less well known. Maybe along the coast path—somewhere that's special to you, or like a special family place, or something like that."

I stare at her. She sounds like she's reciting a speech she's learned by heart. A special family place? Who the hell has a special family place?

I realize I'm still staring, and she's probably expecting a reply.

"I . . . I . . ." I begin. Nope, still not sure where to go from there. She looks disappointed, and I realize I don't want to disappoint her. Then I have a thought. It's not exactly a special family place. But it was special to one member of the family. It was special to Joe.

My hands start shaking at the thought of my brother, so I shove them in my pockets and shove the thoughts down with them and hope she hasn't noticed.

I tell myself it's just a place. Just cliffs, grass, sea. It doesn't mean anything. Taking Erin there might even be a good way to make a new association with it. I can't avoid going anywhere near the coast path for the rest of my life.

In fact, the more I think about it, the more it seems like a good plan. Shut out the past, put it behind me forever, and let in the future. Something like that.

"OK, let's go," I say. "I know just the place."

# Joe

Dust. Or is it sand? In my mouth. Dry. Feels like a rock in the desert.

So thirsty. Lying on my back.

Where am I?

I move, shift to my side. Everything aches. Hurts to move.

How long have I been here?

I drag myself up. Sit for a moment while I get my bearings. Then—slowly, slowly—I stand. Look around.

I know where I am.

I stagger to the edge of the cave. My cave. My rocky hideout. I've been asleep. For—how long?

Bit by bit, it comes back to me. Erin and me in the house. That woman, doing that thing, chanting about—what was it? The light. White light, that's it. The light took me.

I look around again and almost smile. It brought me here.

Brushing myself down, I stumble out of the cave's entrance. The light hurts my eyes, and I can barely see.

Sitting on the rocks, I rub my eyes and try to figure it all out as I blink in the daylight and look out at the ocean.

How long was I in there?

Why have I woken up now?

The sea calms my thoughts—just as it always did. The waves washing over the edges of the rocks low down on the promontory. I breathe in as I turn full circle, looking around. This is my place. If I am here, I will be OK.

That's the last thought I have before I see them.

In the distance at first. Just two blobs, far down the coast path. They're moving in this direction.

I rub my eyes again.

They're coming closer.

It can't be—

I stumble across the rocks. I need to get to them. Need to be sure. There's a steep trail leading up to the coast path from here. I reach the edge of the rocky plinth—but I can't climb it. Something's stopping me. I don't even know what. It's just like when I was in my bedroom and couldn't get out. Held back by an invisible force.

So that's it? I'm here now, a new prison, only stuck all alone this time?

They're coming closer. It's them. It's really them! Together!

I can't believe what I'm seeing. I'm staring so hard, my eyes are watering. Is it spray from the waves? Wind in my eyes? Tears? I don't even know.

"Erin!"

I call out as they come closer. They're talking, their heads close together.

I can't bear it.

*"Erin! Olly!"*

They're looking this way.

"Over *here*!" I'm waving my arms madly—but I'm out of their line of sight.

I scramble over the rocks, try to get as high as I can. They *have* to see me. She has to see me.

*"Erin!"* I call again and again. Nothing.

They're moving away. *No!*

Frustration turns to a disappointment so harsh it's like a knife slicing right through me, through my heart, through my flesh, tearing me apart.

The rocks. I'm slipping and sliding all over them. The waves are getting bigger.

The disappointment is turning into something else. I recognize this feeling. I remember it.

Rage.

And then—as if nature is on my side—the waves increase, the sky darkens. I'm in the middle of a storm. I *am* the middle of a storm. It's right here, inside me, with me. Swirling wind, crashing waves—rocks coming loose.

The cliff path—I see it before they do. Below Erin— she's about to take a step. The edge of the cliff is coming away.

I'm screaming a silent warning to her—but she can't hear me. It's my impotent anger that's causing the problem; there's nothing I can do to stop it.

*No. Please, no!*

"Erin!"

She can't hear me. Can't see me. I'm too far away.

The rocks are coming down like an avalanche now. And then it happens.

She takes the step.

The edge of the cliff comes away.

She slips.

# CHAPTER FOURTEEN

## Erin

The wind is whipping waves into white rollers, crashing onto the rocks in the distance. I'm trying to act as though I'm really listening to Olly chatter away about nothing, trying to give him the correct responses, while all I'm really doing is wondering if by some crazy miracle, I might see Joe any minute now. My head down, shielded from the wind, I'm barely looking where I'm going. Barely listening, barely seeing.

I'm so lost in my thoughts, my loss, that I don't realize what's happening until it's almost too late.

"Watch out here; the path's quite close to the edge," Olly is saying, somewhere on the other side of the dark fog of my thoughts.

I hardly have time to register what he's said when—

"Careful!"

I take a step—the wrong step—slightly off the path, and the rocks below my foot give way. Slipping down the edge of the cliff in an avalanche, they roll away from me and I have a split second to take in what's happening.

I'm going to tumble over the side. My heart is halfway over the edge before the rest of me, and then—"I've got you!"

Olly grabs my hand. He nearly tumbles with me. The pair of us are teetering on the edge.

Then he pulls me—back from the brink, back to the safety of the path. Into his arms. So close I can smell him. A faint scent of aftershave. Soap. A human smell.

For a moment, I let myself give in to the warmth of his contact. My head tilts forward. I close my eyes. It would be so easy to lean against him, stand here with his arms wrapped around me, ask him to keep me safe. The thought takes my breath away even more than the wind snapping around us.

And then I think of Joe, and I know I can't betray him. I can't give up on him. Not yet.

Until I know for sure that he's gone, there's no room for anyone else.

I pull away, awkwardly brushing myself off.

"Thanks," I mumble.

I can feel Olly's eyes on me, forcing me to look back at him. I resist for as long as I can, while I push the twisted mess of thoughts and confused feelings back down. Finally, I raise my eyes to his.

"Are you OK?" he asks.

*No. I'm not OK at all. Nothing about me is OK.*

"Yeah. I'm fine," I say as brightly as I can manage. "Let's go back to town."

We turn back the way we came, walking along the path in silence.

It's only when we're approaching the edge of the harbor that I realize we're still holding hands.

And I know I should—but I don't let go.

## *Olly*

I don't know what it is about this girl. Have I ever felt this way before? I mean, there have been girls. Lots of girls. Too many for a seventeen-year-old, some would say. But if I think about them, this weird thing happens: they kind of melt into one.

And I know that sounds a bit awful. But Erin, she's— she's different from them all. She doesn't want to drag me around the shops, or take constant selfies of us kissing so she can post them on Facebook and Instagram and show off to all her mates.

I mean, she's the one who suggested we go for a walk— where no one would see us.

That means she's interested in being *with* me, not just interested in being *seen* with me. Right?

We get to the end of the coast path, where steps take us

down to the harbor. There's a woman with a young toddler coming up the steps, and I have to let go of Erin's hand so they can pass.

When we're back on the road, Erin's put her hands in her pockets.

"So, d'you want to meet up again?" I ask as we make our way around the harbor front.

Erin looks at me as if I'd suggested we go down to the beach and eat worms.

"I'll see you at school," she says.

I laugh. "Well, yeah. Obvs. But I meant—like, other than that. Like, you know. Maybe a proper date? Or something?" I have never realized until this moment how easy I've found talking to girls in the past. I think I just took it for granted. I've never held my breath while I wait for an answer.

Until now.

Erin bites the edge of a fingernail, in that way she does that I'm already starting to find adorable. "I . . . I don't know. Maybe. I'm not sure." She's moving away, as though I'm some kind of stalker and she needs to get rid of me. "I'll see you at school," she mumbles. "Thanks for the walk."

And before I have a chance to reply, she's turned the opposite way from the harbor and is walking away from me so fast I find myself wondering whether I actually *did* accidentally ask her to sit on the beach and eat worms.

I've clearly done *something* wrong, and I have absolutely zero idea what it was.

# Erin

I've had bad nights before now. Lots of them. Way more than I'd like to remember, in fact.

But I can't remember one as bad as this.

It starts with an hour of lying awake, tossing and turning, too hot, my brain too full, and then too cold and the night too dark and too empty. Eventually I drift into an unsettled sleep, only to wake less than twenty minutes later, drenched in sweat, with half-memories of dreams that leave me feeling desolate and desperate.

The pattern continues in a similar way through the night, repeating and relapsing on a loop of despair and grief. Every time I wake, the thoughts tumble around and around in my head.

*I have to let him go.*

*I can't. I'm not ready.*

*He's gone.*

*But what if he hasn't gone? What if he's waiting for me?*

*I looked. He wasn't there.*

*I have to let him go.*

Finally, I can't take it anymore. I wake for the fifth or sixth time from a dream where I'm falling from a cliff into a dark abyss. Olly is reaching down to me, trying to stop me from falling, but our hands keep missing. Joe is below me, trying to catch me, but he's wearing a blindfold and can't judge where I'm going to fall.

Eventually, I throw the covers off me, sit up in bed, and check the clock. Five a.m. Has a night ever dragged like this?

I get up and grab my notebook and a pen from my nightstand. Pulling a blanket off my bed, I go over to the window seat and draw the curtain aside. It's still dark out. The streetlights are on. There's a shade of lighter gray in the sky, a hint that morning might come, the sun might rise — but the sky isn't making any promises.

I wrap myself up in the blanket and open my notebook.

It's too much — my mind boiling over,
spilling into damp, breathless — awake
      and your face —
your faces — him and you and
         falling —
caught between you both and something
deep inside my chest that hurts . . .
Why?
      I was looking for you in him —
         wasn't I?
Those cliffs, the rush of water
beneath
      I swear I almost felt you again . . .
But that touch,      his touch —
hand in hand replayed over and over —
      that wasn't you.

The heat of the day gets hotter
with each broken sleep, each dream . . .
    OK,
        I like him,
OK,
    that smile, the warmth of an arm
that's here — really here —
    but you . . . with you
I don't know —
        What if I never see you again?
Joe, I think I could die
    and even my bones would miss you.

Writing my feelings down into a poem usually helps. Not this time, though. How can admitting I'm in such pain help anything?

In the past, I needed an outlet, needed to get my feelings out of me, deal with them so I could face the people in my life. This time, I don't need to get the people in my life out of my system; I need the opposite. I need Joe. The need is so strong, it is like a pain deep inside me.

I close my notebook. I have to get out of here.

Padding around my room as quietly as I can, I quickly get dressed and sneak out of my bedroom, softly shutting the door behind me. I creep downstairs, avoiding the creaky floorboards on the landing.

Then I head to the cliffs.

# JOE

What did I do to deserve this? Banished to a rocky ledge with nothing but a cave and endless waves for company. Seeing her in the distance, missing the moment when she might have seen me. Torturing myself with thoughts, memories, regrets.

When will it end?

I am losing myself in my pity. It's drowning me more surely than the waves that are creeping over the point, running into deep pools and filling the crevices between the rocks on a tide that is climbing higher and higher. I wish it could wash me away—but it can't even do that. And I can't even leave this piece of headland.

I turn around in a slow circle, taking in the dark murmuring of the ocean, the rustle of the wind through reeds above me. The utter loneliness of this existence.

I don't know how long I can bear it before I go crazy.

In fact . . .

Maybe it's already happening. I'm seeing things—I must be. My brain is torturing me with pictures that can't be real. It *can't* be real.

I rub my eyes and peer into the murky darkness.

*It's her.*

It's really her. She's coming toward me.

I've got another chance. I know without a doubt that it will be my last one, and I can't let it pass me by.

I scramble at the cliff side, trying to climb it, my clothes tearing on the jagged rocks. Slipping down, again and again. Can't grip the rock, can't climb up, can't reach her. It's like trying to open my bedroom door. I can't do it. I'll never be able to do it. I'm confined to this rocky outcrop, the stage where I get to play out the tragedy of this nightmare I can't call life *or* death.

I fall back, hunched over on the long gray rock that is the only flat part of this place.

I need to think of something. I refuse to let her slip through my fingers again. I have to get to her. I *have* to. I'm not even going to worry about what happens next, how impossible any of this is. All I know is that I need her to see me, just one more time.

## Erin

I don't even know what I'm doing. Now that I'm out here, on an unstable cliff path in almost pitch-darkness with the sea roaring somewhere below me, I have my first flicker of fear.

I didn't realize this was where I was heading till now. Something brought me here. A feeling, an instinct, I don't know—but I owe it to the feeling to give it one last shot, give Joe one last shot, before I give up.

There's a pale-pink line separating the sea and the sky out on the horizon. The world will be waking up soon.

Picking my way along the rough ground, I try to speed up.

I'm coming to the point where I slipped yesterday. I need to be careful. I stop and get my bearings. Behind me, a faint twinkle of lights from the town and the harbor; ahead and to the left of me lies the darkness of the cliffs. To my right, the pink line is growing thicker and deeper, almost maroon now, stretching out as the world wakes from its sleep. A mist is coming up with it, slinking over the water and toward the town, swirling like a genie released from his lamp.

The mist comes in fast from the sea — I've seen it a few times since we've been here.

That's all I need. I don't have a coat, it's dark and cold, and any minute now, I'll probably be standing in the middle of a thick fog.

It's not here yet, though.

I look down to my right. There's an outcrop of rocks, below the path, almost down at sea level. It looks dangerous down there. Waves breaking over them.

I tiptoe closer to the edge of the cliff and look down. There's a straggly path down to the rocks. It's calling to me. I don't know why. It looks steep and tough, and the rocky plinth looks craggy and dark and dangerous. Why would I want to go down there?

I don't know the answer. But something is pulling me, and I need to investigate.

Carefully and slowly, I scramble down the slippery path, feeling for footholds and gripping on to any protruding edge I can find.

I jump the last bit. I'm on the rocks. Wiping salt from my eyes, I pull my hair from my face and look around.

At first, I think I must be imagining it. I'm sure the brain does that kind of thing, kids you that something is in front of you if you've been imagining it and wishing for it so hard. Like a mirage. That's what it is: a mirage.

And then he says my name.

## JOE

I can't move. I feel as if the world has stopped.

I have to find my voice. I force myself to swallow, dry gravel swirling through my throat. Then I give it a go.

"Erin," I say. My voice is hoarse.

She takes a step toward me, slips on a rock. I leap forward and reach for her. I grab her arm.

"You OK?" I ask.

She looks at my hand on her arm. It's only then that I realize—we are touching. Whatever it is that has banished me here hasn't broken our tie. Whatever it is that brings us together isn't letting us go.

She turns slightly so she's facing me. Our eyes are locked—joining us like a bridge across our worlds. I can't turn away. Without shifting my gaze, I run my hand down her arm, feeling for her hand. She grips my hand in hers. Her touch is like a spark inside me. It ignites me. I never thought I would see her again, let alone feel her hand in mine.

Erin lifts her other hand. Slowly, so slowly, she raises it to my face, places her palm against my cheek. I close my eyes—I can't help myself—and press my cheek against her hand. I feel as if I am experiencing human contact for the first time ever. I feel like a prisoner leaving his jail behind after serving a long sentence. I feel like a condemned man who has been offered one last chance at life.

A gasp turns into a sob in my chest.

Erin inches forward. There's a question in her eyes. I let go of her hand, draw my arm around her waist, pull her closer. Her face is close to mine. So close I can see tiny beads of moisture on her cheek. The salt air has tangled her hair; a strand has come loose in that way it does.

I lift my other hand, touch her face. I can feel her breath on my cheek. As I fold the loose strand back, I gently pull her face closer to mine.

I watch her eyes, watch them till the last moment, the last millisecond, when her eyelids softly close. And then I close mine, too.

As the waves wash gently over the rocks, as the seagulls

circle, as the day dawns, as the wind whistles and the mist lifts, our lips finally meet.

I am lost in the moment, in Erin, in this place, in the electricity that feels as if it is crackling around us like a lightning storm.

And I know one thing.

If this is how it feels to be lost, I would be happy never to be found again.

# CHAPTER FIFTEEN

## Erin

I have never been kissed before.

Or at least, that is how it feels. I have been kissed. But I don't know if two snogs behind the gym and one in the back row of the cinema with Timothy Bolton counts. Or that time I thought Dean Smith meant it, and it turned out he was doing it on a dare. I had to feign illness for a week after that, till I hoped everyone had stopped laughing at me.

Not that they ever really stopped laughing at me.

Anyway, if those kisses ever did count, they certainly don't now. Nothing counts now. Nothing even exists, except Joe's lips on mine, his arms tightening around my waist, pulling me closer — so close I am starting to wonder where I end and he begins.

The thought makes me laugh. It's the kind of thing you hear in songs — soppy, badly written, cheesy pop songs that

I've always thought were describing a feeling that didn't exist in real life.

Now I know it does.

Joe pulls away. "What are you laughing at?"

I smile at him. "I'm just happy," I say.

He hesitates. "Are you?"

I step back a little so I can see him properly. "Are you kidding me?" I laugh again. "You're seriously asking me that?"

Joe makes a face. He looks awkward.

"What? What is it?" I ask.

"I just . . . I mean . . . this. Me. Stuck here." He opens his arms to point out our surroundings. "At one point, I wondered if kissing you would bring me back to life, like turning a frog into a prince." He laughs quietly as he looks down at himself. "But it hasn't. I mean, I feel stronger, I feel more—I dunno—alive, I suppose, when you're here. But still, I'm *not* alive. And I'm not . . ."

His voice fades away, his words disappearing into a whisper like a wave washing gently off the rocks.

"You're not what?" I ask.

Eventually, he mumbles, "I'm not him."

"You're not . . ." I begin. Then I realize what he's saying. "Your brother?"

Joe won't look at me. He nods.

I reach out to touch his cheek. Still looking down, he presses his face against my hand. "Joe, look at me."

He raises his eyes upward. I smile at him. "I don't want Olly," I say. "I only went for a walk with him in the hope that it might help me find you."

"Really?"

I nod. "*Really*. Joe, I only want you."

Still half looking down, he smiles at me. His shyness makes me bold. I slip my arms around his neck. Draw him closer, reach up to whisper into his ear. "If you knew how much I've wanted this moment, how I haven't stopped thinking about you since you went, you wouldn't doubt me."

Joe replies by pulling me closer still. This time when our lips meet, the urgency of our kiss takes away any doubt, any fear, any worries. Nothing exists — in this world or any other — except this moment, this kiss, us.

## Olly

Thursday morning I wake up, get showered and dressed as usual. But as I do, I'm aware that there's something different about the morning, or about me.

The first clue is when I catch myself whistling in the shower. When did I last do that?

I glance at myself in the bathroom mirror, and that confirms it. I'm smiling.

I stare at the face looking back at me as if it's a stranger's. That's when I realize what the feeling is.

It's something like happiness; something like optimism.

The realization stops me in my tracks. Do I have the right to feel either of those things?

Before I get used to it, the usual feelings of guilt, shame, and grief engulf me. This time, they hit so hard, I find myself falling backward. The emotion is like a sharp, well-directed punch in my gut.

Grabbing the sink for support, I sit on the edge of the bath and catch my breath.

*I am allowed to feel happiness, I am allowed to feel happiness, I am allowed to feel happiness.*

I say the words over and over to myself.

Even though they are a lie, the mantra calms my heart rate down enough that I figure I can stand up without passing out.

I throw cold water on my face, check that I've got my happy-go-lucky expression back in place, and head downstairs for breakfast with Mum and Dad.

Half an hour later, I'm out the door and hurrying to school. I want to get there before her.

I'm hanging out in the yard, kicking a ball around with Tod and Matt and some of the others, pretending to be interested in the game but mostly looking for her.

Zoe and her little gaggle are hanging around the school

entrance, preening and gossiping and fake-laughing at one another's jokes as usual. I give Nia a nod as they pass me. She's not as bad as Zoe and Kirsty. I don't really know why she hangs around with them.

"Oi. Olly. Ball," Matt calls over.

I'm about to turn for the ball—and then I see her. "Carry on without me for a bit," I call back to Matt. I jog past Zoe and her crew and over to Erin. I spot all three girls turn to watch me, feel three sets of eyes on my back as I pass them.

In the past, it would have been Zoe. I'd have kissed her and slung an arm over her shoulder and been as happy as her to strut into the school with the best-looking girl on my arm.

How could I have been so shallow?

I don't care about any of that now. Let their eyes burn into my back. Erin's the one I want now. And I don't care if they know it.

She looks up as I approach. I fall into step beside her.

"So. Hey," I say.

She gives me a half-smile and raises a *Seriously?* eyebrow.

We head toward the school doors. Zoe and her crew watch us walk past them with their jaws hanging open. I don't care about them. I care about Erin.

"OK, maybe that wasn't my smoothest line ever," I admit.

She laughs, and I feel like I've won a prize.

"Come out with me," I say, seizing the moment.

Erin stops in the doorway and looks at me. Zoe and the others walk past, heads craning so far around to look at us, you'd think their necks were made of elastic, Zoe's eyebrows raised so high, they practically form a part in her hair. Forget Zoe. "On a date," I add. "A proper date. This weekend, maybe."

The girls have passed us now. So have most of the others. I think the bell's rung and we should be heading to homeroom. Neither of us moves.

"I . . . what?" Erin stammers. "I—I mean, that's really nice of you," she adds.

I laugh. "I'm not saying it to be nice. I'm saying it because I like you. So, what d'you think?"

Erin lets out a breath. Then she shakes her head. Very slightly. Just enough to pierce my hopes. "I'm sorry," she says eventually. "Thank you, but I—I'd better not."

She starts to walk away, and I trot along beside her like a confused puppy. "What's up?" I ask. "I thought you liked me. We had a good time yesterday, didn't we? I mean, we don't need to rush it. We could just—"

Erin stops walking again. Looks me in the eye. Her forehead creases for a moment. She looks like she's weighing something in her mind. Then she speaks again. "I just can't," she says. "I'm sorry. I—I already have a boyfriend."

And with that, she turns and walks away, leaving me standing on my own, feeling like a fool.

# Erin

Did I actually just do that? I mean, how many firsts was that in one go?

First time I've actually been officially asked out on a date.

Judging by the look on his face, I'd say it was the first time a girl has said no to Olly.

First time I've called Joe my boyfriend out loud.

I am also aware that it was the first time the rest of Nia's friends have noticed me since I arrived here.

All of which leads me . . . where? Rushing to homeroom with my brain in a jumble is mostly where it leads me. My head is still full of thoughts of Joe. My lips are still tingling from the feel of his mouth on mine. How could I even think about going on a date with anyone else? I can't.

There are three or four chairs free when I get there. Before I've thought about which one I might pick, I spot Zoe Philips nudge Nia and nod at the seat on their row, next to Nia.

Nia smiles at me and pulls the chair out. "Sit here," she says warmly.

"Thanks," I mumble, and sit down.

I try to spend the next ten minutes making myself as invisible as I can. Old habits die hard. I rummage through my bag, pretend to be looking for something, pull out a notebook and pen, pretend to scribble down something important. It's my default behavior. It's what's got me through hundreds of homeroom periods before now. It's how I block out the giggling, the name-calling, the prods in my back. The notes being passed around the class about me.

I still see them, though. Which is how come I spot Zoe scribble something on a piece of paper, then tear it out of her notebook and fold it in half.

Here we go. The whole thing was a ruse. Get me to sit with them so they can pull me to pieces and make fun of me more effectively.

I straighten my back, try to make myself ready for it.

And I am. I will be. I have been many times before. But it turns out I'm not actually ready for what *does* happen, as the next few seconds take me completely by surprise.

Zoe passes the note to Nia and nudges a thumb toward me.

The note is for *me*?

Nia slips the note to me under the desk.

My heart is banging so hard I'm wondering when someone's going to mention it. Surely they can hear it?

What do I do? Open the note? Ignore it?

If I had a hundred pounds—which I don't—I would bet it on the probability that Zoe's note is going to say something like "Who d'you think you are, loser? Lay off Olly. He's MINE!"

Good thing betting isn't allowed in school, then.

I unfold the note.

> Hey, sorry we've not met properly yet. I'm having a sleepover on Saturday. Wanna join us? Luv, Zoe

It's just as well I'm sitting down, or I would probably have fainted in shock. I have to read the note three times before I'm sure I've got it right.

I might not be the most popular girl in school, but I'm not an idiot. I know that Zoe wouldn't be interested in being my friend if she hadn't just witnessed one of the school's A-list boys talking to me.

But even so. Is it really superficial of me to be glad? Is it wrong to be aware of how nice it would be to fit in? To think that, regardless of her motivation for asking me along, once they get to know me, they might actually want to be my friends anyway? That I could ever actually be part of a group of girls? That I could be one of the gang?

Is it so awful to want those things?

I don't think so.

Which is why I open my notebook and turn to a blank page. Hunched over my desk so it looks as if I'm working, I scribble on the corner of the page.

*That would be amazing!!!!*

No. That's no good. Too eager. Way too many exclamation marks. I check that no one's looking, then I rip off the corner, crumple it up, and try again. *Be cool, Erin.*

*I'll check with my parents and let you know.*

*Really?* I want Zoe to think I'm a little kid who has to get her parents' permission?

In the end, I surreptitiously rip a third piece of paper out of my notebook and keep it as real as I can.

*I'd love to. Let me know the plan
and I'll see you there.*

Do I sign my name? I mean, it's not as if she doesn't know who it's from. On the other hand, she signed hers. She even put *luv* on it. In the end, I scribble my name, add a couple of kisses, and pass the note to Nia.

She passes it to Zoe, who opens it, smiles, and gives me a thumbs-up.

I can't help smiling back.

I know I should keep my feet on the ground. I know that if I don't, it'll be my face falling flat on the ground instead. I know, I know, I know.

But just for once, I've decided to forget. I've decided to fit in. I've decided to toy with the idea of being part of a group of girls. And not just any group. The popular group.

And as Nia joins me on the way to English and links my arm while she tells me about the kinds of things that happen at Zoe's sleepovers and the laughs they have together, I've decided I like it.

# CHAPTER SIXTEEN

## olly

I'm not ready to let her go yet.

I've been asking around. Just a bit. And I've discovered why I hadn't noticed her till now.

Turns out she only moved here a couple of months ago.

Which means that the boyfriend probably lives in her old town.

Which means he isn't here.

Ergo: fair play, I say.

I manage to engineer it so that I happen to be hanging around outside the school doors as she's leaving.

She's with Nia and Kirsty. I didn't realize she was friends with them. That throws me off my stride for a moment. Zoe's not around, so at least I don't have to deal with her *trying not to look like she cares* stares.

I wander over.

"Hey," I say, trying to sound as casual as I vaguely remember once being.

Nia spots me first and nudges Erin. "I'll leave you to it," she says with one of those knowing winks that girls give each other when they've been discussing boys. She and Kirsty move away. "See you tomorrow," they trill with a little wave.

And we're on our own.

"You don't give up easily, do you?" she says as we walk across the yard.

"Nope."

"Even when I told you I've got a boyfriend?"

I nod. "Even then."

She bites her lip. Makes my heart do a stupid little jump. I want to touch her lip where she's biting it. I am actually shocked enough that it stops me in my tracks for a moment. I want to kiss her.

I haven't felt like this since before . . .

"So, look, I've been thinking," I say quickly. Anything to stop my mind from going where it was about to go. No point in ruining a potentially good moment with my morbid thoughts.

"No one ever told you that's bad for you?" she says drily, and I laugh.

"Look. We can be friends," I blurt out.

She raises an eyebrow. "Friends," she says. There's a half-smile dancing in her eyes.

"Yeah. Why not? Just 'cause you're a girl and I'm a boy, that's no reason why we can't hang out. Is it?"

She tilts her head to the side as she thinks. "I suppose not."

I lean closer, looking at our feet walking in time. I lower my voice. "I figure this boyfriend of yours must be a long way away, and what he doesn't know won't hurt him, right?"

Erin stops walking and looks at me. Her face is . . . I don't know. She looks different, suddenly. Which is when I realize how all this might sound. Like I've been looking into her background. Like I'm some kind of stalker.

"Look, I didn't mean — I meant — I was just guessing, I mean, you've only just started here, right?" I babble ridiculously.

She turns away again, walks more quickly. We're nearly at the gates at the end of the yard. Last chance. "Look. No strings, no funny business. Just meet me this weekend. Saturday night."

"I'm busy Saturday night," she says quickly.

"Friday, then. Tomorrow night. We can go for a burger or something. Or go to the amusement park or the cinema. Whatever you want. I just want to get to know you."

Erin stops at the gate. I stop, too. She raises those big sad eyes and meets mine.

"Why?" she asks softly.

"Why what?"

She shrugs. "Why me?"

For a moment I'm stumped. I mean, she's right. *Why* her? Is it just my pride? I don't like being turned down? Is that what this is about? Am I *that* shallow? Or is it something more than that?

Is it that the things that used to matter so much to me now feel so meaningless that they've forced me to look in different places for any possibility of happiness? Is it that she seems so much like a girl Joe would have gone for that I think she'll somehow make me feel closer to him? Is it that I want to be a better person, and something about her makes me think she could help me get there? That she can give me absolution or something?

Is it all of those things, or something else entirely?

Either way, she's got her eyes trained on me, and I know for sure that the last thing I'm going to tell her is the truth.

So I shrug right back at her and reply in the only way that I can without feeling like I'm coming apart at the seams.

"Why not?"

## Erin

I stare at him for another moment or two. What is it with this guy? Why the hell is he interested in me? And why now? Why, when I've finally found Joe again and am not remotely interested in anyone else, am I suddenly attractive to the kind of guy who has never in the whole of my life paid me the slightest bit of attention?

And why do I want to say yes? Is it that being seen with him seems to be my passport to actually being part of a group of friends for once in my life?

Is it that I want an excuse to find out more about Joe, and Olly is my only access to that information?

Well, yes. It is; it's both of those things.

But the truth that I would *really* like to hide from if I could, but that unfortunately I don't think I can, is a bit simpler than that.

I like him.

Not in the way I like Joe. Joe is like the other half of me. He makes me feel whole. He's like the answer to the questions I've been asking all my life, the ending to the sentences I begin that have always gone nowhere till I met him.

No one could come close to what Joe means to me — not even his brother.

But Olly makes me feel . . . I don't know. Light, I guess. He makes me smile. He makes me want to have fun. And I can't help wondering if it's really so wrong to let myself do those things occasionally.

Which is why, finally, I smile at him. "All right, I give in," I concede. "We can hang out together. But just as friends, OK?"

Olly grins back at me so widely, his smile makes his eyes dance. He gives me a Boy Scout salute. "Just friends.

All clear. So shall I call for you tomorrow? I don't even know where you live."

"I—" I'm about to give him my address, but I stop myself just in time. I can't tell him I live in his old house! I don't like being dishonest with him, but there's no way I can start complicating things like that. "Let's meet in town," I suggest.

Olly nods. "OK. How about meeting me outside Mr. Fish at seven?"

I already know Mr. Fish. It's Phoebe's favorite fish and chips place. I might actually have plans that my little sister would be jealous of, for the first time since we got here. Probably for the first time ever.

"Sounds good," I agree.

"Fab. It's a date."

I give him a stern look.

"What?" Olly looks confused. "Oh. Sorry. No. It's not a date. It's definitely not a date. It's just hanging out. With a pal. Is that OK?"

I laugh. I can't help myself. "Yeah, that's cool," I say.

We've reached the school gates, and he turns to walk the opposite way from me. "See you tomorrow, then," he says before giving me one more flash of that big smile.

"Yeah, see you tomorrow," I reply. And despite myself, despite wishing I wasn't, despite hating myself for it, and despite knowing it's wrong, I can't help admitting to myself that I'm looking forward to it.

# Olly

She likes me. She does. I know she does. I'm sure she does. I think. I mean — the way she smiles. The way she kind of looks at me from under her hair, like she's trying to hide, trying not to smile, trying not to enjoy my company — all of it, I love it.

It's like a challenge — but not the kind of challenge the old Olly would have wanted. The kind that's all about the chase and the winning and the telling the guys I scored again.

It couldn't be further from that kind of challenge. It's not about notches or scoring. It's more a challenge to myself. A challenge to be a better person, to be as good as she is, to be worthy of her.

She's good for me. She's going to be good for me. I can tell. She's already changing me. She's already given me the first feelings of hope and optimism and even — dare I say it? — happiness that I've felt in over six months.

And I don't want to tell the lads. I don't want to tell anyone, in fact. I want to keep it to myself, keep her to myself.

Yeah, OK, she's got a boyfriend. If I'm honest, if I think about it, that makes me feel bad. But like I said to her, we're just friends. Where's the harm? I'm not asking her to cheat on him. And if, in time, he starts to fade and she realizes she likes me more — well, that's up to her.

In the meantime, we can hang out. I can allow myself that. Can't I?

To hell with it. I'm doing it, I'm seeing her. Erin is a way for me to leave behind my grief over Joe, my guilt, my suffering. She's got nothing to do with any of that. She's the first person, the first thing, that has come along and given my heart and my mind respite from all that pain. She's like a fresh breath and a new start.

Erin could be my future. My way to a better future. And I'm not going to lose out on that.

## Erin

Friday morning I'm up at five o'clock. I set my alarm when I went to bed, but I'm awake before it goes off.

I get dressed and creep out of my room. I can hear Dad snoring as I pass their bedroom. Aside from that, the house is silent. I slip downstairs, let myself out as quietly as I can, and head for the cliffs.

Pulling my coat tight and flicking my flashlight on, I tread carefully along the path, watching every footstep and praying he'll still be there.

As I approach the rocky outcrop where he is—Joe told me last time that it's called Raven's Point—I look out toward the horizon. There's a thin line of light between the sea and sky. Dark clouds above it seem to be holding it down, stopping the day from arriving too soon. Good. I want the next hour to pass as slowly as possible. Until we can work out anything better, this is my only chance to see Joe, and I want to make the most of it.

"Erin!"

I look down. He's there on the rocks, waiting for me. The sight of him feels like air, filling me with lightness and space. It's as though I spend my days walking around buckled into a tight, heavy suit of armor, and Joe unbuckles me from the metal and releases me from it — and from a need for it.

I pick my way down the stony trail to join him. In an instant, his arms are around me. His breath is warm in my ear. "I've missed you so much," he whispers, pulling me close.

His embrace eliminates the outside world. I wrap my arms around his neck, leaning close and pressing myself into his chest.

His hands stroke my hair. "I can't bear only seeing you like this," he says. "It's not enough."

I move slightly away to answer him, but as I glance up at him, the look on his face removes any words I might have had. His eyes — they're full of longing and pain. Searching mine. I wish I could take the pain away. Wish we could figure out a way to be together properly, not just a stolen hour of darkness before the rest of the world has woken up. For a moment, I'm hit by the futility, the impossibility of our situation. Life and death. There couldn't be a bigger barrier between us.

And it's not the only barrier. I can't bear the fact that I'm keeping something from him. I had intended to tell Joe as soon as I got here about my plans to see Olly. I don't want to lie to him or hide anything from him. Olly is just a friend — and he's Joe's brother. Surely Joe would understand that and be glad for me. For us both.

But when his eyes are so dark and so filled with pain, I lose my nerve, and I can't tell him. Not now. Not yet. I convince myself there's no need, and no time. We have an hour together. I don't want to waste it talking about other people. I just want to focus on us, on here, on now.

I reach up, put my hand on the back of Joe's head. My fingers in his coarse hair, I pull him toward me.

A moment later, his lips meet mine, and I stop thinking or worrying about anything.

## JOE

She brings me to life. Not in the way I'd hoped. Not *actually* back to life. But closer to it than I am when she's not here. When I'm alone, I feel as intangible as the air around me. I feel as if I could dissipate at any moment, like the spray of the waves. But when she's here, when the feelings between us are strong, I come into being; I'm almost real.

But it's not enough. Of course it's not enough. I could spend every waking moment with her, lie by her side every night, and it still wouldn't be enough. I would always want more.

Because I love her.

I want to tell her. I need to tell her. Can she tell? Can she see it in my eyes? I feel as if the love is leaking out of me, pouring out through my eyes and my kisses. It's making me more real but emptying me out at the same time.

Does she know? Does she feel the same?

But even though loving her feels like the best thing I've ever done, it feels selfish, too. My love is keeping her from having a life. It's holding her in this half-living place with me. How can that be fair?

Then I lose myself in her pale-blue eyes, and I know I will never willingly let her go.

"Come, look, let me show you my place," I say. I take her hand and we pick our way carefully across the rocks and the crevices, over the boulders, over the dark pools teeming with tiny bits of life. Across the rocky stage that is the only bit of the world I can exist on.

"Under here." We duck down under a large precipice. It's like a roof, a canopy. I let go of her hand so we can tread single file through the crevice under the rock. On the other side, I point to the cavern in the side of the cliff to our left.

Erin stops and peers in. "Wow. This is it?" she asks. "Your poetry cave?"

I smile and open my arms across the entrance as if I'm welcoming her into my mansion. "Come on in," I say, as I lead the way.

Erin ducks down to squeeze into the cave and follows me to a ridge along the side. I sit down and pat the rock next to me for her to do the same.

She sits and looks around.

I point at the corner of the ceiling, where damp drips plop from the end of a triangular rock that protrudes down. "There are a couple of stalactites here."

Erin nods. "Very cool."

I point at a low, flat rock in front of us. "Coffee table," I say.

Erin laughs and leans into me. I put an arm around her shoulder. With my other arm I point out through the doorway. "And the sun rises around about there."

Erin follows the line of my hand. The cave's entrance is like a frame. Beyond it, a hint of light is starting to edge over the horizon. A speck of light, with pink veins growing out from it. A few fluffy clouds above it are growing into pale bruises.

"I love it," Erin says.

She turns to look at me. I hold her eyes, holding my breath at the same time. I need to say it, need to tell her, need to have it out there—however crazy or hopeless it is.

"Erin, I—" I begin. My mouth is as dry as the rocks in

the dark corners of the cave. My throat feels as if it is filled with them, too.

Erin's eyes are on mine, she's holding me here, like a fly pinned to a wall by its wings. She's taking my words away. "I . . ." I try again.

But she stops me with a kiss. And then I forget what it was I wanted to say after all. It can wait.

The time is going too quickly. The tiny spark of light peeking up from behind the horizon is growing fatter and rounder.

We watch it grow brighter, the clouds turning into fat peaches above it.

"I need to go," Erin says softly. "Everyone'll be awake soon."

She gets up to leave. "I wish you didn't have to go," I say.

"Me too," Erin says at the doorway. Then she stops and turns to face me. "Joe, I . . ." she begins. Then hesitates.

I know what she wants to say! I can see it on her face. She feels the same! Of course, she does. But I don't want her to have to say it first.

"I love you," I blurt out.

For a moment, Erin looks startled. She even falls back on her heels a tiny bit.

That was what she was going to say, wasn't it? Her silence is making me doubt it.

Then she smiles. A beautiful, slow smile that spreads

more light than the sunrise behind her. "I love you too, Joe," she says softly.

A moment later, we're in each other's arms again, and this time our kisses are even more intense. I want to hold her tighter and closer. I want to crawl into her and live just underneath her skin, be part of her forever.

And I know that when she leaves me in a few minutes, I'll feel like a rag doll with its insides taken out, and my day will spread out like an eternity.

She pulls away first. "I really need to go," she whispers. Then, with one last kiss on the end of my nose, she wriggles out of my arms and turns to leave.

She stops at the cave's entrance and turns back. "See you tomorrow?" she says.

"What about later today? Come after school, this evening?"

"I—I . . ." Erin's face reddens. "I can't. I've got to do this thing. Meeting up with some friends."

I shrug. Try to act as if I don't care, despite knowing how pathetic it is to even try. I've spread my heart out on a cliff edge for her. "OK," I say. "See you tomorrow, then. I love you."

She smiles. "I love you."

And then she's gone. And I'm left standing in a cave watching the sun climb into the sky and wondering how I can make those three words keep me going for another twenty-four hours.

# CHAPTER SEVENTEEN

# Erin

I'm a terrible person. How can he not see that? Every step I take along the path home is punctuated with a mental kick. Why didn't I tell him? How can I be so deceitful? How can he love me?

I was going to tell him. I know he wouldn't like it, but at least it would have been honest. There's nothing in it at all. Olly and I are just friends. We're barely even that. But we might *become* friends. Why is that so wrong? If there's nothing in it, why do I feel so guilty?

Other than the fact that I kept it from Joe?

I was about to say it. I opened my mouth. The words were right there, ready to slip out, ready to be laid bare for him — and then he went and told me he loves me.

Which is amazing.

Which is wonderful.

Which is how I feel about him, too.

But now all I can think is that maybe he wouldn't have said it if he knew the truth. That the reason I can't come back to see him this evening is because I'm meeting his brother.

I'm an awful person.

The feeling follows me all the way home. It's like a shadow that I can't shake off.

I don't like it. I've been here before. I know this cloud; I'm familiar with this shadow. It was a fairly permanent feature of my life for years, following me everywhere, growing lower and lower and closer and closer until it swallowed me up and I couldn't see my way out of it.

Is that what this whole thing will do to me? Is it ultimately the craziest thing I could ever have chosen to do — to fall in love with a dead boy? What does that say about me? About my commitment to life? Other than the fact that Joe's love makes me feel more alive than I've ever felt.

So why am I now tearing that apart by messing around with someone else?

I don't know the answers to any of it, but even the questions are freaking me out. I can't afford to focus on this. I'm not going there again. I need a strategy.

As I sneak back into the house and up to my bedroom, I go over a plan in my head.

1. I'll tell Olly this evening that my boyfriend says I can't see him again.

2. I'll tell Joe I met up with Olly but that I'm not going to see him again.

3. I will *not* give in to the dark cloud and will dodge it by keeping myself busy.

4. I'll focus on nice things, like the fact that I've got a sleepover with my new friends tomorrow. (And will not let myself get nervous about this, either.)

By the time I go downstairs, yawning and stretching and dressed for school to join the others for breakfast, the cloud has already turned into a light mist and started to move away.

I manage to banish it for the whole day. In fact, it's probably the best day I've had since we arrived here.

Zoe passes notes to me in homeroom, reminding me about Saturday and confirming that I can come. Nia saves me a seat in English, and we work together on a poem and chat and giggle our way through class. I even get told off for laughing at one point, and Nia instantly apologizes and says it was her fault. I don't think anyone has ever done something like that in school before.

Kirsty beckons me over to join the three of them at lunchtime, and I do my best to keep up with the gossip and the chat. Any time Zoe mentions someone I might not know, Nia gives me a nudge and explains the background. I have to keep stopping and telling myself it's really happening. I'm really part of the group—I've got actual friends.

And in between all of it is the best thing of all. The memory of this morning, of Joe's words, the fact that he loves me.

I've never known a school day to pass so quickly or so happily. By the time I'm getting ready to go out with Olly, I've almost forgotten the person I used to be—the shy, awkward, anxious person who barely spoke to anyone through five years of high school.

In fact, as I'm walking around to the harbor front to meet Olly, I make another decision: that girl is gone and she's not coming back. I won't let her. I don't need her. I am pretty sure that a whole new life is starting for me.

For the first time since we moved here, I am truly happy—and truly ready to leave the past behind me.

Olly is there before me again.

He smiles as he sees me coming, and I don't know why—and yes, I hate myself a bit for this—but my stomach gives a little flutter at the sight of him.

It's not like the way I feel with Joe. Nothing could ever come close to that. The way I feel about Joe is the most all-consuming thing I've ever felt. It's true love. This isn't even in the same league. Olly's just a friend.

He's just a friend.

But there's no denying that he's attractive, and he *is* fun to be with. As a friend.

"You look lovely," he says, looking me up and down in a way that makes me feel like I'm blushing down to my feet. I'm not used to being complimented in that way. Not even by Joe. With Joe, it's as if the outside of me isn't even relevant. He sees all the way through to what's inside. Olly's eyes are definitely traveling the length of my body. He makes me feel exposed—especially as for once I put on a closer-fitting shirt with my jeans and left my beanie hat at home. He's making me feel like I should have put on another layer of clothes to hide inside.

"You don't look too bad yourself," I find myself replying, to cover my embarrassment and take the focus off me. A second later, I wish I could rein the words back in. That was so flirtatious! I'm not meant to be flirting with him; he's a friend. Just a friend.

"I mean. I—I like your top," I add quickly, in a pathetic attempt to backtrack. "It suits you." *Really?*

Olly gives me a sideways look. Then he pulls a mock-serious face and says in a formal voice, "Well, thank you kindly. And please allow me to compliment you on the quality of stitching in your jacket."

I can't help it. I burst out laughing. "Oh, God, I'm sorry. That was really lame, wasn't it?"

Olly shrugs. "A compliment's a compliment." Then he takes my hand, lifts my arm and pretends to study my jacket sleeve. "But you know, it really is a very fine piece of needlework."

I punch him on the arm. "OK, enough. Come on, where are we going?"

"Fish and chips, a movie, stroll along the harbor front?" he suggests.

"You want me to choose?"

He thrusts his hands in his pockets, kicks a stone away as he looks down. "Ah. Well, actually, I meant all three."

All three? Isn't that sounding a bit too much like a date? Am I kidding myself if I try to convince myself that it isn't a date anyway?

"Well, I'm starving, so I'm definitely up for fish and chips. Why don't we take the rest as it comes?"

Olly grins and his smile seems to fill me with air. Being with him makes me lighter. "Sounds good to me," he says, stepping aside and waving me ahead of him into Mr. Fish. "After you."

As I step inside the restaurant and study the board above us, I focus as hard as I can on the menu and try to convince myself I can't feel his hand touching my back so lightly I could almost be imagining it.

## Olly

We make our way over to the end of the beach with our fish and chips. When we reach the wall at the far end, I take my coat off and lay it on the sand.

"Your table is ready, madam," I say with a flourish as I sit down and pat the space next to me.

Erin sits down on my coat, her feet out in front of her on the sand. I shift slightly, pretending to get comfortable but really using it as an excuse to shuffle closer so our legs are touching. I don't know if she notices; she doesn't move her leg, so I guess I've gotten away with it.

"Careful of the seagulls," I warn her as we open our dinners. "They're greedy little buggers—they'll grab your food right out of your hands. Look, you have to cover it like this."

Erin follows my lead as we each make a roof with our wrappers and sneak our dinner out from under them, one french fry at a time.

"So," I say, as casually as I can, "how's the boyfriend?"

Erin takes a couple of mouthfuls before replying. Then she covers her food up and looks at me. "Yeah, I need to talk to you about that," she says.

"Seen the light, eh?" I joke. "Decided it's time to ditch him and go out with me?" My smile feels wooden, but I need to hold it in place. I promised her we'd just be friends, so I need to keep it light and make her laugh. Not get heavy. Not act like a boyfriend.

"It's kind of the opposite," she says. "I was talking with him this morning—"

"He's here?" I ask her. Damn. I thought he was in her

old town. For the first time, I realize I don't even know where she moved from. I know barely anything about her, in fact.

She shakes her head.

"You spoke on the phone?"

Erin pauses. "It's complicated," she says. "But we both agreed that we're not splitting up. Far from it." She looks me right in the eye then and says, really softly, "I love him."

My heart skips at the sound of that word on her lips. It's completely crazy. I've never used the word *love* with a girl, ever. But she makes me want to say it. I hardly know her, hardly know anything about her. Plus she's got a boyfriend. I need to leave her well alone. I *should.* But I can't. I'll take whatever she's prepared to offer me.

"He's OK about us being friends, though, isn't he?" I ask hopefully. Then I realize I'm sounding a bit intense. "I mean, obviously I'm bound to be a better catch," I add jokily. "But as long as he doesn't know how good-looking I am, then there's no need for him to see me as a threat, is there?"

Erin laughs. Then she shakes her head. "I like you, Olly," she says.

"Well, that's a start."

"But it can't be more than that. And no, I haven't told him yet—but I will." She pauses to eat a couple of fries. Then she leans back against the wall and screws her forehead up. "I don't get it, though."

"Don't get what?" I ask.

"You. Us. Not that there is an 'us,' but you know. This. I don't understand it."

"What d'you mean?"

She shakes her head. "Come on. You could probably get any girl in the school. I know you went out with Zoe, and I get the impression she doesn't go out with just anyone."

I can't help it. I'm pleased. She's been talking about me with her new pals. Mind you, when one of those pals is Zoe, God only knows how the conversation might have gone.

Erin's still talking. "I just don't get why you'd want *me*, is all."

I look at her, wait for her to return my look. When her eyes meet mine, I hold them for a moment. I'm on a high wire, trying to work out how to make my next move. Mess about, play the fool, dance around on the wire? Or take one very careful step and be honest?

And yeah, I know it's the dangerous choice, and I could end up falling hard from a great height, but I decide to go for option B.

"You're right, I guess," I begin carefully. "I suppose you're not the kind of girl I usually go for. Or used to, anyway. You're more the kind of girl . . ."

I stop. I suddenly have this awful thought that I'm going to start crying if I continue. I haven't cried since he died. Not once. I can't cry now, not in front of Erin. I don't deserve the relief of tears.

She reaches out, touches my arm. "More the kind of girl . . . ?" she prompts me gently.

I swallow and look away. The waves are washing onto the beach, white froth tickling the sand, sucking pebbles away. It's one of my favorite sounds: the jangle of pebbles on a beach. I want to tell her, want to share stupid things like that.

I pick up a handful of sand, letting it run through my fingers as I go on. "More the kind of girl my brother would have gone for," I say woodenly. Then I realize she might not even know about Joe.

I risk a glance at her. Her eyes are fixed on me; she's waiting for me to go on. She knows. I can tell. I know that look. Sympathy.

I don't want her sympathy. I want something different from her. I know there's only one way I'm likely to get it, and that's by continuing along this high wire of honesty and hoping she'll be there to catch me if I fall.

"Like . . . all the girls I've been out with before, they're mostly concerned with superficial things," I continue. "They wanted to go out with me because of how I act, how I look."

Erin nudges my leg with hers. "Don't flatter yourself!" she says with a laugh. It breaks the horrible intensity of the moment. Makes me laugh, too.

"Yeah. Sorry," I say, cringing at how I must have sounded. "But it's true. They liked me for what they saw on the outside. For how the world saw me."

Do I dare admit something I have never in my entire life admitted out loud? I risk another glance at her. She's nodding. "Go on."

"I . . . I was always kind of jealous of my brother," I say, talking to the hourglass of sand running through my fingers. "I mean, he thought he was rubbish with girls."

"Wasn't he?" Erin asks.

I laugh. "Well, yeah, he was."

She laughs, too. I like making her laugh. I love the way her eyes crinkle at the edges and her head goes back. I want to make her laugh every day. But I want to be honest with her, too. She makes me want to open myself up, climb out of the suit of armor I've been busy building since Joe died.

"But girls liked him. He always had a whole group of them around him. He didn't realize how much they liked him, you know?"

She nods. "I suppose we always think everyone else does things so much better than we do."

"Exactly! He used to think I had it made." I shake my head. "I never got the chance to tell him how wrong he was. How I'd have traded with him if I'd gotten the chance."

Erin looks surprised. "Really? Honestly, you'd have swapped with him?"

"Well, obviously I wouldn't have given up my looks and my body for his," I quip. Erin punches my leg and laughs again. Another point for me.

I pause to think about her question seriously. "But, yeah. If I'd ever thought about it properly, I'd have swapped with him any day of the week. The girls who hung around him liked him for what was on the inside. I guess I never realized it at the time, but if all they're interested in is how many times they can photograph you snogging so they can post it online and show off to their friends—well, it's like they're saying that what's on the inside doesn't count or isn't good enough or something. And that's not a great thing to realize."

I stop talking and let out a breath. Have I scared her off with too much honesty? Am I being too intense? I don't dare to even look at her. But there's more. There's something else I want to say.

I squeeze the sand tighter, so it slips from my palm a grain at a time. "You make me look inside," I say, my throat squeezed as tight as the sand in my fist. "And I like it."

Erin doesn't say anything. Instead, she moves nearer to me, snuggles up to my side, her head on my shoulder. She slips an arm around my waist. I know she's just comforting me like a friend, but I can barely breathe.

Before I can stop myself, I put an arm around her shoulder and pull her closer. I tilt my head so my cheek grazes her hair. The softness makes me feel like I'm melting. A faint scent of coconut. Something fruity, too. I don't know what it is. I don't care.

Right now, I really don't care about anything much,

other than how perfect and right it feels to be sitting here like this, snuggled up on a coat, looking out at the waves with Erin. I don't want the moment to end.

# Erin

## TEN THINGS I LEARN ON SATURDAY, IN CHRONOLOGICAL ORDER

1. If I forget to set my alarm on Friday night, I will not wake up in time to sneak out and see Joe before everyone else wakes up.

2. Not seeing Joe after an evening with Olly makes me feel (a) completely desperate and as though I am being torn in half, and (b) if I'm truly hand-on-heart honest, a little relieved that I don't get the opportunity to tell him I've seen Olly.

3. Getting a text from a boy who is actually alive, who other people can acknowledge the existence of, and who, OK, yes, is very good-looking, telling you that he enjoyed his evening with you, feels good.

4. Feeling good—especially about things like the above—leads to enormous amounts of guilt, shame, and self-hatred.

5. Guilt, shame, and self-hatred are easier to ignore when you are having a good time.

6. Zoe and Kirsty are hilarious and fun and friendly and not the sullen posers that some people seem to think they are.

7. Nia is starting to feel like the nearest thing I've had to a best friend since . . . well, ever.

8. Feeling part of a group of friends is really, *really* nice.

9. I quite like hard cider, and it turns out that after two pints of it, I think I'm rather good at singing, dancing, and air guitar. Even if the video results prove I am very much mistaken in that belief.

10. I might be having the biggest laughs in the world with the best new friends I've

ever had, but no matter what I'm doing, I cannot get Joe out of my head for even one minute, and all I want is to be with him again and share the night's stories with him. Joe. Not Olly.

Closing thought: If Zoe is under the (mistaken) impression that Olly and I have started dating, and if that gives me some kind of membership card to this new group, well, it's not exactly an unforgivable crime if I decide not to put her right on that.

Is it?

# JOE

My mind has been to dark places before. I remember more of them every day. Not just the dark places. The good ones, too, even if they feel like tiny dots of sunlight sprinkled over the gray sky that was my life.

Feelings I mostly remember: inadequacy, loneliness, sadness, despair.

So, yes. I am familiar with the sensation that my insides are a smoldering pit of embers that will not burn out. I have experienced something like that feeling before. Many times.

And yet, I don't think I have ever felt it like this. This

bad. The embers smoldering as hot as this. So hot they are almost white.

It's been two days. More than two days. I saw her Friday morning, and now it's Sunday evening. The day is almost over. I'm tiring. I think maybe I'm fading. I don't even know. Is she the only thing that keeps me here? Without her presence, her feelings for me, will I fade away forever? Does she set me free, or does she tether me to a world that is trying to release me?

I don't know the answers. I'm even losing my grip on the questions. I'm losing my sense of who I am. Each memory I gain from the life I lived feels as if it's taking away another piece of the me that exists now.

Ha. *Exists.* What a word. How could I even think I have earned the right to use such a grand word to describe what I do? What I am.

I am losing myself in misery. Every day I ask myself, Is this the end? Surely it can't last much longer. I feel as though a time bomb is ticking away inside me. What will it take to make it finally go off and be done with me for good? Is there a hidden sequence, a combination, a puzzle that needs completing, that will set me free from this nightmare?

And then . . . in the middle of my massive self-indulgence trip, I look to the rocky path for the millionth time, and this time I see something. I see someone.

Erin.

And as if it had never been there at all, the darkness

dissipates. The smoldering smoke of the genie is back in the bottle, taking the dark traitor with it. I am real again. As real as I get.

I hurry across to the bottom of the trail. As soon as she picks her way down it, I'm there, and she is in my arms. My hands in her hair, our cheeks pressed together. I want to pull her closer, I want her to become part of me and never leave me again. I am full of want. I am nothing but wanting her.

She holds me close, kisses me back, smiles, talks, tells me she missed me. But she's not the same. Something has changed. It's as if there's a barrier between us. Is it in her words or in her touch as well?

Are my thoughts and questions just another part of my growing madness? Is it simply that nothing she says or does will be enough for me now? These snatched moments certainly won't be.

"Come on, it's a nice evening. Let me show you one of my favorite spots," I say as I take her hand. I need to keep moving. Shake my doubts away.

We pick our way across my rocky stage, and for a moment I indulge myself in a fantasy that this is normal life, an everyday couple hanging out by the sea, having a romantic walk, sharing their lives.

I have to stop myself. I want that life so much, the thought of it feels like arrows directed at my heart.

"Here," I say, keeping it light, keeping it fun, doing all

I can not to betray the intensity that's burning inside me. I don't want to scare her off. I think I have done that already. She's different. She's definitely different.

"Are you OK?" I ask as I lead her to the grassy knoll that sits below a massive rock. It faces out to sea and is soft like an expensive cushion. Best seat in the house.

She answers too quickly as we sit down. "I'm fine. Why?"

I narrow my eyes as I study her face. "Really? Are you sure? You just don't seem quite yourself."

Erin laughs—but it's a laugh I haven't heard before. It's false, too high, too sharp. "Who else am I going to be?"

Am I being paranoid? Has this almost permanent solitary confinement finally gotten to me, or is she hiding something from me? I need to know. "Erin," I say softly, hoping she'll hear from my voice that she can trust me. "I know you. If there's something wrong, you can tell me."

She takes a sharp breath, then slowly, slowly lets it out. Pulling her knees up and wrapping her arms around them, she turns away from me and looks out to the horizon.

Then, in a tiny voice, so quiet I could almost believe it was a rustling of wind through the gorse—and believe me, I wish it were—she says, "I've been seeing Olly."

My mouth replies before my brain allows the words to sink in properly. "You mean at school? You mean, like in the corridors? You mean you've seen him in passing, just like everyone else there? That's what you mean, isn't it?"

She glances at me from under her hair in that way I always thought just meant she was shy. Now I wonder quite how much she hides behind those bangs of hers.

Then she shakes her head. Quickly. Efficiently. Staccato.

"There's nothing in it," she says. "We're just friends. But we've gone out."

There's a storm inside me. I'm trying to keep it down, but I don't know if I can. I'm watching the waves below us. It was flat calm out there only moments ago; now the water is beginning to simmer and bubble, whitecaps coming into the bay, waves breaking in fans across the rocks.

"You've gone out?" I force the question past the lump in my throat. "Like on a date?"

Erin turns to me, takes both my hands in hers. I force myself not to snatch them away. "No, of course not on a date. I would never do that to you. Joe, I love you."

She loves me. *She loves me.* Her words are like a balm to my broken body and my tortured mind. I stroke her fingers with mine. She feels real again. Warm. The touch of her skin seeps life into me, like a drip.

"But I like him," she carries on. "I like his company, and I want to be friends with him."

I drop her hands. Do I do it on purpose, or has the contact broken? I don't even know. I can't think straight. The medicine of her words has turned sour; I feel like I'm choking on it.

"We have a laugh together. We're just friends. OK?" she says, somewhere in the distance.

I take a moment before replying. If I speak right now, I think my words will come out like fire from a dragon—and I don't want to burn her with them.

"I don't want you to see him," I say. My voice is lower than I mean it to be. It sounds like a threat. "Please," I add in an attempt to soften the intensity of emotion that I'm failing to hide.

Erin stares at me. I can't hold her gaze. I turn away.

"He's just a friend," she repeats. She moves around so she's in front of me, forces me to look at her. "Joe. I have never felt this way about anyone before. The way I feel about you. I am yours. You know that, don't you?"

I reach out to touch her face. Yes. She's there. She's here. Stroking her cheek, I nod slowly. My voice is gravel. "I know. I believe you."

Erin tilts her cheek against my hand and smiles. "Good. You shouldn't doubt me."

And I know I believe her. I know she wouldn't cheat on me, or lie to me. I know that. But still. The darkness won't subside. The swirling isn't going away. In fact, it is churning more frantically inside me. Something is building. A memory, a feeling.

"I don't doubt you," I tell her. "I believe you. But if you love me, please do something for me."

"Of course. Anything."

"Stop seeing him."

Erin pulls away. Her voice is sharper. "Joe, I've told you. He's just a friend. Don't you want me to have friends?"

"Of course I do."

"Really? You're sure you don't just want to keep me for yourself? Have no life except the times I have with you?" She's getting to her feet, walking away from me. "It's not fair for you to tell me I can't have any friends."

She's stomping away, down toward the flat rocks below us. My rage is creating whirlpools in the water between the rocks. Witches' cauldrons, bubbling with heat.

I follow her down and try to grab her arm. My hand goes through her. I can't get hold of her. I'm losing her.

"I've been under a black cloud for so long," she cries. "It's been like waiting for my life to begin. And then I finally make some friends, start to have some fun — and you want to stop me."

"Erin, I don't want to stop you from having fun. I don't want to stop you from having friends. Just . . . just not *him*. Not Olly."

"But why not? I'd have thought you'd be happy to think that your brother's got a friend as well. He sure needs one right now."

Her words slap me in the face so hard I actually raise my hand to my cheek.

Erin reaches out to my face, closes her hand over mine.

This time we make contact again. "I — I'm sorry. I just mean that he's grieving, Joe. For you. He loves you, like I do."

Her words harden something inside me, locking down a sheet of metal around my heart. "Don't talk to me about my brother loving me," I say in a voice that even I don't recognize.

"But *why*?" Erin insists. I need her to stop asking, to stop pushing, to just do what I say. "He's your brother, for God's sake! You sound like you hate him. Why can't I be his friend? Just give me one reason, and I'll stop. One reason — if you have one."

And then it is there. The truth comes up from inside me, so ferociously it shocks even me.

"Because he killed me, Erin!"

My words crackle across the sky like a thundercloud. I didn't even know they were there until they came out of my mouth. But I do now, and I will never be able to hide from them again.

I didn't realize it had started raining, but my cheeks are wet. Tears mingling with big, fat raindrops plopping down on us. *Can I cry tears?*

And then I'm on my knees, my head in my hands. The sudden knowledge has floored me. "He killed me," I repeat, my words burning my throat as they seep out of me. My hands around my knees, Erin's arms around me. "He killed me. He killed me."

# CHAPTER EIGHTEEN

## Erin

Sunday night, I shut myself away in my room. I don't want to see anyone. I need to think. I need to be on my own.

Lying on my bed, I stare at the ceiling and try to get my head around what happened today.

*He killed me, Erin.*

I can't get Joe's words out of my mind. If I hadn't seen his face as he said them, seen how sure he was of his facts, I would not have believed it possible. I asked him over and over what he meant, how he knew, how it had happened, but he had nothing. Except those words: *He killed me. He killed me.*

Olly. The happy-go-lucky guy who makes me laugh and always has a smile. But now that I think about it, maybe that's weird in itself. I mean, his brother died only months ago. How can he smile at anything?

The thought makes me shiver.

Maybe that's even more proof that Joe is right. Olly killed him, and he doesn't even care. He has no remorse, no shame. How else could he go around smiling and joking the way he does, as if he hasn't got a care in the world?

But, really? Olly—a murderer? It's not possible; it can't be.

The pieces simply don't add up. And so I make three decisions.

The first is that I'm going to find out what happened. Joe couldn't remember any facts about his death—just the knowledge that Olly was responsible. He can't remember how he died, where, even when. Up till now, he's never asked, never wanted to know. We've been too wrapped up in each other to worry about anything else. And maybe this is the moment. The turning point. What we do now could change everything. Maybe this is our chance to be together. I know it's ridiculous; I know I'm kidding myself; I know it's idiocy on a level I would laugh at if someone told me. But what if the truth is the key that will unlock everything? That will somehow bring Joe back for good? What if . . . ?

I had promised Joe I wouldn't look into it, way back when we first met. He didn't want me to—and neither did I. I didn't want to run the risk of seeing something I couldn't un-see. Even without Joe telling me not to, I wasn't confident enough that I could cope with the certainty of that knowledge.

But things have changed. I need to know now, and so

does Joe. I'm going to find out all of it. I don't care what it takes. And I don't care if someone ends up in prison—even if it's his brother. I'm going to get justice for Joe.

The second decision is easy. I'm not going to see Olly again. The thought of being near him makes my skin prickle with fear and disgust. I'm not going to talk to him, I'm not going to talk about him. I'm having nothing to do with him.

My third decision is that until I've gotten to the bottom of how Joe died, I'm not going to rest. It is the only thing I will give my time, my thoughts, and my attention to. That and being with Joe. Those are the only things that matter to me now.

## Olly

I wake up on Monday morning feeling good. Erin was busy with her friends and family all weekend, so I haven't seen her since Friday night. I can't wait to see her, find out how her weekend went, see what she's been up to. Hang out.

I half expect to bump into her in the school yard before homeroom, but she's not there. Maybe she's late.

I look for her at break. Can't find her anywhere.

Lunchtime, I figure I'm bound to see her in the cafeteria. She'll be with Zoe and the others.

She isn't.

I text her, but she doesn't reply.

Is she home sick? Maybe I could go around and take her some soup after school. That's what you take people when they're sick, isn't it?

Except I don't even know where she lives. Plus I don't know she's sick at all.

So I do something I haven't done for months and could quite happily never have bothered doing again: I approach Zoe.

"Hey, is this seat free?" I ask, sauntering over to her table with a sandwich and a packet of chips. Kirsty and Nia glance at me, then back at Zoe, their eyes like saucers.

Zoe, on the other hand, is cool as anything.

"Sure," she replies without even looking at me as she swallows her mouthful of food and waves a hand over their bags, stacked on the bench opposite her. "Nia, shift our stuff and let Olly sit down."

It's really not what I want to be doing, but I sit down next to Nia, opposite Zoe, and try to think of how to make small talk.

Zoe saves me the bother. Picking a french fry off her plate and waving it suggestively in front of her lips, she smiles a slow smile at me. "So," she drawls. "To what do we owe this honor?"

"I—um, I just thought we haven't chatted for a while and—"

"Let me guess." Zoe cuts me off. "You're wondering where your new girlfriend is."

"She's not my girlfriend. She's just a friend," I say, my voice steel. I'm not going to let her get to me.

Five months we went out. I don't know how I did it. Well, yes, I do. Fancied her like crazy. She sure knows how to switch it on, pull all the right moves, keep a guy wanting more, act the part to perfection.

And that's the problem. She's just one big act. She hardly ever lets the real Zoe out, and the acting gets tiresome after a while. Still, she's my best chance of finding out what's happened to Erin, so I need to keep it cool.

"OK," I admit after a pause. "Yeah, I'm looking for Erin. Know where she is?"

Zoe turns to the others, holding her arms out in a *told you so* gesture. "And there was me thinking Olly here actually wanted the pleasure of our company."

Kirsty laughs — too loud. Nia doesn't really respond. Her dark cheeks flush a little and she goes back to eating her lunch.

I force a laugh. This is going badly. "Of course I want your company," I insist, not convincing anyone. "It's been ages since we've hung out."

Zoe raises an eyebrow. "Yes." She bites the word out. "It has."

I'm not sure she actually has the right to be acting so miffed. I don't think she was ever into more than the *idea* of us as some kind of perfect couple. But we weren't, not really. Spending time with Erin has made me realize even more that Zoe was never really interested in me as a person.

On the other hand, I don't want to alienate her right now. I decide to go for the sympathy card. It's true, anyway.

"I've kind of had things on my mind this year," I mumble. It does the trick. Zoe at least has the decency to look embarrassed by her high-and-mighty attitude.

"I know," she says, biting the edge of her lipsticked mouth. "And if there's anything you ever want from me, anything I can do, you'll let me know, won't you?"

I don't know if she's actually being genuine, if she actually cares about me, or if she's playing a part again. Either way, I appreciate the gesture. "Yeah. I will. Thanks."

Zoe goes back to her fries. "Anyway. Library," she says in an offhand voice.

The rapid change of subject catches me out. "What about the library?"

"That's where your girlfriend is."

"She's not my girlfriend," I insist.

Zoe shrugs. "Whatever."

But she's right. I've got the information I came for. I haven't really got anything else to discuss with her. With any of them.

I get up from the bench and grab my sandwich and chips. "Well, I'll see you around, then," I say.

"Not if I see you first," Zoe says.

"See you, Olly," Nia adds. Kirsty gives me a wave.

The library. I can't even remember the last time I went there. Not sure I've even been near it since being in the sixth form. It's in a separate building from where all my classes are.

I check my watch. There's still half an hour before afternoon classes. I hurry down the corridor and across the yard. I just hope she hasn't left before I get there.

# Erin

I could quite easily stretch my arms out on the desk, put my head down on them, and fall asleep. I stayed up too late last night, tossing and turning and planning. And the first thing I have to do is find out Joe's last name. Turns out that when you've been so busy discussing important things like poetry and love and waves and cliffs with someone, and so busy having a laugh with their brother, weeks can easily go by without it occurring to you that you don't even know their surname. I'm sure someone must have mentioned it at school, but if they have, I've forgotten it.

So I've ended up in the library, scrolling through yearbooks. My eyes are on the verge of closing when I see it.

A photo of Joe.

Gardiner. Joe Gardiner. That's his name. That *was* his name.

For a ridiculous moment, I find myself trying out the

sound of *Erin Gardiner* in my head. I like it. Too bad, as I'll never get the chance to use it.

Now that I know his name, a flash of panic goes through me. What's my next step?

I decide to try Facebook. See if there's an account linked with his name.

I don't get very far with that idea. School computers don't allow access to Facebook and phones are banned in the library, so I'll have to check when I get home.

So I'll just look him up. Just put his name in Google and see what comes up.

I type his name into the search bar, but my fingers are reluctant to hit the Search button. I'm still too scared of what I'll see.

My hand is hovering over the mouse, my brain trying to force it to click the button, when I hear a familiar voice behind me.

"There you are!"

Without stopping to think about it, I hit the x in the top corner and close the page.

I don't turn around.

Olly sidles up next to me, pulling up a chair.

"What are you up to?" he asks, glancing at the computer screen, which is now completely blank. Did he see? Oh, my God, did he see what I was doing?

"I'm busy," I say without turning to look at him. I only feel slightly ridiculous pretending to be engrossed in a computer screen that has absolutely nothing on it. Mostly I feel a mixture of revulsion and anxiety at him being so near to me.

"Erin?" he says, a question mark hanging off the end of the word.

What do I do? I don't want to look at him. I certainly don't want to talk to him. I force myself to turn my head. "Look. I haven't got time to chat," I insist. "I've got to get some homework finished for this afternoon."

Olly looks at the screen, then back at me. "Really? 'Cause I'm no technical expert or anything, but it doesn't look like you've got a huge amount going on there right now."

Then he does that thing he does. It's like a smile that's aimed right at you like a dart, or an arrow. Or a bullet.

Which only reminds me of Joe's words.

*He killed me.*

"I just closed a page," I say, relieved that at least he almost definitely hadn't seen what I was doing. "But I need to get on with it." Then as an afterthought, because his face drops like a puppy's who's just been told he can't go for a walk, I add, "Sorry."

Olly doesn't say anything for a moment. Part of me wants to change my mind, tell him I don't mean it, abandon what I'm doing and hang out with him. I want to pretend he's just a regular guy, I'm a regular girl. Pretend Joe hasn't said anything about him. I want him to make me smile and make me laugh, take away my sadness—or at least distract me from it for a while.

But the other part of me keeps hearing Joe's words.

*He killed me. He killed me.*

Whatever exactly happened between them, Joe's words are enough to tell me that if it wasn't for Olly, Joe would actually be here in real life. He'd be in the same class as me. I would have met the real, *alive* Joe, right here in this school. We'd have met, and gotten together. We could have had a normal life, could have gotten to know each other and fallen in love without it feeling like torture.

The thought of it makes me gasp for air. The library suddenly feels too small, the air too tight, and with Olly sitting next to me, it feels dangerous, too.

"Please, Olly. I need to get on with it," I say, although I know I can't do any more looking online. Not now. Not with my head feeling like this. I know this kind of feeling, I've been here too many times before. It starts with a flicker of nerves in my stomach. Before I know it, I'm in the throes of a full-on panic attack, panting and gasping for air.

I can't let Olly see how I feel.

Eventually he stands up. "OK," he says. "I can take a hint." Then he adds, with a glimmer of humor in his voice, "Not that it was a hint exactly. More of a sledgehammer."

He's waiting for me to laugh and tell him I'll see him later.

I don't.

"OK. Right." He's still there. "I'll see you later? Like, maybe get together after school?"

I shake my head. "I don't know, Olly. I'll see you around, OK?"

Olly laughs. But it's not a normal laugh. Not the kind that I've enjoyed hearing. Not the kind that sounds happy. This one sounds bitter, dark.

"*I'll see you around?*" he repeats. "Really?"

I shrug. "Sorry," I mumble.

He doesn't say anything else. Instead, he softly places his chair under the desk in a way that is more sinister than if he'd thrown it across the room. So controlled. Mixed with Joe's words that are repeating and repeating on a constant loop in my head, it makes me wonder what he's capable of. What he's done.

I hold my breath until he's left the room.

When I hear the door close behind him, I finally let my breath out. My eyes are stinging with tears. I'm not going to cry them, though. Not for him. Not for the person who killed the boy I love.

I will *never* cry a single tear for him.

# Olly

What the hell? I mean, seriously, *what the hell*? Did that actually just happen?

She completely cut me dead.

*I'll see you around?*

In other words: get the hell out of my life, and don't wait by the phone, 'cause I won't be calling.

I march down the corridor, my brain a dark cloud, my body coiled and ready for a fight. I slam through the doors at the end of the corridor and head out into the yard.

People are everywhere. Year sevens playing with a jump rope, giggling in high voices. Older girls gossiping in a corner. Gangs of boys slouching around the place, trying not to look as lost and stupid as they all know, deep down inside, they are.

I hate them all.

The darkness is growing in my mind. The black mist that covers everything and takes away reason. I know this feeling. I've hidden from it for a long time, kidded myself it's not there. But it's always there, underneath.

It is not a good feeling.

In the far corner, a group of lads are messing around on the soccer field. There are fifteen minutes of lunch left.

I make my way over to them. I know from experience that the only way to get out of a mood like this is to kick a ball around as hard as I can—and hope that no one gets in the way.

# Erin

I can't concentrate all afternoon. Double psychology. An hour and a half on child cognitive development. Seriously.

It's all I can do not to run out of the class. Somehow, I manage to deep-breathe my way through it, repeating my mantras over and over, drawing on all my techniques. Taking slow breaths into my stomach. Gaining control and composure. Calling on all my strategies.

I make a list.

### THREE REASONS I DO NOT NEED TO PANIC

1. Olly has never done anything to make me feel nervous or scared in any way whatsoever.

2. Even if he did, he can't get me on my own. I have people around me all afternoon, and I'm walking home with Phoebe.

3. I took a self-defense course last year. If it turned out I had any reason to feel threatened—which I am fairly certain I won't—then I figure I've got fifty-fifty odds of fending him off.

I'm calming down—and starting to feel slightly ridiculous for thinking along those lines. I mean, I can't suddenly start painting Olly as some kind of ax-wielding maniac. There might still be an explanation for all this. But until I know what it is, I don't want to be near him again, especially when I'm on my own.

At the end of the day, it's as I expected. I'm waiting by the gates for Phoebe when he shows up.

I turn the other way, pretending I haven't noticed him, in the hope he'll go away.

Fat chance. He comes to stand right in front of me. "Erin."

I don't turn my head.

"Erin, can't you at least look at me?" he says. I haven't heard him talk like this before. He sounds pained, sad, desperate.

He sounds like Joe.

I turn to face him.

"What have I done?" he says. "Have I done something to upset you?"

*What, you mean apart from kill your own brother?*

I shake my head.

"So why won't you talk to me? I don't understand. I thought we were getting on really well."

I can't answer him. I don't want to listen to him. Hearing the pain in his voice makes me want to soothe him—and I can't do that. I'm not going to comfort Joe's killer. I'm not.

He reaches out to touch my arm, and I pull away as though he were on fire.

"Jesus, Erin!" He steps back. "What the hell is the matter?"

"Don't get angry with me," I snap.

"I—I'm not angry. I'm—look, I'm sorry. I just don't understand what's going on. Tell me what I've done. Whatever it is, I'm sorry. I would never intentionally upset you. You're . . ."

His voice trails away. And despite myself, despite everything, I want to know the end of the sentence. "I'm what?" I ask.

Olly shrugs. "You're, like, my favorite person right now."

I have a sudden memory. Dad loves cheesy old films, and we used to watch all these black-and-white B movies with him. I remember this one about a group of evil kids who could read people's minds. The town decided that it had to get rid of them, and the teacher volunteered to do the deed. All he had to do was keep them in the classroom without them finding out that they were all about to be blown up, or set on fire or something.

The teacher was taking a risk. The plan was that he would escape at the last minute, but he knew there was a chance he'd perish in that classroom along with all the kids.

So he's there, teaching his lesson, and the kids are trying to pierce his mind, see what he's really thinking. He forces himself to think of nothing but a brick wall. You see the wall, high and firm against them. But the kids are powerful, and they start getting through the teacher's defenses. It shows the bricks starting to fall, while the teacher's silently saying to himself, over and over again: *a brick wall, a brick wall, a brick wall.*

That's what Olly's doing to me. I thought I was firm against him, thought I could keep him out. But I'm weak. Yes, I admit it. I want to believe he's innocent, want to think that Joe got it wrong—even if I've never seen him as certain about anything as he was about this.

But what if, what if . . . ?

The bricks are tumbling. Toppling one by one and breaking up on the ground.

Out of the corner of my eye, I can see Phoebe heading this way, swinging her bag as she walks and chatting to one of her classmates like she hasn't got a care in the world. I envy her so much.

I don't want Olly to see her, don't want him having anything to do with her.

"Look, just meet me, please," he's saying. "I've got soccer practice now, but how about tomorrow? Just to chat. We could go for a walk or something."

Go for a walk? Go out on the coast path on my own with him? Along the edge of a cliff? Not in a million years!

"I don't want to go for a walk," I reply steadily.

"OK. Come for a milk shake or a juice or coffee, then. Just for, like, an hour or something. Just for however long it takes for me to convince you that I'm really, really sorry for whatever it is I've done."

*It'll take longer than an hour to do that.*

Phoebe's nearly caught up to us. I need to get rid of him. "OK, whatever," I agree hastily.

Olly's smile is so wide, I feel guilty.

Wait. How is it fair that *I'm* the one who feels bad here? That I'm the one feeling sorry for *him*?

Nothing about this is fair.

"Cool. So, meet me tomorrow at five o'clock at Pam's Parlor. Best shakes in town. You know the place?"

I don't, but I'll find it. I need to get away. Phoebe's ten steps away. "Yeah," I say quickly. "I'll see you there."

And before he has the chance to say anything else, to make too many bricks tumble from the wall, I turn away and head over to join Phoebe.

As we walk home together and I listen to her chat away about her day, a thought occurs to me, and I can't shake it off.

I can't remember how Dad's film ended. Did the teacher get away, or at the last moment did the kids pull down all the bricks and make sure he perished in the classroom along with the rest of them?

# CHAPTER NINETEEN

*Olly*

I can hardly concentrate at soccer practice. I keep missing passes and giving the ball away to the other side after the lamest tackles.

All my usual feelings are locked in the back of my mind. Mostly the grief. That's always in there. But the guilt is never far away, either. The part I played. The things I did. The things I'll never forgive myself for.

But I'm not letting any of it out today.

All I want to think about is her. Twenty-four hours and I'll be alone with her. The thought makes my stomach flip over with nerves.

Seriously?

When did I ever get nervous like this before? What even is it about this girl? I've known her — what — two weeks? A few conversations, a walk on the coast path, fish and chips on the beach. How is that enough to make me feel like this?

And how the hell *am* I feeling anyway?

As if I didn't know.

I've sometimes wondered if I was capable of it. Had a couple of girls wonder the same thing, too.

*The only person you love is yourself, Olly.*

*All you care about is the thrill of the chase, Olly.*

Yeah, they've thrown it all at me, and more. And they were right. I never did feel it for them.

But I feel it now.

And even though it's turned my heart inside out and my brain upside down and thrown my schoolwork out the window and messed up my social life with the lads, I wouldn't swap this feeling for anything. And I'm not afraid to say it, either.

I'm falling in love with her.

# Erin

I do my best to make small talk with my family over dinner. I must be convincing them that things are OK. Yeah, I catch them giving me the odd sideways glance. But mostly, I think they've decided we're all right now, that the exorcism never happened—certainly no one brings it up or refers to it. Our new lives have truly begun.

Happy family.

As soon as we've done the dishes and Mum and Dad

have settled down in front of the telly, I make my excuses and scuttle upstairs. I've got a job to do.

I power up my computer and consider where to start. I figure Facebook is as good a place as any, especially since I couldn't get on it at school.

I put his name in the search bar, and within seconds a list of Joe Gardiners comes up. One of them has his photo.

Just seeing him come up in my search bar sends a cold flash through me. I don't know if I can handle it. My hand hovers over the link for ages.

What have I got to lose? It's not going to change anything. Nothing on this page can bring him back. It can't take him further away, either. It can't harm me. Plus I doubt very much that anything about this page could be worse than knowing that tomorrow evening I'm meeting up with his killer.

I click the link and it opens his page.

The first thing I realize is that it's been turned into some kind of tribute to him. A memorial page.

I scroll down the page. It's not actually scary at all. Mostly it's trite words from people who sound like they barely knew him but wanted to get in on the sympathy act when he died.

> I can't believe Joe has gone. We had Art
> together for three years.
> I never really talked to you at school, but my
> heart is breaking for you now.

> I know I hardly knew you, Joe, but I can't stop crying.

> RIP, Joe. You're in a better place now, mate.

> Never knew you irl, but you were the best Facebook pal in the world. I'll miss you so much.

*Get a life,* I find myself thinking. The irony makes me laugh softly as I scroll through the photos. There aren't many. Just a handful. But I can't stop staring at them.

It's Joe — my Joe — only he looks so different. So . . . I guess the only word I can think of is *alive.*

His face is fuller. His hair looks like he might have washed or at least brushed it at some point in the last century. His face is stubble-free.

My chest aches with how much I wish I'd had the chance to know him in real life.

*Irl.*

In fact, it hurts too much. Way too much. This is why I haven't done it up to now. Each screen I look at is like feeling a knife slicing through another layer of my heart.

I don't need old photos and empty words that others have written about him. I need to see him. I need to be with him. I need to be in his arms. We *have* to find a way to be together properly. There *has* to be a way. I can't bear the impossibility of it any longer.

I exit Facebook, shut down my computer, and go downstairs.

Mum and Dad are at opposite ends of the sofa. Dad's engrossed in one of those auction programs where people scrabble around yard sales, trying to make a little money out of someone else's unwanted junk. Mum's half watching the telly and half reading a book.

"I'm just popping out," I say casually.

Mum looks up. "Really? Again?" she asks, barely hiding the shock in her voice.

Thanks, Mum. Nice way to let me know that the thought of me having something resembling a social life is the most bizarre thing you can imagine.

"Is that OK?" I ask.

"Done your homework?" Dad asks, glancing up from the telly.

"We haven't got any," I assure him. "I'll only be out an hour or so. Some of the girls at school are meeting at the harbor."

Mum's expression changes from shock to delight. "Oh, that's lovely, darling. Of course. Go on, have fun."

My feelings turn from irritation to guilt. I hate lying to them. For the millionth time, I think about how much they've done for me. The number of times Mum was the one by my side, passing me brown paper bags to breathe into when I was mid–panic attack and gasping for air; she was the one who drove me to every therapy appointment and never asked a single question about what was said in there; she was the one who had the idea of leaving our lives behind to make a fresh start.

And how am I repaying her? By lying through my teeth so I can go out and meet up with a ghost she helped expel from the house.

There just isn't any way I could ever begin to explain that to her. So I don't even try. Instead, I lean over the back of the sofa and plant a kiss on her cheek. "Thanks, Mum," I say, and then in a whisper, I add, "for everything."

Before my swirling emotions confuse me so much that I'm in danger of breaking down and telling her all of it, I grab my coat and head out of the house.

As I hurry through town and climb over the stile that takes me out along the coast path towards Raven's Point and Joe, I figure out a plan.

I'm not going to tell Joe I'm meeting Olly tomorrow. It's not lying; it's protecting him.

Olly is the last person — literally the very last person in the world — that I want to be meeting up with. But I'm not doing it for Olly. I'm not doing it to see his smile or to listen to him try to win me over.

I'm doing it because I need to get to the bottom of what happened to Joe. Meeting up with Olly is my best chance of finding out. And until I've got some answers, I'm not going to make things any worse for Joe than they already are.

Because, frankly, being stuck out on a bunch of rocks with no one for company ninety percent of the time and in love with a girl who has to lie to everyone so she can sneak out and see you for brief visits, not to mention actually being dead and having just remembered your brother is the one who killed you—well, I think that's pretty much enough horribleness to be dealing with.

I'm *not* going to be the one to add anything else to that list.


# JOE


The light is fading as she comes into view across the cliffs.

Why does that feel so fitting?

What did they call it in English class? In that book we were studying? There's a word for it. I know there is. Or a phrase.

What was the book?

Everything is fading. My sight is getting dimmer. The sounds around me seem to be coming from far away. The energy in my body is down to reserves. If I were a car, the red light on the gas gauge would be on by now.

Not quite running on empty.

Not quite.

Why? What's happening? Am I nearly through with this? I'm almost ready for it to be done now.

And yet, as Erin climbs down to the rocks and smiles at me, I am refueled. As she comes into my arms, she breathes oxygen into my lungs. As she kisses me, my dark, gray body turns to at least a watery pastel shade.

She is my breath. She is the only thing holding me here.

Is it fair to keep her here? To tether her to such a lack of hope, prospects, future?

I don't know, but as if to prove what a loser I am, I refuse to let her go. If she wants to be with me, I am too weak to be the one to cut her free. I hate myself for it. But my hate is nowhere near as strong as my love for her. And so, if she wants to be with me, I won't be the one to send her away.

While she holds me, talks to me, laughs with me, kisses my mouth, I am more alive than I have ever been—even when I *was* alive.

Maybe there's hope for me. For us. Maybe. When my brain feels awake like this, I wonder if there's a chance. If there's a place we can meet, if we can ever be together properly. I want to believe there is. I tell myself we'll find it.

I'll tell myself as many lies as I need to in order to get through this. And I'll believe her lies, too. And if there's something odd about her when she tells me she can't see me tomorrow and doesn't really explain why, or if I notice a hint of red in her cheeks, or if I suspect she isn't telling me everything—I won't let that get in the way. Our time together is too precious for me to squander a moment of it doing anything but loving her.

I remember it as she leaves. The expression I was looking for.

Her footsteps literally take away the light, and I retreat to the blackness of my cave, the harshness of this jagged plinth, the lashing of the waves as they attack the rocks beneath my feet.

*Pathetic fallacy.* That's it.

How apt. As the night enfolds me and I know that I won't see a soul for another two days, I know that I have never felt quite as pathetic as I do in this moment.

# CHAPTER TWENTY

## Erin

My mouth is as dry as sand as I walk into town to meet Olly on Tuesday.

I debated lying to Mum and Dad again. I thought about telling them I had an after-school club to go to. I just couldn't think of one that wouldn't open up more questions than I could face coming up with answers for.

So I told the truth. Or at least part of it. I didn't say, *"Hey, Mum, Dad, I'm off to meet the murderer of this super-hot dead boy that I'm dating—and guess what, he's his brother, too!"*

I just said I was meeting a boy.

You'd think I'd come home with four A stars in my A levels from the beam on Mum's face.

I refuse to feel guilty. For the millionth time, I remind myself I haven't done anything wrong. Olly is the one who's got the explaining to do. *He's* the one who's done something very, very wrong.

Which is why my throat resembles the texture of the beach at low tide as I push open the doors of Pam's Parlor and spot him sitting at a table at the back.

As he looks up and beams at me, my stomach flips over a little, too.

Just nerves.

He jumps up from his chair and stands there awkwardly for a moment, like he doesn't know how to greet me. I have no intention of inviting any kind of physical contact. My body is a steel wall against the possibility of a hug.

Eventually, Olly takes the hint and steps back a little. Shoving his hands in his pockets, he half smiles, half frowns. "I didn't think you were going to come," he says.

I shrug. "I said I would."

"Yeah, I know. I just . . ." His voice trails away. He looks like a little boy who doesn't know what to do next, and I can't help it—I feel sorry for him.

"It's nice to see you," I find myself saying.

What the hell? Why did I say that? How can I even think it? I am ashamed of my disloyalty, but I can't take the words back. And when Olly's smile returns in full force and he says, "You too. I've been looking forward to seeing you all day," I can't help a teeny, tiny, horrible, fickle little corner of myself being pleased.

Olly touches my elbow. "Come on, let's get some shakes," he says, and I let him lead me over to the counter.

We order our drinks and take our seats at the back table again. I'm glad. No one will bother us here.

But it's only when he's looking me in the eye and says, "So. Tell me what I've done, and I promise you I will do everything I can to make up for it," that it occurs to me that perhaps I should have thought about this bit.

I mean, how am I meant to get the conversation started? It's not exactly the kind of thing you can slip into conversation. *"I'll have a three-scoop strawberry shake, please — oh, and did you by any chance murder your own brother?"*

I figure I haven't got much to lose, so I decide to get the ball rolling.

"You haven't exactly done something wrong. Well, not to me, anyway," I open hesitantly.

"OK. Well, that's a relief. I tell you, I've been racking my brain for the last twenty-four hours, and I couldn't think of anything I'd done wrong, either."

"I said, not to *me*."

Olly opens his arms wide, in a cheerful surrender. "OK. Fair enough. So who *have* I upset? Tell me, and I'll apologize to them, too. I'll do anything if it gets me back in your good graces."

I'm looking down into my lap, trying to figure out where to start. I have absolutely no idea.

Luckily for me, the waitress turns up with our drinks and gives me a moment's respite.

"One double-dip chocolate, one pineapple and strawberry?" she asks.

Olly points to me. "She's the healthy one. Chocoholics Anonymous for me, please."

The waitress laughs, and a spike of anger shoots through me. Does he have to charm the pants off every female he speaks to?

Olly takes a sip of his drink, closing his eyes as he draws through his straw. "Mmmm. Best shakes in the world," he says.

"Really?" I can't help myself. "So you've had a milk shake in literally every ice-cream parlor in the world?"

Olly shrugs. "Well. Actually, I don't think I've ever even had one outside of this town," he admits. "But I bet no one makes them as well as Pam."

I can't do the small-talk thing anymore. I suck on my drink while I pull my thoughts together. Then I let out a breath and say, "Olly, can I ask you about something? About someone?"

"Shoot. Of course you can."

My hands are shaking. I grip my glass to try to stop them. I can feel my heart rate speeding up. I hate that feeling. Too many negative associations with it.

I take three deep breaths, calming my breathing down

till I can't feel it pounding against my ears anymore. Then, in a voice that feels about as thin and as shaky as a reed, I say, "It's about Joe."

# Olly

That was the last thing I expected her to say.

I mean, she's only just moved here. She wasn't even here before . . . before he . . .

I can't even say the word now. Can't even *think* it.

She wasn't here. She didn't know him.

That's why she's such a breath of fresh air to me, or at least partly why. Being with her has no associations for me. She is fresh pastures.

But something hits me harder than that. And this one makes the breath catch in my throat so harshly, I have to reach for my drink to smooth it down. Swallowing the foamy drink that suddenly seems to have lost all its flavor, I try to figure it out.

But I can't. I have no option but to ask her.

I can feel my voice shaking as I struggle to find the words. *Come on, Olly. Just ask.*

"I've just realized something," I say, looking right into her eyes. That way, I figure I'll be able to tell if she's lying when she answers me.

"Go on," she says softly. I know that voice. It's the one

that the therapist used with me afterward to show me she was on my side, make me open up to her, share my feelings. Not that it worked.

"You only moved here in the summer, right?"

"Yes. Why? What's that got to do with—?"

"The first time we met. First time I ever saw you, in the school yard—you said his name."

I can see it in her eyes, just before I say it. I've caught her out. What the hell is her game?

I hold her eyes while I gather the words together, phrasing them in my head. Ignoring the pounding in my ears, the anxiety that envelops me at the thought of saying his name out loud, I lean forward, and in a low voice that comes out much more raspy and urgent than I intended it to, I ask her, "If you only moved here in the summer, how the hell did you know Joe?"

# Erin

He's waiting for me to reply. I look away while I figure out what to say. I don't like the way he's looking at me. As though I've got something to hide. As though I'm the one who's done something wrong, not him.

I can't help kicking myself. If I'd thought ahead, I would probably have been able to come up with something.

*Here's an answer I prepared earlier.*

But I didn't, and I haven't. And if I think about it, I'm not entirely innocent here, either. I've lied to Olly from the start. The fact that he's done something even worse doesn't make my actions OK.

To buy myself a few moments to think, I say something that definitely isn't a lie.

"You wouldn't believe me if I told you."

Olly sits back in his seat. "Try me."

"OK," I say, with absolutely zero intention of actually doing that. And then, almost without even thinking about it or planning what I'm going to say, the words start to come.

"We met online."

Olly raises a *Really?* eyebrow, and his doubt annoys me so much that it fuels me to continue. "We met on a website, a forum, for . . ."

I gulp down my nerves. Is it safe to get this near to the truth? Safer than the *actual* truth, I guess, so I carry on. "For people interested in poetry and music and stuff."

Olly's expression changes. His eyes have gone from disbelief to — I don't know what it is. Fear? Panic?

"We'd connected online. That was all," I continue. "And then one day, he just wasn't there anymore. I didn't know what had happened. Didn't know where he lived or anything. All I had was some exchanged messages and a photo he'd sent me. Then we moved here and — well, you know the rest."

"Really?" he asks. "You actually did know him?"

"Yeah, I really did. We used to share poems that we'd written," I say, more comfortable now I'm not *totally* lying through my teeth.

Olly allows himself a smile. "Sounds like him," he murmurs. Then the smile disappears. "Why did you keep it from me?" he asks, his voice gravel. Why didn't you tell me the truth?"

"I . . ."

"Look. It doesn't matter. Just be honest with me now, OK? Promise me you haven't made this all up?"

I stare at him. Has he seen through me so quickly?

"Wh — why would I have done that?" I manage eventually.

Olly laughs softly. "As an excuse to talk to me," he smirks. "Because I'm so devastatingly attractive."

My milk shake literally bubbles out of the glass as I laugh down my straw. It's a relief to laugh. Breaks the horrible tension for a moment.

I glance up and meet Olly's eyes. He's looking back at me, all innocent confusion. "What?" he asks.

I just keep laughing. "You really thought that? I mean, seriously?"

He holds my gaze for a couple of seconds, then his face relaxes and he laughs, too. "Well, obviously, now that I know you a bit better, I know that you would never resort to yelling my brother's name across a school yard just to speak to me."

"But it was your first thought?" I say, no longer smiling.

Olly turns serious, too. "Yeah. Because that's the kind of game-playing I was always used to." He holds my eyes, and I feel like a butterfly pinned to the wall. "Till you came along," he adds.

I can't help it: my insides flutter under his gaze.

Eventually, I look away and go back to sipping my drink. But this is good. He's opening up. We've mentioned Joe. Maybe this is it. My chance to get in there. I can't risk letting the moment pass, so before he says anything else or breaks the mood, I take a breath and say, as calmly and gently as I can, "Tell me more about Joe."

Olly looks down at the table and shakes his head. He doesn't say anything. I'm tempted to jump into the silence, tell him it's OK, not to bother, change the subject. I'm scared. Now I'm on the brink of hearing what he has to say, I don't know if I want to.

The silence stretches out, sharp and tight like a taut wire.

And then, in a low voice, so quiet I have to hold my breath to hear him, he starts to speak.

"It's the summers I remember the most," he says. "When we were really little. We were best mates, back then. Messing around on the beach, building sand castles, jumping over waves, chasing each other across the sand."

He pauses for a microsecond. Then he shakes his head

again and lets out a huge breath. "It changed as we grew older and we realized how different we were."

"In what ways?" I ask.

"I guess I didn't grow up all that much. I still liked messing around on the beach, mostly surfing, a bit of volleyball. Then I got into soccer and didn't care about much else for a few years. Till I discovered girls."

"Ha. Yes, I was going to mention that."

Olly grimaces. "Yeah, that's when we really went in different directions. Joe became more and more introverted, going off on his own with a notebook, sitting at home, playing his guitar." He allows himself a wry smile. "And I guess going online and chatting to strange girls."

I slurp heavily on my milk shake, hoping he can't see my burning cheeks.

"Not that you're strange, of course," he adds, and I glance up to see him smiling at me.

I wish he'd stop. Each time he casually refers to my lie, I feel as if a layer of my skin is being slowly shredded. As if he'll see the real me underneath if he keeps going. I need to move the subject back to Joe and Olly.

"And what were you doing in the meantime?" I ask.

"Me? Mostly just having a good time. Parties, girls . . ." He stops, as if his words have run into a barrier.

I wait.

Eventually he says, "And drugs."

That stops me short. I mean, it's not as if I've never heard of drugs. I know some people take them. I expect half the people in my year at school have tried them at some point. I haven't, though. The thought of it scares me — especially after what I went through last year. I could never see pills as entertainment. But it doesn't mean I'm judging him for it.

He shrugs. "Helped make Saturday nights even better, you know? It was just what we did. Just a bit of fun." Then he adds, "Which was all fine while it stayed that way."

"What d'you mean? What changed?"

"Joe changed," he says simply. "And that was my fault." Then in a voice that cracks with so much emotion, it sounds like a superhuman effort to get the words out, he adds, "If it wasn't for me, he'd still be alive."

A streak of lightning runs through me, turning to ice as it travels around my body. I'm getting closer to what I've come to find out. This is why I'm here.

But now that I'm so near, I'm terrified to hear it.

"What do you mean?" I ask, half wanting him to continue and half wanting to run out of the café with my hands over my ears.

He doesn't say anything for ages. Then he looks at me. His eyes are familiar. They look a bit like the eyes of the dogs in those ads, begging someone to adopt them. But more than that, they look like Joe's. The same pain, the same loss, the same helpless desperation.

He reaches a hand across the table. And no, maybe I

shouldn't, but I put my hand out toward his.

I hate myself for the feeling I have when his fingers close around mine. How can I want him to do this? How can I want his touch?

"I've never talked to anyone about this before," he says, and my heart literally leaps into my mouth. OK, maybe not literally. I don't think that's even medically possible. But if it were, then, believe me, it would be doing that.

He's about to confess to killing his brother—the boy I love—and I'm sitting here holding his hand and comforting him while he does.

"Go on," my disloyal mouth somehow manages to croak.

"I used to rag on him, tell him he had no life, he was no fun, he'd never get a girl. Stupid things like that."

"Nice."

"No, I wasn't nice. I was awful. Thought I was so cool, so clever, thought I had it all. Thought Joe was such a loser, when actually it was the other way around."

"How so?"

"I was the one thinking life was about getting high, going to parties, snogging girls whose names I can barely remember. He was the one who thought about things— really thought about them. Felt things. He lived life on a level that meant something, while I skated along the edges of it, telling myself I had it all."

"So what changed?"

"I guess one day he'd had enough of me ripping him to pieces and decided to put an end to it."

"Put an end to it? How?"

"Called my bluff. Said he wanted to come to a party with me. So I took him along that weekend." Olly absent-mindedly strokes the back of my hand as he talks. I don't ask him to stop. I don't want to. Again, I hate myself.

"We hung out together for a bit. Well, I say 'hung out together.' What I mean is, Joe followed me around like a lapdog for an hour or so, till I spotted Zoe and told him to get lost so I could be alone with her."

He falters and looks at me. "You knew about me and Zoe, didn't you? That we dated?"

"It's fine," I say. "Go on." Lying again. It doesn't feel fine at all. It feels . . . what? I can't even work out *how* I feel about what he's telling me. My emotions are a tangled ball of string. My heart hurts at the thought of Joe being sent away, lost, awkward, and lonely in a room full of happy, smiley people. But there's another feeling too, knotted with the rest of it. Knotted so tight, I don't want to pull it out and look at it, or the whole of me will come undone.

Jealousy. At the thought of Olly with Zoe.

I push my mixed-up, messed-up feelings aside and listen as he continues.

"Zoe and I had gone upstairs." He glances at me again, and quickly adds, "I came downstairs after a bit."

I don't ask him what the "bit" entailed. I don't want to know.

"To be honest, there were a lot of drugs around that night. Half the people there were popping pills or sharing spliffs. I'd had some weed earlier and half a pill of something at the party."

He mistakes my ignorance for judgment.

"I know it's dumb," he says. "It's just what we did. I didn't question it back then."

"Go on," I say softly.

"I couldn't find Joe. I looked for him all over. Started panicking a bit. Partly because I felt responsible for him, partly because I was still a bit out of it and didn't want to start getting paranoid. I was picturing him sitting on his own in a corner, writing poetry or something. I got a bit angry at the thought. Like, my reputation was at stake, and I didn't want him messing it up with his loner-boy ways."

"So where was he?"

Olly smiles. I can almost see him reliving the memory behind his watery eyes. "He was in the room at the back of the house. The room with the loudest music. The room with the bouncing floor. He was the one in the middle of the dance floor, hands in the air, sweat dripping from his hair, grinning from ear to ear as he danced like he was on hot coals."

Despite myself, and despite my shock, I smile at that.

"Someone had given him Ecstasy. He'd had at least one

pill—maybe more—and it turned him into a party animal. It was as if he'd had a complete personality transplant."

I'm trying to picture it, trying to imagine Joe like that, and I can't. For the life of me, I can't.

Olly's on a roll now. He barely notices me, other than my hand, which he's gripping tightly, as if he knows I want to pull away and he won't let me.

"That was it, then. He came to everything with me. Every weekend, he wanted to go to a party, wanted to get out of his head, didn't care what it was—usually Ecstasy. We got into a bit of a routine. Got close, in a weird sort of way. It was the first time in years that we'd hung out together. It was like we were best mates again, not just brothers."

"That must have been nice."

Olly's mouth turns up ever so slightly at the corners. "Yeah," he says. "It was. It was really nice. I'm glad I've got those memories. I mean, was it smart? No. Was it legal? No. Was it healthy? Probably not. Well, definitely not, as we found out. But would I trade those weeks of hanging out with my kid brother, laughing together, dancing together, flirting with girls together? Nah, not for anything. Well. Not for anything except to have him back."

The mixed-up ball of string inside me turns to wire and scratches me so hard, I want to scream. I don't know which bit bothers me the most.

Yes, I do. All of it. Every word. Joe flirting with girls.

Olly flirting with girls. Joe alive. Every single thing he's telling me grates at my insides.

I want him to stop, but it's too late. He's not stopping now. Not for me, not for anything. He needs to get this out — I can see that as clearly as I've ever seen anything. And to be honest, the thought of walking out on him now feels like throwing him out of a speeding car on a busy highway.

I can't do it to him. I couldn't anyway. This is what I'm here for. I have to find out the truth.

So I grip his hand as hard as he's clutching mine — only stopping for a millisecond to wonder which of us is clinging more desperately to the other — and then I grit my teeth and quietly say, "Go on. What happened next?"

# CHAPTER TWENTY-ONE

*Olly*

The words are pouring out of me, and I can't stop them. I don't want to. It's as if I've spent these past months building a dam inside me, holding everything back — and now she's come along and pulled down all the defenses I've put so much effort into building.

"Go on," she says gently. "What happened next?"

And I accept her invitation.

"I guess I had slightly mixed feelings about it, even then."

"About Joe taking the drugs?"

I nod. "I mean, I know it's not smart. It feels like it is at the time. Feels like it gives you entry into the fun club. But really it just messes you up. I know that now. But it was even worse for Joe."

"Why?"

"There was something different in the way he did it — in his relationship with the drugs. I'd drop a pill or two at parties, bought it myself sometimes. But I only bothered with them if I was in the mood. Joe — well, it was like he *had* to have it. Without the pills, he was the same old quiet, shy, withdrawn loner, sitting in a corner with his notebook. In fact, even more so. When he wasn't high, he was virtually a recluse. When he was high, he was the life and soul of the party."

"One extreme or the other," she murmurs.

"Yeah. Exactly. And the *need.* It was scary."

"Scary? How?"

I let out a breath. I don't know if I can do this. I pull my hand away from hers and rub my chin.

Erin gets out of her seat. "Hey, where — ?" I begin.

"I'm not going anywhere," she says, stopping me. Coming around to my side of the table, she pulls out the seat next to mine and puts her hand back on mine. "Go on," she coaxes me as I close my other hand over hers.

My throat is taut and on fire, but I want to go on. I need to. I have to get this out now that I've started.

"He had these rages," I say, hating myself for how disloyal I sound, but knowing that I won't be free of this unless I tell her everything. "He'd always had them. When he was little, he'd throw things around. Then he discovered poems and songs, and all his feelings went into writing those instead. But toward the . . ." I stop. There's a rock inside me. I can't get past it.

"Toward the end?" Erin says gently.

I nod. The rock softens a tiny bit. "He stopped writing so much. He didn't have the patience for it anymore, so he wasn't getting the rage out of him. It was like the writing was part of what he needed to do for his life to work. D'you know what I mean?"

Erin smiles. "Yeah," she says. "I totally know what you mean."

From the way she says it, I get the feeling she has a story of her own here. And I want to know it. I want to know everything about her. But not yet. Not till I'm on the other side of this and I've found out if she still wants to know me.

"So one weekend, we'd been out to a party as usual on Saturday night, and the next morning, Joe woke up with the worst headache in the world. Mum and Dad had gone out for one of their long Sunday walks, and Joe came bursting into my room."

"I'm guessing you were sleeping off a hangover yourself?" she asks.

"Yup. It was all pretty much par for the course on a Sunday morning. The weekends had developed a bit of a pattern. Get in after Mum and Dad had gone to bed on a Saturday night so they couldn't see how wasted we were, then sleep in all morning on Sundays while they went out for a long walk. Twelve hours' sleep and a massive breakfast, and we were normally fine by lunchtime."

"But not this time?"

I shake my head. I don't want to go back there. Don't

want to relive *any* of this. But I can't stop now. I feel like I'm on a one-way track to the edge of a cliff. There's no way out, and there is nowhere to turn around and go back.

"He was clutching his head and screaming, said he was in agony. His screams woke me up before he'd even come into my bedroom."

"What did you do?" she asks.

I don't know if I can answer her. She'll judge me. I know she will. But then, she could never judge me more harshly than I have judged myself every single day. I twist around in my seat so I'm facing her. "I've never told anyone what happened next. Not even Mum and Dad. No one."

Erin swallows. "You can trust me," she says hoarsely.

I nod. I'm at the end of the track. It's time to take a leap of faith.

I hold her eyes, turning them into a promise. "Yeah," I say. "I hope so."

## Erin

"You can trust me," I tell him, and as I say the words, I know they're true. At least, I think they are. But what does that mean? If he confesses to killing Joe, does it mean I've just promised not to report him to the police? Does it mean I can never tell Joe what I am about to hear? Never tell anyone?

Even as I think the words, they sound crazy in my mind. Olly isn't a killer. He *can't* be. He just can't.

But then why is Joe so convinced he is?

"I hope so," Olly says, breaking me out of my thoughts. It sounds like he has as much doubt as I do about what we both mean by the word *trust.*

But we're in it now, and I can tell he needs to say this as much as I need to hear it.

Olly looks down, talking to the table. "Joe came into my room, complaining about his headache." He swallows hard. When he talks again, his voice is so strained, I can barely hear him. "I pulled my comforter over my head. Told him to go away."

"And did he?" I ask.

Olly shakes his head. "He kept talking about it. Said he couldn't bear it, and he needed something stronger than Tylenol. So I . . ."

I stroke his arm, encouraging him to go on.

"I told him I had some pills in my bag." Olly's words come out in a strangled sob. I can only just make out what he's saying. "Told him to help himself and leave me the hell alone."

He looks up at me. His eyes are pools of tears. "It was the last thing I ever said to him, Erin. The last words he ever heard from me."

He stops trying to talk. He's crying openly now, and I know there's nothing I can say to make him feel better. I wish there were. I want to pull him to me, hold him close, tell him it'll all be OK. But I can't. And it won't. I can't take his pain away.

Olly swipes the back of his hand across his eyes. "So he took the pills, and he left me alone. Like I told him to. I went back to sleep. Didn't wake up till Mum was at my door, telling me it was nearly one o'clock and lunch was on the table."

"Everything OK here?" The waitress is suddenly at our table. The incongruity of her presence is like a jolt to my body.

Olly swiftly looks away. I hold his other hand tighter. "Yeah, everything's good, thank you," I reply. The waitress clocks our linked hands and gives me a little nod before turning away. She probably thinks we're having a lovers' tiff.

As the waitress leaves, I notice there are a few other people in the café, too. I'm glad we're in the darkest back corner. The others are at the front, looking out the window. No one's bothered about us.

"Go on," I say to Olly.

Olly covers his mouth. He looks as if he's trying to hold the words back, trying to stop them from coming out, trying to stop them from being true.

I stroke his hand. It's the only thing I can think to do. I can't rescue him from this, however much I wish I could.

"Mum said she'd tried to wake Joe up, but he was . . ." He stops, holds a fist against his mouth. The rest of his sentence comes out in a choke. "She said he was 'dead to the world.' Those were her words."

"Oh, Olly." My hand still holding his, I close my other hand around it.

Olly shakes his head. "I told her he had a bad headache and that we should just leave him to sleep it off."

He looks at me with an expression of utter helplessness that I have never seen before. Not on anyone, anywhere. "Even then," he says, tears dripping into his mouth. "Even then, he might have lived. If we'd known. If we'd called an ambulance. If we'd done something."

"If you'd known what?"

Olly takes his hand away from me and pulls the napkin from under his glass. He loudly blows his nose, then shoves the napkin in his pocket and reaches out for me. I take his hand in both of mine again.

"Joe had a brain aneurysm," he says.

"He *what*?" For the first time in the whole conversation, Olly has completely thrown me. No matter how hard I try, I can't attach his words to something that I had expected to come from this.

Joe had a medical condition? He was ill? I mean, it's not as if I was expecting Olly to tell me he'd hacked Joe to death with an ax. But I thought — I don't know — maybe that they'd both been completely out of it and gotten into a fight, Olly had gone too far, something like that. But this . . .

Maybe it isn't Olly's fault at all. Maybe Joe got the whole thing wrong.

"No one knew," he's saying. "According to the doctors, loads of people have them. Something like one in fifty. Most people never even know they have one. You only know about it if it ruptures."

"What does it mean if that happens?"

"Well, your odds are pretty much divided in three. A third survive and go on to lead normal lives. They're the lucky ones. Another third survive but with brain damage . . ."

"And a third don't make it?"

Olly bites his lip. "Yeah. Guess which third Joe was in."

I don't have to guess.

"Turned out his headache wasn't a hangover at all. The aneurysm had started bleeding. That was why his headache was so bad. If we'd known he had an aneurysm, we'd have known what to look out for." Olly exhales heavily. "If we'd known he had one, I would never have let him touch the pills."

"They made it worse?"

"Oh, yeah. The rush of Ecstasy—it raises the blood pressure. It was about the worst thing he could've done."

I don't know if I'm being disloyal to Joe with my next thought. Am I?

Who knows? What I do know is that Joe isn't here and Olly is—and he needs me. "But he *wanted* you to take him to the parties," I insist. "*He* took the pills. You didn't make him."

Olly stares down at his drink for a full minute at least. Then he drains the dregs, takes the straw out, folds it in half, and in half again.

Only then does he look at me. "No. I didn't make him take anything at the party," he says. His eyes are dark holes, deep wells with no end. "But it was the pills he took on the Sunday morning that blew the aneurysm apart. The ones *I* gave him. I had really strong painkillers in my bag, 'cause I get muscle spasms sometimes from soccer. But that wasn't all I had. I had other pills in there, too, left over from the party the night before — and those were the ones he took."

Olly breaks away from me to rummage in his jeans pocket. Then he pulls out a pill bottle.

"What's that?" I ask.

"It — it's what I kept my pills in," Olly replies carefully. "So Mum and Dad wouldn't suspect. It's exactly the same as the bottle my painkillers were in, except I took the label off this one."

I stare at the bottle. It's just a normal pill bottle from the pharmacist. "He took those pills instead of the painkillers?"

Olly nods. "They were both in my bag. I didn't tell him which ones to take. I didn't tell him to be careful — I just said take the pills from my bag. I basically told him to take poison."

"Olly, you—"

He shakes his head and carries on. "And when Mum looked in on him and told me she couldn't wake him up—when *I* was the one who told her to leave him—he wasn't asleep. He was unconscious."

His last words come out as such a hoarse whisper, I can barely hear them. He clutches my arm as he says them, as if I can save him, as if holding on to me will stop him from sinking. "I killed him, Erin. I killed my own brother."

The starkness of his words, the way they almost mirror Joe's . . . For a moment I am speechless. The shock and, yes, the relief are overwhelming. Because as far as I can make out, what Olly's just told me means that he *isn't* responsible for Joe's death.

"It wasn't your fault," I say. "You didn't know."

Olly's shaking his head. I let go of his hand and reach out to touch his face. Tears stain his cheeks, running down them in tracks.

"Olly," I whisper. Eventually, he turns to face me.

"It wasn't your fault," I say again.

Olly tries to look away, but I'm holding him too firmly. His jaw is tight. His cheeks—so unlike Joe's—are smooth, apart from the tear tracks. I hold his eyes as firmly as I'm holding his face.

I want him to know I am holding him. I want him to feel the safety of me. Because he *is* safe, and I won't let him do this to himself.

Joe's been dead for over six months. That's over six months of Olly carrying this guilt like a prisoner's chain around his neck.

"He's in here," he whispers. He's still holding the bottle.

"He *what*?" I stare at the bottle in his hand.

Olly swallows. "I know, it's a bit grim. We—after he was . . ." His voice trails off.

I suddenly realize what he's telling me. "Cremated?"

For a moment, my brain feels as though it's been put through a spin wash, twisted around and around like a knotted ball of string, and churned out through a potato masher.

I'm staring at a bottle that contains Joe's ashes. Joe. The boy I love. The boy I see nearly every day—the reality of him is a bottle full of ash.

I can barely take it in.

Somewhere outside of my messed-up brain, Olly is still talking. I drag my attention back to him, back to here and now.

"Yeah. Mum and Dad spread his ashes at Raven's Point, his favorite place. I couldn't go with them. But I asked if I could have some for myself." He holds the bottle out in front of him, stares at it. "I kept them in here so I'd never forget what happened—why it happened. So I'd always have him close."

"And keep your guilt even closer," I say.

"I dunno. Maybe. Yeah, I suppose." Olly lifts a shoulder.

"I've never told anyone any of this." He looks so lost. I want to give him something in return.

I don't have much to offer.

"I understand," I say carefully. "I once carried around something similar." My breaths are coming out short and sharp. I plow straight on before I talk myself out of it. "A pill bottle as well," I continue. "I—I went through a bad time, and I had some painkillers from an injury. I used to look at the bottle every day. Emptied it out and counted the pills every night. It sort of became a habit, a compulsion. The counting. Like I had to do it to keep me safe."

I can hardly believe I'm telling him this. I haven't even told Joe that part. But suddenly I need to share myself with Olly. And I want to. I want to give him something of me, something real, something deep and painful, like he's given me.

"You didn't . . . ?" Olly takes my hand.

"It's a long story," I say. He doesn't need the whole story. Not now. "But even after . . . the worst had passed, I kept the bottle. Kept it till we moved here, in fact."

"In case you needed it?" he asks.

I shake my head. "No. I kept it to remind me of my darkest time. As a warning never to go back there."

Olly grips my hand more tightly. "I get that," he says. He's staring at me so hard, it feels as if he's looking right inside me. As if he can see all my secrets, all my lies, my past, my fears, the bits I haven't told him.

I feel exposed. I feel opened up now, as though I have no defenses, as though he can just walk right in and have whatever he wants of me.

But it's even more dangerous than that. The really dangerous thing is that I *want* to open up and let him in. I want to close myself around him. I want to be with him.

I want him.

And I guess I'm not doing a good job of hiding it, because in the next minute, he does the most dangerous thing of all. Reaching out to touch my face more softly than I think I have ever been touched in my life, he leans toward me, closes his eyes, and kisses me, as gently as a wave stroking the beach on a hot summer's day.

And if that isn't dangerous enough, I'm kissing him back.

My last thought as he wraps his arms around me, pulling me closer, his hands in my hair, his lips pressed against mine, his kiss making me lose myself completely, is a question I can't answer.

*Can you be unfaithful to a ghost?*

# CHAPTER TWENTY-TWO

## Olly

This is it. I can feel it. I'll look back on this in years to come. I'll picture the scene. I'll remember the taste of my milk shake, and the taste of hers in her kiss. I'll remember the distant sound of the waves outside. I'll remember the couple in the corner, the peeling paint on the wall. And I'll remember that this was the moment my life started to go right for me again.

I break away from the kiss. There's something I need to tell her.

"Erin," I begin. I need her to know this. "I've never done this before."

"You've never kissed a girl? Um, I find that a bit hard to—"

"Not that," I add, with a laugh. "I've never cried. Over Joe. Not once."

Erin pulls away a little — or she tries to. My arm is still around her waist, and I'm not about to let her go. "I've wanted to, hundreds of times. Every day, probably. But I haven't allowed myself."

"Why not?"

I pause for ages, trying to get the words right. Finally I say, "I didn't think I was entitled to."

"Oh, Olly. You've been going through as much hell as him."

I squint at her. "Huh? As who?"

Erin's face flushes, and this time she *does* pull away. She looks down and bites the edge of her thumbnail as she carries on. "The hell that Joe went through, I mean," she says hurriedly. "At the end. The nightmare it must have been for him. You're going through a nightmare, too."

It's true. I would never have looked at it like that, but she's right. She makes me look at things differently. She makes me look at *myself* differently.

There's something else I need to tell her — and I can't hold it back.

"Erin," I say again.

"What?" She looks up at me from under her bangs.

"I . . ."

I catch my breath. This is a first for me. First time I've felt flustered with a girl. First time I've said these words. "I think I'm falling in love with you."

I'm not sure what I expect her to do or to say. I know I don't really expect her to say she loves me, too. Sure, I hope for it, but in my heart I know that's not where she's at. Not yet.

But I know what I don't expect.

I don't expect her to freak out.

Erin's face has drained of color. She looks as white as the walls. Whiter, probably. She gets up from her chair.

I reach out to grab her arm, but she pulls away.

"Erin, I—"

"I can't do this," she blurts out, waving a hand to ward me off. "I—I'm sorry, Olly. I want to help you—I do. I won't tell anyone what you've told me. And I'll be your friend. But I can't be more than that. I can't."

I'm out of my seat, too. "Erin, wait. I'm sorry. I shouldn't have said that. Please, come back, let's talk."

Erin shakes her head. "I can't. *I'm* sorry."

Then, before I have the chance to say anything else, she's pushed her chair under the table, grabbed her coat, and practically run out of the café.

And I'm left sitting on my own at the table as the darkness gathers outside, wondering why the hell I couldn't have kept the words locked up inside me, along with everything else.

# Erin

I can't believe what I've done.

There have been times in my life when I've had a pretty low opinion of myself, but they've never come close to how much I hate myself right now.

I'm in love with Joe. What the hell was I doing, kissing his brother?

And what the hell was he doing, telling me he loves me? He has no right to love me. I never said he could. He doesn't know me. He knows a lie. A pretense.

What would he think if he knew the truth?

What would *anyone* think?

I don't need to ponder for too long. The answer is obvious. They'd think I was crazy.

In love with a ghost?

I can feel familiar sensations creeping around my body as I stumble home along the cobbled backstreets. My heart rate speeding up, hands shaking, breath catching in my throat. I can't let it happen. Can't start panicking now.

But how can I do anything else but panic? I have literally *no one* I can talk to about this. After the betrayal I just played out with Olly, I certainly can't talk to Joe. Not yet, anyway. I'll have to find a way to tell him all this—not the kiss, but the details of how he died. But I need to think of a way of doing it without telling him how close Olly and I have gotten. That would hurt Joe more than anything else I could do to him. I'll tell him soon. Not yet. Not till I've figured out how to do it without tearing him apart even more.

What a mess.

Eventually, I make it home and stagger through the door.

Mum's in the kitchen. She comes into the living room when she hears the door. I'm leaning against the wall.

"Hi, darling. I wasn't expecting you home so soon," she says. Then she looks more closely at me. "Erin?" She takes a couple of steps toward me. "Are you OK?"

I wave her away and stand up straighter. I just need to act for a couple more minutes. "I'm fine, Mum."

Big wooden smile.

She's giving me that look. The one where it's as if she's trying to pry inside my head to weed out the truth.

"Honestly, Mum. I'm fine. Just a bit breathless from the hills."

Mum narrows her eyes. "You're sure?"

Then I have an idea. A plan. A way to avoid everyone for a couple of days.

"OK, to be honest, I'm not feeling all that great. I think I've caught a stomach bug. There's one going around at school." The lie comes so easily. The more I tell, the better I'm getting at it.

"Oh, sweetheart. Shall I make you some oop?"

*Oop.* Mum's special tomato soup that she's always made for me when I'm sick. Just the word is enough to make me want to break down, throw myself on the floor, and cry myself dry.

"That would be lovely," I manage to croak.

Mum takes another couple of steps toward me and opens her arms. I fall into them and she strokes my hair.

"Oh, sweetheart, you poor thing," she says, kissing the top of my head. "Go on upstairs and I'll bring you some oop when I've made it. It'll make you feel better."

I drink in her comfort, trying to pretend to myself that a bowl of tomato soup really can make me feel better. It has done so many times in the past.

I'm not sure *anything* can help me this time.

## JOE

I'm fading. I can feel it happening.

I can't remember when I last saw Erin. It's been days, I know that. Maybe two. Three? I'm losing her. I'm losing everything. This is it — I know it.

I sleep at the wrong times. I sleep *all* the time. And then I wake disoriented, confused. I don't think I slept before. Did I? Maybe I did. I no longer know anything for sure.

Each time I wake up, it takes so much energy to remind myself where I am, who I am, what's happening, that by the time I've done all that, I'm ready to go back to sleep again.

I haven't got the energy to clamber over the rocks anymore, so mostly I stay in my cave.

I sit.

I watch the sunrise. When I remember. When I am awake.

I say her name, over and over.

Erin.

Erin.

Erin.

I wait.

She'll find me. When she comes.

I hope she comes.

# Erin

I manage to convince everyone that I'm sick enough to stay out of school for two days. Mum fusses around me, bringing me comfort food, playing Scrabble in bed with me. Dad pops his head in from time to time, to check if I'm OK. Phoebe hurls herself through my bedroom door when she gets home from school, giving me the usual running commentary on her day.

Olly sends texts. I reply to half of them. If I ignore him, I'm scared he'll just turn up at the door. As far as I know, he still doesn't know where we live, but what if he finds out? What then? I can't even think about how I'd explain that one to him, so I give him the same line I'm giving everyone else.

> So sorry. Had to leave. Got a stomach bug.
> Home in bed. See you soon. x

I can't face Joe. I want to see him so badly, but I can't—not till I've figured out what's going on with Olly and how I feel about him.

So I divide most of my time between wanting to hide away from the entire world forever and wishing there were someone—anyone at all—I could talk to.

Every day I summon an inner army to fend off the rising panic. I've only got myself to get through this. Every coping strategy I've ever had, every piece of advice that's ever helped—I need them all now. I can feel myself slipping down into the dark well, and I need to find a light from somewhere, or a stepping-stone to help me out. I need a reason to *want* to get out. The darkness of the well feels too inviting right now.

I have to fight it. But I need something—or someone— to help me. I need someone to talk to, someone I can trust.

I'm in the middle of wondering if I could ever consider telling my parents any of this, and deciding that the answer is a definite *no,* when my phone pings with a text. It's an unknown number.

Hi. Heard you're sick. Hope you're better
for the weekend. Sleepover at my house on
Saturday? x

Another text comes through half a minute later.

Forgot to say—it's Nia. Got your number
off Olly. Hope that's OK. Missing you at
school. x

I stare at the text for about five minutes. Then I read it again. And again.

Nia cares. She wants to see me. She's missing me. She texted just when I needed someone.

Suddenly I don't want to hang around in bed any longer. I've had enough of moping. And no, I have no idea where this will lead, what I'm going to do, who I will ever be able to talk to about any of it—but I am feeling something mostly unfamiliar to me. Hope.

I might not have a clue how to unscramble my screwed-up head and my messed-up love life, but I've got something that I've never had before. I've got a group of friends who actually want to hang out with me. I might even have a best friend—who knows?

I don't want to hide away in my bedroom any longer. It's time to shake myself out of this and figure things out.

I've got friends. And if anyone's going to make me feel better about all of this, it's them.

So I text back.

> Yeah. Stomach bug. Nearly better now. Yes
> please to Saturday ☺ ☺

And then I get up. I'm ready to face up to my life again and see if I can at least focus on the one tiny corner of it that is going right.

# CHAPTER TWENTY-THREE

*Olly*

I've made a decision. I'm not going to worry. Not going to sweat it.

She's not feeling well, and she doesn't want to see me, and that's fine. Maybe that's why she ran out of the café so suddenly. Maybe she was going to be sick or something. It's not exactly what you want to happen the first time you've kissed someone new.

Especially if it was the best kiss you've ever had in your life. Which it was—for me, anyway.

It crosses my mind just to turn up at her house with a bunch of flowers, and then I remember I don't know where she lives. I asked her in one of my texts, but she must have missed it, because she didn't reply. For a second, I even consider asking the admin ladies at school. They're not meant to give that kind of information out, but one of them has a soft spot for me, and I think she might tell me if I asked.

But that's maybe a shade too stalker-ish.

So I'll wait till she's better. I'll try not to text her ten times a day, try not to keep checking my phone to make sure I haven't accidentally muted the volume and missed a text from her.

And I'll try to remember that in some vague corner of my mind, there was a time when I used to coast through life. I'll try to remember to be cool.

Even if I have just told my deepest, darkest secret to a girl I didn't even know existed two months ago.

And even if she is the only thing I can think about, every minute of the day.

Cool, Olly. Play it cool.

Yeah, right.


# Erin


"Here—your glass is empty." Zoe nudges me to hold out my glass for her and tops it up from the bottle she sneaked into the house past Nia's parents.

I take a few quick gulps and enjoy the feeling of it going to my head.

"Someone's thirsty!" Kirsty says with a laugh.

I laugh back and hold my glass out for another top-up.

"I think this has been the best night of my life," I

announce, barely caring that my words are coming out slightly slurred.

And it's true. Or at least it feels like it is. The four of us had dinner with Nia's parents. Her mum made us an amazing Kenyan curry, which we took up to Nia's bedroom and ate like a picnic on the floor. Family recipe, apparently. All I know is that it was a bit hot for me, which meant that I gulped down my first pint of beer fairly quickly.

I'm not sure what number pint I'm on now. Three? Maybe four.

Which, for someone who barely drinks, is quite a lot.

So my inhibitions are at an all-time low when Zoe announces that we should play a few rounds of Truth or Dare. "I'll go first," she adds.

"OK, truth or dare?" Kirsty asks.

Zoe rubs her chin. "Hmm. Let's think. OK, I'll start off with a truth."

Nia looks around at us.

Kirsty smiles slyly. "I know." She turns to Zoe. "How far did you go with Olly Gardiner when you were going out with him?"

I bury my face in my glass and take another hefty swig. I don't want any of them to see my reaction. I don't even know what my reaction is going to be.

Zoe grins brazenly. "On a scale of . . . ?" she asks.

"One to ten," Nia suggests.

Zoe screws up her nose. "Well, let's see. That would have to be an eleven, then. We did everything. And I mean *everything*!"

I drain my glass and let the booze cloud my thoughts. I don't want to have any thoughts. Or feelings.

We continue, going around one by one. Kirsty chooses a dare, and we make her stand in the window and lift up her top for five seconds. Nia chooses a dare, too, and we make her go downstairs and sneak a couple of bottles of wine back to the bedroom without her parents finding out. We open the first one and fill our glasses.

And then it's my turn.

Zoe looks me in the eye. "So. New girl," she says. She's smiling, but something about her smile is a bit off. A bit false. Unless it's just the alcohol, which it could well be. I'm not sure I'd trust my own judgment about anything right now.

"Truth or dare?" she asks.

To be honest, I'm terrified of being dared to do anything. My worst fear would be to make a complete fool of myself with them before I've properly cemented myself as one of the gang. So I have no choice.

I take a big slug from my wineglass. "Truth."

I drain the rest of my glass as the girls huddle together to discuss what they most want to know from me. The room is starting to sway.

"We barely know you," Kirsty says. "So how do we know what to ask you?"

Nia wags her finger. "OK, I know. How about this. Tell us a secret that you have never told anyone!"

Her question turns me cold inside. And terrifies me. And excites me.

*Can I do it? Can I tell them?*

All this time with Joe, I haven't been able to talk to a soul about him, and here's my chance. I feel like I'll burst if I don't. But then, if I do and they laugh at me, what then? I couldn't bear that.

Zoe reaches out for my hand. "We're your friends," she assures me, giving my hand a squeeze. "You can trust us."

"What's said in Nia's bedroom stays in Nia's bedroom," Kirsty adds. And even though she pronounces *bedroom* "bezhroom" and is slightly swaying as she says it, I believe her. I want to believe her.

Zoe waves her arm at Kirsty. "Fill Erin up," she instructs her. "Her glass is empty."

Kirsty lumbers toward me and pours me a huge glass of wine. I take a gulp of it, and then another.

"Tell you what," Nia says. "To make you feel better, how about one of us has to do the same thing first?" She looks around at the others. "Tell the rest of us something you haven't told anyone."

"OK, I'll do it," Zoe says. She takes a swig of her drink

and wipes her mouth. "But this is a serious secret, and you have to *promise* not to tell anyone."

We all promise.

"OK, so you remember that substitute we had for PE in year eleven?"

"The fit one?" Kirsty asks. "What was his name?"

"Mr. Barratt, wasn't it?" Nia adds.

"That's the one," Zoe confirms. "Nathan Barratt."

"What about him?" I venture, taking a slug of my wine. My glass is nearly empty again. Zoe waves at my glass and Kirsty tops me up yet again. The wine sloshes over the top as she pours. I don't know if it's from her pouring or my drunken swaying.

"Well, let's put it this way: he had me working out a *lot* more than I'm used to. . . ."

Nia claps a hand over her mouth. "You didn't!" she exclaims.

"Oh, yes, I did. First time I've ever enjoyed physical education in my life!"

Kirsty leans across me to high-five Zoe, and my glass spills a bit more. I can't believe it! Zoe's just admitted to having sex with a teacher. She could get expelled for that. He could go to prison!

OK, that's it. I'm telling them.

I drain my glass. "I've seen a ghost," I declare.

Everything stops as the three of them turn to look at me. I can't breathe. Oh, God, have I made a mistake? Should

I tell them I'm joking? Then I think about Zoe admitting something so serious, and I feel like I'll be letting her down if I back off.

Zoe grabs the wine bottle from Kirsty and leans in farther as she tops me up again. "Tell us more," she says slowly.

And I do. I tell them everything. Or most of it. I tell them about moving into the house, about seeing Joe in my room, talking with him, getting to know him. I tell them about that awful woman coming over to expel him from the house. I tell them I've seen him since then out on the coast path.

I stop short of two things. I don't tell them exactly where he is now, and I don't tell them that we've kissed or said we love each other. But other than that, I tell them pretty much everything.

When I finish speaking, I swear they all have the same expression on their faces. Jaws wide open, eyes so wide and round that I'm a tiny bit worried they're going to pop out of their sockets.

Nia is first to speak.

"That is incredible!" she says. "I mean, God, it's amazing. Wow! I mean—wow!"

She turns to the others to see if they agree. Zoe shakes herself and answers first. "Yeah," she says carefully. "You swear that's true? You're not just, y'know, trying to make fools of us?"

I shake my head and try to ignore the sloshing feeling

inside my head. "You told me to tell you a secret," I say, swaying slightly. "And I have. That's my secret. I haven't told a single soul till this moment. And I've told you pretty much every bit of it. That's it. That's my secret."

Kirsty is unscrewing the top from the wine that Nia sneaked upstairs. "This calls for a refill," she says. She fills all our glasses, and we hold them together in a toast.

"To sleepovers!" says Kirsty.

"To sharing," adds Nia.

"To secrets," offers Zoe.

They all look at me. As I clink my glass against theirs, I say, "To meeting the best friends I've ever had."

And then we knock back our drinks in one.

Nia throws an arm around my shoulder and gives me a squeeze. "I'm so glad we're getting to know each other," she says, while the other two go off to choose some music. Zoe's decided we're going to have a disco. "You've made this group ten times better than it was before you came along."

Her words warm me up inside even more than the glassful of wine I've just swallowed in one.

And for the first time in weeks, I feel as if I've taken the weight off my shoulders. I've told them what's going on—and the world didn't end. The sky didn't fall in. They didn't laugh me out of town.

As I laugh and drink and dance and sing the rest of the night through, the outside world melts away. All of it. Joe, Olly, everything and everyone beyond this room. Just for this one night, just for these few hours, I am a normal girl, hanging out on a Saturday night with her new best friends.

As I finally fall into a loglike sleep, squashed on Nia's sofa, a wave of optimism enfolds me. Everything's going to work out fine. I absolutely know it.

# JOE

I think I'm hallucinating.

I'm in my cave. I hear a noise. Loud. Like thunder, maybe.

I crawl outside like an animal, on my hands and knees. Squint into the sunlight. It's creeping up behind the night. It lights up like a match, a spark shooting upward. Gunshot. Makes me jump back.

I'm going crazy.

Can't even gather my . . .

Anyway. Then it's later.

I've worked out what day it is. I've been counting. I can't remember what it was that I was counting. Days, I think. I've figured it out. It's Sunday.

People walk by up there on Sundays. With their dogs.

There's a family now. On the coast path. Heading this way. Man, woman, two girls?

I hide under the roof of my cave, squint at the daylight. I see them.

A girl breaks off from the others. She's only a silhouette at the moment.

She's coming toward me. Clambering down the slippery path that leads into the watery dungeons of my world. My stage. My arena. Where my drama is played out. My tragedy. My comedy that isn't funny.

The girl calls out. I'm hiding behind a rock. A really big one.

"Joe!" she calls.

It must be her, then. It must be . . .

So I creep out from behind the rock. And it is—it's her!

"Erin?" I ask, tiptoeing toward her. My mouth feels like the underside of a rock that has been in the desert for a thousand years. When did I last use my voice?

Erin smiles. "Joe!" She picks her way across the boulders toward me.

She's here. I reach out. I can't—can't touch her. My hand slips through her.

Why can't I make contact with her? What's happened to me?

"Joe," she whispers. Her voice breaks. There are tears on her cheeks.

I try again. My fingers reach out, like someone feeling their way through the dark. She holds out her hand. This time it works. We make contact.

Closer. She comes closer to me. Then she's in my arms, and I am whole again. As whole as I can be.

Her aliveness seeps into my deteriorating body as I hold her, and smell her, and feel the warmth of her skin. "Erin," I whisper.

She pulls away. "I haven't got long," she says, pointing up to the coast path. "My folks said they wanted to go for a family walk. I know it was risky, but I sneaked off. Said I wanted to be alone for a bit, to write a poem."

"Poems," I say, like a foreigner trying out a new language for the first time. "I write those too, don't I? I write— I wrote them. Didn't I?"

Erin narrows her eyes. "Joe, are you OK?" she asks.

I nod my head vigorously. I don't want her to know what's happening. She might not come back if she knows I'm only half here. Maybe not even that much. Maybe next time I'll be less.

I force a laugh. "Yeah. Just messing around," I say.

Then I pull her closer again.

She whispers in my ear. "I just wanted to see you. I've got lots to tell you. Important stuff. But not now. I haven't got long enough. Next time, OK?"

"Next time," I murmur into her hair. I like the idea of a next time.

"But I just wanted to see you. I wanted to check that you're OK."

I pull her even closer. "I am now," I say.

She holds me, too, but it's not—I don't know. It's not the same. Something's changed. I think. Is it her? Am I losing her? Am I losing everything? Is death finally folding itself around me completely and taking me away? Maybe I was left in limbo for a reason, and whatever it was has been accomplished. Fallen in love — perhaps that was what I was meant to do. Experienced it for the first time. Now that I've done that, is this half life finally releasing me for good?

Before I can figure out how to put my jumbled thoughts into a coherent sentence, she's pulling away. "I've got to go, before my parents decide to come after me or something."

I lean in to kiss her lips — but I'm too late. She's kissing me good-bye, and her kiss feels so brief.

"I'll see you soon," she whispers.

"Yeah, I hope so."

And then, just as suddenly and as strangely as she had arrived, she is climbing over the rocks and up the path, and out of sight.

Gone.

Did I imagine her?

*I'll see you soon,* she said.

Is that enough to keep me here?

# CHAPTER TWENTY-FOUR

## Erin

Monday morning, Phoebe and I chat and laugh all the way to school. We play stepping between the lines and hopping for one block and all the games we used to play when we were both little.

"You seem different," she observes.

"Yeah, I feel different," I reply.

We get to the school gates. "I like it," she says before giving me a kiss on the cheek and running off to join her friends.

For once I don't mind; for once I'm not jealous. Because I'm going to join my friends too.

Except I can't find them. Not immediately, anyway.

They're usually hanging around in the yard before we go into homeroom.

Maybe I'm late. No biggie.

I get my phone out of my pocket to check the time. Nope, it's normal time. They'll be here somewhere.

Then I have a thought. I haven't really heard from any of them since the sleepover. I mean, it's only one day, but— well, I sent a group text to them all yesterday morning saying what a laugh it was and how I'm looking forward to doing it again, and other than a quick "Me too" from Nia, I didn't hear back. I didn't think about it much yesterday.

To be perfectly honest, I was too busy with my family. And thinking about Joe and Olly. Trying to work it all out in my head.

Anyway. I'm not thinking about that now.

I glance around the yard, looking for them.

Is it my imagination or . . . ?

A couple of younger kids are looking at me. I'm sure they are. They turn away as soon as I spot them, but they're laughing.

At me?

No. Why would two kids I've never met before be laughing at me? Paranoia. Old habits die hard, I guess.

But then it happens again. More than once. In fact, as I cross the yard, it's as if people are turning to look at me all the way. And laughing. Some more openly than others. They're sniggering behind their hands.

*What the hell is going on?*

My stride feels wooden as I reach the doors into the main building.

Two boys walk past me. One of them throws his coat over his head and makes a *"Whooooooo!"* noise as they pass me.

The other boy punches his arm, and they both slink off, laughing.

You know the expression about someone's blood running cold? You think it's a cliché, till it happens to you.

It is as if someone has poured freezing-cold water into my veins. Running through my body, turning me to ice from the inside.

I can hardly walk.

I can barely breathe.

I don't want to believe it. I won't believe it. Not till I'm sure.

Which I am, about five minutes later when I walk into homeroom.

The teacher isn't here yet, but most of the class is.

Zoe is in the center of the room, perched on the edge of a desk. She has her back to me, so she doesn't know I've come into the room.

I don't think she would care, though.

Her arms are flailing dramatically as she holds court. I don't hear much of what she says. Partly because the frozen blood in my body is pounding so hard in my ears that I can scarcely hear. Partly because she stops when one of the girls nudges her. But I catch a bit of it. I catch enough.

"So first of all, I come up with this ridiculous story that

is *so* obviously made up, just so she'll tell us all her secrets in return. And then she's, like, 'OK, here's the thing. I'm hanging out with a ghost. He's, like, my best friend. We go for walks together and everything. Me and my ghost boy-friend.' And we're, like, 'Oh, OK, yeah, sure, we believe you.' Whatever!"

The gaggle of girls bursts out laughing.

Then, one by one, like a row of dominoes, they nudge each other and glance up at me. Some of them look embarrassed; some of them try to hide their giggles behind their hands.

Last to notice me is Zoe.

She turns her head, oh, so slowly, and smiles at me as if I'm in on the joke rather than the butt of it.

"Oh, hi there, Erin," she says, kicking a chair out from under the desk she's sitting on. "Come and join us."

And for a tiny, stupid, delusional moment, I think maybe I've got it all wrong and things aren't as bad as they seem.

And then she adds, "We were just talking about you. It's *dead* interesting."

And the room spins so hard, I have to clutch the door to steady myself.

A couple of the girls laugh as they watch me nearly lose my balance. Yeah. It's so hilarious.

I don't care. Not now. Why bother caring about them? Why care about anything? It'll always end the same way.

I take a couple of breaths as I steady myself against the door.

"No, thanks," I somehow manage to say.

Zoe shrugs. "Suit yourself," she says. "We were only hanging out with you to find out what Olly saw in you. Thought there must be something there if he was interested. And it turned out there was." She grins, a nasty, evil, cold grin. "Just not in the way we thought."

And with that, she turns back to her flock of worshippers, and I stumble out of the classroom and into the corridor.

As the door closes behind me, I try to block out the laughter still coming from inside. But despite the blood in my ears, I can't get rid of it.

The laughter. The jeers. The gossip, the whispered comments behind cupped hands. I've seen it before. I've *been* here before. It nearly destroyed me.

I just don't think I can take it if it happens again. I don't think I could survive it.

## Olly

I texted Erin this morning to check if she'll be in school today, and she said she will be. Mum was having a bad morning, though. Not for the first time since Joe died, although they have been getting a bit less frequent. But I

337

don't like to leave her when she's like that, so I stayed home longer than usual to be with her till Dad got in from his night shift. Which means I'm late, and I can't find her.

I can't start the day till I've seen her, till I know we're cool. So I'm the first out of homeroom, and I take the scenic route to my first lesson — that is, walking up and down every corridor in the place till I'll "accidentally" bump into her.

I'm walking past the lockers for the hundredth time when I see Nia turn the corner at the end of the corridor. She's heading my way.

"Hey, Nia!" I call her as she gets near.

"Olly! I was looking for you," she says. She looks shaken.

"Why, what's up? Have you seen Erin?" I ask.

Nia glances over her shoulder, like she wants to make sure we're not being watched. "That's why I was looking for you," she says. "There's something I need to tell you. It's about Erin."

## Erin

I don't even know where I'm going. I am half blinded — but by what, I don't even know. Tears? Terror? Panic? Perhaps the blood pounding around my head is forcing my eyes closed.

I'm stumbling along the corridors, each step cranking the anxiety up another notch. Every corner I turn means new people in the next corridor. Each new person I see means another person who knows my secret, my shame, my humiliation. Means more laughter. More sniggers. More stares.

I'm going around in circles.

I can't do this. I need to get out of here.

I turn another corner and I see someone ahead of me. It's Nia. Thank goodness. She'll help me. At least I think she will. Can I even trust her? Out of all of them, she's the one who —

And then I see who she's talking to. Olly! They haven't seen me. I duck back around the corner and listen in on what they're saying. They're near enough. I can't face Olly. Not right now.

"There's something I need to tell you," Nia is saying to Olly.

*No. Not you, Nia. Please don't let it be you who's going to —*

"It's about Erin," she adds, and the corridor starts to rotate around me. "There's something you should know — something bad . . ."

Nia. The one person who I thought might have been genuine. The one out of them all who I thought was a true friend, was maybe even my best friend. I thought I could trust her. And it turns out she is the first one to go running to Olly to spill my shame.

She was playing me all along. She played me better than even Zoe did. And she's cashing in on the prize before anyone else can beat her to it.

Zoe's words were like a slap in my face, but Nia's are like a punch in my stomach. You can only be really hurt by someone if you care about them. Or if you thought they cared about you.

Well, there's no point in caring about any of it now—or any of them. At least I know the truth now: that none of them cared about me. And Olly will soon join the rest of the school in their laughter.

No. He won't laugh. He'll just hate me. He'll think I'm making fun of him and his dead brother. Either that or he'll think I'm crazy—or a liar. How could he feel anything but anger and disgust either way?

How could Nia be so cruel?

How could I be so stupid?

I can't risk them seeing me like this. I can't risk them seeing me at all. I have to stop wallowing and formulate a plan before they come past and catch me here, leaning against a wall, panting, disheveled, and ashamed.

Feeling my way along the wall like a first-time ice-skater gripping the boards, I stumble down the corridor.

Eventually, I find the bathroom. I run into a stall and slam the door shut.

I sit. I try to remember all my strategies.

Breathe. In, two-three, and out, two-three.

No. Can't do it. Not working. I can't find the breaths. They're just not coming. There isn't enough oxygen in this cubicle. In this building.

Tears are rolling down my face. Panic coursing through my body.

Next strategy. Five good things about the situation.

One . . .

My mind is blank.

I will never trust happiness again.

Next strategy. Paper bag. Dammit. I felt so good when I left home this morning, I didn't even think to bring a bag to breathe into. I thought those days were finally behind me.

The thought brings it all back. I've circled all the way back to the beginning.

*Bag Lady.*

*Do us all a favor.*

And that's when I have the thought.

No.

I don't want to have that thought. I promised Joe I would never again let anyone make me feel this way.

I can't put my family through that again.

But once the thought is there, it takes root. I don't want to hurt them—but I'll do that anyway once they find out about this. How long will it take? I imagine Phoebe will know by the end of the day—and she can't keep anything to herself.

I thought I couldn't feel any more shame than I did

already, but the idea of my parents hearing about this takes me further down that well than I realized I could go.

The depths of the darkness that is engulfing me seem to have no limit. No base. No floor. Nothing to stand on, to hold me up.

I've got nothing.

I *am* nothing.

And then it hits me. For the first time since arriving at school this morning, I have a glimmer of hope.

I *have* got something. I've got someone. Someone who loves me for who I am, who will never laugh at me, never leave me, never shame me.

In fact, the more I think about it, the more I realize the truth: he is *all* I've got.

I know what I have to do. I know how to get away from the bullying and the baying and the laughter, once and for all.

And I finally know how to be with the boy I love—forever.

# JOE

I feel different this morning. Don't know why. Like I'm revived, back in the room.

Ha. Room? Yeah, that's quite a grand title for a dark, damp, cramped, cold cave.

I crawl to the entrance and look out. Sun's up already.

What there is of it. It's mostly hidden behind black clouds. It's raining out at sea. From here, I can see the wind blowing a storm across the horizon, darkening the world as it travels from left to right, like a heavy curtain being drawn across the sky.

It's coming closer, too. The first drops have started dripping just outside the entrance.

I need to get out. I'm getting claustrophobic.

The sea is high today. Only the tops of the boulders are visible, and even those are being washed clean, over and over again, by the waves crashing hard against the rocks at the end of the point.

I carefully step outside my cave and stretch. Every bone is aching. Every muscle is tight. If I could have one wish right now, it would be a comfortable bed. Just for one night.

No. If I could have one wish, it would be that Erin would come. The aching in my bones is nothing compared with the aching need in my heart to see her.

I can picture her more clearly this morning. Maybe it's the rain, washing me clean as it gets heavier. I stretch my arms right out and tilt my head upward. Big fat drops fall on my face, cleansing me, fall into my mouth, reviving me.

I run my hands through my hair—and a memory comes to me. Standing at the water's edge, on a beach, up to my knees. Running hands through wet hair. Splashing in the water.

I never liked the sea all that much. It was Olly's thing.

He was the cool one who had all the moves on the water. At the end of every summer, he'd be bronzed, bare-chested, with his floppy hair bleached blond by the sun. Me—I'd be pale and freckled, sitting in the shade with a notebook.

Did I waste my life?

The question slices through me like a flash of lightning. Electrifying me, crackling through my body while the rain continues to shower me, harder, faster. I wish it could wash away my memories, my regret, my need.

The only thing I really need now is Erin. I wish she would come, but she won't now. Not today. If she's not here by dawn, she won't be coming. Somehow I have to make it through another day on my own.

I watch the swells break over the rocks, covering the entire plinth in white, foaming water, the rain throwing darts at the ocean, poking holes in it.

My senses are growing sharper and sharper. It's almost as if I'm coming back to life.

*Is* that what's happening? Could it possibly be . . . ?

The hope is an explosion in my mind. I want to share this feeling with her. I wish so badly that I could.

I clamber back to my cave and continue to watch. As I look out at the net curtain of rain lashing against the entrance of my little house, something else comes to me.

Another memory. Sitting in here in the rain when I was alive. I think I did it many times. I kept my notebook and pen in here somewhere. Where did I keep them?

I turn away from the rain, the waves breaking so hard that water is seeping inside. There are parts of this cave I haven't explored yet, and now that the thought is there, it eclipses all the others. Where is my notebook?

I need to find it. I need to connect. I need to write my feelings down. The thought fills me with determination.

I get up to look for it. I know it's here somewhere.

I know what I need to do.

## Erin

The weather changes almost as soon as I step onto the coast path. Within seconds, I'm drenched. Maybe I should have brought my coat, but I wasn't exactly thinking about practical things like that. It won't matter soon anyway.

I watch my feet as I walk. The path is muddy, rivulets running across it already. They're like the tears I won't cry. I'm not wasting my tears on any of those people.

Especially not Nia. Especially not Olly.

She'll have told him everything by now. Will he go back to Zoe? My phone beeps. I pull it out of my pocket and glance at it. It's a text from Nia.

I don't open it. I just about stop short of throwing my phone over the cliff. I shove it back in my pocket instead. I refuse to give her the satisfaction of having her mocking, jeering words read.

What will Olly think when he knows it all? What's he thinking now? He'll either think I'm completely crazy or that I was using the story of his dead brother to make myself sound important to the girls.

He'll hate me. He'll have every right.

Well, it doesn't matter. Not now. None of them matter anymore.

I climb over the stile, and I'm on the headland. My heart speeds up as I reach the path down to the rocks. Nearly there. Nearly with him. My love.

The track down to the rocks is a river of mud. I'll be filthy when I get down there.

I laugh out loud. Who cares? Joe won't care about any of it. I know that. All he'll care about is that I'm here. That I've chosen him.

I can hardly believe I was ever tempted away from him—tempted into being with Olly, with my so-called friends, tempted by the thought of having a real life. At least I realize the truth now: Joe was the only person who knew me. He's the only one I need. I won't forget it again.

The rain is lashing harder. I try to pull the hair back off my face, but the wind keeps whipping it back into my eyes and mouth. I didn't even bring my hat.

I swipe my arm across my eyes. I need to see clearly. The rain is pouring down the track like a waterfall. It's little more than a death slide. I don't know how to get down it.

The sky is virtually dark, even though it's only mid-morning.

I pause and look out to sea in time to see a flash scorch across the horizon. Black clouds growing like an army of anger. I count the seconds, holding my breath as I do.

One, two, three . . .

The thunder booms. Three seconds. The storm is three miles away.

I let my breath out. I need to do this. Need to get to him.

"Joe!" I yell, looking across the rocks to see if he's there. The rocks are whitewashed by frothing waves. Of course he's not there. He'll be in his cave. If I can just get down this path, I can inch my way along the back edge of the rocks and get to him. Then I'll never need to leave. If I slip and fall on the rocks, well, that'll only speed up my plans.

I'm going to try. I crouch down, turn around, and dangle my foot over the edge, looking for the foothold. This is it.

I stretch my foot downward.

*I'm coming to you, Joe. We're going to be together, for good.*

## JOE

What was that?

My stupid, overeager mind is playing tricks on me. I thought I heard a voice. *Her* voice. She called out my name.

I shove the notebook under the bench, pull my ragged,

damp shirt closer around my shivering body, and crawl out of the cave. Picking my way along the edges of the rocks, I crane my neck to look for any sign of her.

The sky is almost black. The waves are getting higher and angrier with every lashing of the rocks. I cling to the sharp edges of the cliffside even harder, placing each foot as carefully as I can.

The lightning comes out of nowhere. Strobe lighting screaming across the sky. Less than two seconds later, the thunder unleashes itself so loud and long, it is as if it is coming from the core of the earth, booming out its pain.

I've never seen a storm like this. It feels as if the world is being ripped apart. I think I am in the middle of it.

*"Joe . . ."*

Again.

It's her, I'm sure of it.

I need to get to her. She's coming to me. I want to run, want to throw myself at her, but instead, I have to watch every footstep, inch my way across the bank to get to her.

"Erin, I'm coming!" I call back.

Waves lash the rocks on every side of me. I don't care. Nothing can stop me.

I'm nearly there. I can see her! Her back to me, one hand clutching the top of the cliff, one leg stretched down, the other perched on a tiny rock jutting out from the headland.

She's searching for the foothold with her lower leg. I

scramble across the rock. Another wave is coming. It's the biggest of the set. I remember now. Olly used to count them. He said that one in seven is always bigger than the rest. This is that one.

And then—

I see it.

The edge of the cliff is all mud. She's feeling around for a foothold, but there isn't one. She's going to slip. She can't fall! I need to get to her.

"Erin! No! You're going to fall! You'll kill yourself!" I scream uselessly—my voice is ripped away from me by the wind, thrown out to sea like trash.

"I don't care!" she calls back.

She's letting go, leaning backwards—

And then it happens.

A hand comes over the top. Grasps hers. Holds tight. Saves her.

A face appears over the edge of the cliff, blond hair plastered to the head with rain, a face filled with a level of anxiety and need and love that is only matched by my own. A face that belongs to someone who can save her, not just stand by and watch her fall.

*Olly.*

# CHAPTER TWENTY-FIVE

# Olly

Erin's dangling off the edge of the cliff. Both legs kicking frantically, searching for a foothold. I'm gripping her wrist so tightly, she couldn't let me go, even if she wanted to.

I shuffle as close to the edge of the cliff as I dare without risking sliding over the precipice myself. Then I hold my other hand out.

"Take it!" I call.

Erin keeps flailing.

"Erin! Take my hand!"

"I don't want to!" she yells back at me. "Let me go! I don't need you!"

I grip harder. I'm not letting her fall, no matter what she says.

"Erin, please! Just come back up and let's talk."

"There's nothing to talk about!"

"I don't care what you've said. I don't care why you said it. I'm not judging you. Just please, let me get you back to safety."

"I don't care about safety," she says. "I don't care if you judge me. I don't care about *anything* anymore. It's too late to care."

She's slipping. She's going to fall in a minute. I can't hold her indefinitely. It's a long way to the bottom, and the waves are coming thick and fast. She won't survive it.

I'm not losing her now. Not after running all the way here, getting to her just in time. I won't let it be for nothing.

My face is wet. Tears hiding in the rain that's falling so hard, it's almost blinding me. Through the tears, I'm aware of her disheveled state, the wind and rain lashing at her as she scrambles to get away from me. The top buttons of her shirt have come undone, and something glints against the rain lashing down.

No. It can't be.

A silver surfboard around her neck.

She's wearing my necklace!

The shock of it almost makes me drop her hand. I grip harder as my brain ticks around. I lost it a couple of years ago, when I was snooping around in Joe's closet. He was out and I wanted to know what he got up to in there, what was so special about that dark corner of the house. The leather was a bit worn, and I realized a day or so later that I'd lost it. I was always convinced I'd lost it in there, but I never found it. Since Joe died, I've thought of it sometimes. The loss of my beloved necklace mixed with the loss of him.

And now it's turned up again. Around Erin's neck.

It's too much to figure out right now. I need to focus on what's happening here. "Erin, please just take my hand." My words come out in a sob.

And then —

A voice.

A voice I know almost as well as my own.

"Erin, take his hand."

I allow my eyes to flicker away from Erin for the briefest of moments.

It can't be.

*"Joe?"*

I can see him, below us, hauling his way across the rocks as fast as he can. It's really him. It's Joe. Erin stops struggling for a second, and I reach down and grab her other hand. As soon as I do, she's fighting me again.

"You promised you'd never . . ." Joe's voice drifts up to us. "Erin, please. Let him save you."

For the first time in months, I'm grateful for all those hours I spent in the gym. I tense my body and hold Erin firmly. "Keep hold of my hands and walk up the rock," I instruct her. "Just do it. We'll figure everything out. All of it. Just let me get you to safety."

Eventually, Erin sighs and shakes her head. Then she does what I say. Three steps up and I heave her over the edge, holding on to her. She's safe.

I can breathe again.

As soon as we're clear of the ledge, she pulls out of my arms and starts yelling at me. "Who the hell told you I was here? Why did you follow me? Why are you stopping me from being with the only person who really cares? The only one who understands me?"

"*Seriously?*" I yell back at her. "You're angry with *me*?"

She looks at me. "I . . . I . . ."

And suddenly I can't help myself. There's too much inside me, and it has to come out. "Nia told me everything. You moved into *my house*! The house we left because it was too painful. You sleep in his room! My brother's room! All this time, all the things you've said to me, it was just a pack of lies—all of it. You lied to my face for weeks—and *I'm* the bad guy?"

I pause and draw a ragged breath. Stare down the cliff at the ghostly figure clambering over boulders, coming toward us. I can still barely believe my eyes. "Is it true?" My voice is hoarse. "That crazy story Nia told me—that you had seen Joe's ghost in the house. Is it true? Were you just using me to find out about him?"

She hangs her head, and I know that all of it is true. Every impossible bit of it.

"I didn't use you," she mumbles eventually. "I liked you. I like you."

"How many lies did you tell me?" I ask. My voice is gravel.

"I don't know. More than I should have. More than you deserved. I didn't want to," she says. "But what could I have said? I told you I had a boyfriend. I could *never* have told you more than that. You wouldn't have believed me."

Her voice is like a thin reed, stretched, scratchy, broken. "You could have tried," I say weakly, my anger already deflated.

She pushes back a damp strand of hair from her face. "I know. I'm sorry. I really am."

"Erin," Joe calls to her. He's nearly reached us. "I can't climb up," he says, leaning across a boulder below us.

Joe. My brother.

Pale, gray, deep dark eyes, rain plastering his hair to his head, arms hanging uselessly by his sides. The sight of him takes my last bit of anger away.

Erin turns toward him. "I'm coming, Joe," she says.

I take a step toward her. She steps back. No. No!

I can't stay angry at her. I don't care what she's done. I love her. We'll work it out.

"It's OK," I say. "I forgive you. Just . . . let's talk. We'll figure it out. All of it."

I hold out my hand, and she inches back. She's getting

closer and closer to the edge again. "It's too late now," she says, almost calm now. "I'm going to him. I'm joining him. I'll be with him in his world. This one hasn't got anything for me anymore."

And before I know what's happening, she's clambering back down the track. She works quickly, holding the edge just long enough to get a foothold this time. Letting go. Half stepping, half slipping down the muddy track. She's nearly at the boulder where Joe is waiting for her.

I can't lose her. I can't let her go to him.

I have no option but to go after her.

## JOE

I remember. I remember it all. Everything.

My life has come down to this moment, and it is all clear. The three of us together, linked by grief, shame, denial . . . love.

The surfboard. The electricity of the storm.

I was wrong. I see that now.

I see everything now.

I've theorized about it all so many times, going over and over it in my head.

What else did I have to help me pass the hours but my thoughts?

I thought perhaps I was here because of love. I had to

experience real love before I could leave. That my life was not truly over without it. And yes, I think that is true. But it's not the only thing.

I see that now as well.

It was about *this,* too. This guilt. This forgiveness.

Loose ends. Unfinished business. Call it what you will. I remember now. I was wrong. I'm not the only one who needs releasing.

He has to know.

And she has to live.

# Erin

I'm here. Finally. Here with Joe. He steps toward me and takes my hand. I want him to hold me, want him to wrap me up in his arms and tell me it's all going to be all right.

But he doesn't. In fact, he barely seems aware of me. He's looking past me. He's looking at Olly.

"You can see me," Joe says, almost in a whisper. The wind whips his words away as soon as he's spoken them.

I turn to see Olly behind me. "Olly?" I ask. "Is he right?"

I'm expecting him to say, "Is who right? There's no one here."

But he doesn't. He looks straight at Joe. And then he says, "Yes. I can."

The moment stretches on as the realization settles around each of us. But we can't afford to stand here gawping at one another too long. The next wave is coming. It's going to wipe us all off the boulder in a minute.

Is that what I want? It was. I know it was. I'm *sure* it was. Is it now?

Joe pulls me to the side. "Follow me," he says and leads the way across the boulder. Snaking along the edge of the cliff, we follow him to the grassy dip on the other side of his rocky ledge, out of the way of the waves. "We'll be safe here for a bit," he says.

The three of us huddle on the grassy knoll as the waves continue to whitewash the rocks.

"I don't know how long we've got," Joe says.

"How long for what?" I ask. Joe's got this weird look in his eyes. Like — I don't know. Calm. Serene. Like he's come to some kind of decision. Acceptance. I haven't seen him look like this before.

"Joe." Olly clears his throat. "I don't know what this is, don't know if it's even real — but if it is, and if we haven't got long, and if this is my only chance, there's something I need to say."

"Me too," Joe says. "You first."

I look from one to the other, as if I am a spectator at a tennis match.

Olly takes a breath. Then he pulls himself up straighter and looks Joe in the eye. "It was my fault," he says. "You had a headache. I was so hungover and just wanted you to leave me alone, so I told you to take the pills out of my bag. I wasn't thinking straight. I forgot that I'd put the other pills from the party in there. You took them—and they killed you." Olly's voice cracks. As it does, a retreating growl of thunder rolls across the sea ahead of us. "Joe, I killed you. It was all my fault."

At this, Olly breaks down, sobbing so hard it almost sounds as if he's going to be sick. Every part of me wants to comfort him. But I can't. Not here, in front of Joe. Not when I'm going to leave him, leave everyone, to be with Joe.

So we let him cry.

And when he pauses, when his tears have finished racking his body and he looks up, he drags a muddy arm across his face and reaches into his pocket.

The pill bottle.

"I've carried this with me everywhere," Olly says. His voice is hoarse and gravelly; it sounds like it's being dredged from the seabed. "I've carried *you* everywhere." He looks down at the bottle. "Maybe it's time to let you go."

Joe is staring—but not at Olly. He's staring at the bottle.

"Olly," he says, "now I have to tell *you* something." Then in a whisper so quiet I could easily have mistaken it for the wind whistling through the grass, he adds, "I took the wrong pills."

"I know." Olly nods. "That's what I'm trying to say. It was all my fault. You weren't to know which ones to—"

"No," Joe breaks in. "I knew exactly which pills I was taking." He waits for that to sink in. "I took the wrong ones on purpose. I didn't remember that before. I do now. I remember." His voice is so strange. Kind of peaceful. At peace. Like — I don't know. He doesn't quite sound human. It's weird. His voice is like a song. Like — like an angel. Was this how he sang? It's beautiful.

Olly looks at him. "What?" he asks.

"It wasn't your fault," Joe says simply, steadily. "I was ill. You didn't know it. No one knew it. And I took the pills. Nobody made me."

"But I didn't check. I had painkillers in my bag, too. You took the wrong ones. I killed you, Joe."

This time when Joe speaks, his voice not only stills both of us; even the storm seems to take a breath and hold back for a moment.

"I thought that, too," he says. "I thought it for a long time. The belief ate away at me, gnawed at me like a starving animal demolishing a carcass. But I remember it all now." He points at the bottle. "Seeing the bottle. The three of us here together. I don't know. It — it completes things." He shrugs. "I remember."

"What do you remember?" Olly asks, his voice barely more than a whisper.

"I knew what I was doing. I saw the pills, both bottles of them, and I chose which ones to take."

Olly just stares at him.

"Joe," I interrupt. "You told me that —"

"I know." His eyes still on Olly, he goes on. "You told me to take the pills and leave you the hell alone. I remember that."

"Joe, I never —"

Joe waves a hand to stop him. "It's OK." Joe finally turns to me, takes my hand. "I was wrong," he says. "I told you Olly had killed me. I thought he did, but I'd remembered wrong. He didn't." Turning back to Olly, he repeats, "You didn't kill me."

Olly rubs the back of his hand across his eyes. "Joe, you're not just saying this to —"

"To what? Make you feel better? You think I would do that? Dude, I'm the one who's dead here. You get to live. Why should I take pity on *you*?"

Olly laughs softly. "Not lost your sense of humor, then?"

Joe shakes his head. "I went into your bedroom. I asked for pills, and when I saw them, I had a choice. Get rid of my headache, or get completely wasted and not care about anything. I chose the latter. I think on some level, I knew there was something really wrong, knew I was too far gone for pain relief. The only relief for me was oblivion — and I was the one who chose that. None of us knew what the repercussions would be."

There's a pause, and I can see Olly taking this all in. Joe nods slowly. Then he lets go of my hand. Instead, he puts a hand on each shoulder and pulls me close. "Go with him," he whispers in my ear.

I pull away from Joe, shocked. "You're sending me away? You don't want me? I thought you loved me."

"I do love you," Joe says. "And that's why I'm sending you away. I have nothing to offer you." He holds his arms wide to encompass the rocks, the sea. "There's nothing for you here. Nothing but death, and I won't let you choose that."

"But there's nothing for me in life, either," I insist, taking hold of his hand. "I can't face any of them. I have no friends, I have nothing."

"You have got friends," Olly says. "You've got me and Nia, for starters."

"Nia? My friend? She couldn't wait to come gossiping to you the first chance she got."

Olly stares at me. "Is that really what you think?"

"I — well . . ." My voice trails away, and I'm suddenly filled with doubt for the first time. That *was* what Nia was doing, wasn't it? I overheard her. . . .

Should I have read her text?

"Nia wanted to tell me before I heard it from anyone else. Before it reached me on the school-gossip grapevine. She wanted to help you. She said she was going to text you. Didn't you get it?"

"I . . ."

I reach into my pocket and grab my phone.

"Read it," Olly insists.

I open Nia's message.

Oh, God. I can't believe what Zoe did. Are
you OK? I made sure I got to Olly before she
could. He's gonna stand by you. So am I.
Zoe's a bully and I'll never talk to her again.
Let me know where you are and I'll come
find you.

A sob leaps into my throat. I can hardly believe it. Nia is choosing me over Zoe?

"Erin, she cares about you." Olly reaches out to take my hand. "And so do I."

I stand there for a few moments before I realize I'm holding hands with both of them. One on each side. I don't know which way to turn.

We stand like that for what feels like forever. Then I realize that Joe's hand is no longer solid in mine. It's insubstantial, like air. I try to grip it, but I can't.

"Joe!"

He smiles at me. "It's done now," he whispers. "I'm free to leave."

I try to grab his hand again, but I can't. My fingers clutch at air.

"No!"

Joe bends toward me and closes his eyes. A second later, the briefest touch of his lips on mine. I try to touch his face, but it's fading.

"Go with Olly," he says. Then he looks at Olly. "Promise me you won't hurt her."

"Never," Olly croaks.

"Thank you. You're my best friend. You're my hero. You always were."

I can barely see him. His face is swimming in and out of my vision. He's fading. He's slipping away. "I love you," he whispers. "I love you both." But the words are little more than the whistling of the wind across the surface of the sea.

Olly holds me close as we watch him. Smiling. Smiling all the way. As Joe fades, as he melts, as he becomes the sea and the sky and the air.

## Olly

The tide is retreating. So is the storm. We're perched on the farthest rock we dare clamber on to.

"Ready?" I ask.

Erin nods.

I open the bottle and hold it out. Tipping it sideways, I let the wind take its contents out to sea.

I let go.

"Good-bye, Joe," I whisper.

Erin grips my hand tightly. "Good-bye, Joe," she echoes.

Her voice cracks on his name, and I put the empty bottle back in my pocket and wrap an arm around her shoulder.

We stand there a while longer, watching the wind dancing on the tips of the waves, watching the sky's black anger melt to gray, watching till there is nothing left to watch.

"Come on, I want to show you something," she says. We turn away from the sea, and Erin leads me to a cave in the rocks. She tells me it was Joe's cave.

I never knew. He always said he had a secret place around here. I tried to find it so many times after he died. Didn't even know what I was looking for, so I gave up in the end. I was never really sure I wanted to find it.

But I'm glad I have.

We snuggle together on a stone bench inside the cave. "Come here." I pull Erin toward me and shuffle along to get even closer. As I do, my feet kick something under the bench. I reach down to pick up whatever it was that I'd kicked. It's a book.

I hold it up and look at it. Stare at it. I know this book.

"D'you think it's Joe's?" Erin asks.

I nod slowly. "I *know* it's Joe's," I tell her. "I bought it for him two Christmases ago."

Erin reaches out for it. "Can I?" she asks.

I pass her the book. As she opens it, I lean close so our shoulders are touching.

She leafs through the pages, and I read each poem with her.

She turns the last page. This poem is different from the others; the writing is scratchy and desperate, the lines dipping and slipping, the ink patchy and blotchy. I can no longer see through my tears, so, instead, I listen as she reads it aloud.

With each line, I release my brother, piece by piece, from my grasp and from my guilt and from myself.

And with every word Erin reads, I fall a little bit more in love with her.

# CHAPTER TWENTY-SIX

# Erin

The door opens within about half a second of my knocking.

"Sorry. That was a bit overeager, wasn't it?" the woman on the other side says. She's quite tall. Slim. Blond hair. She's wearing stylish jeans that women her age can't normally get away with, but she does.

She's got pale-green eyes. Just like Joe's.

She reaches out to shake my hand.

"Hi, Mrs.—"

"I'm Lisa," she stops me.

"OK, um, hi, Lisa," I say. "I'm Erin."

She laughs. "I know." Then she pulls her hand away. "Oh, forget that. Come here." And before I can argue, she's pulled me into a hug. "It's lovely to meet you," she says. "You're the first thing to make him smile since . . . well. You've made him happy."

She stands aside to let me into the room. "Come on in, love. I'll call him down."

She leaves me standing in their living room for a second while she goes into the hall. "Olly! Erin's here!"

While she's out of the room, I have a glance around. Photos on the mantelpiece. I can't resist.

There's one of two young boys, the younger one sitting on the beach, the other pouring sand over his legs, probably age about six and seven. It makes me smile. There's another: two boys again, a few years older, arms slung around each other's shoulders, squinting as they smile into the camera. There's a third. The same two boys. The younger one is holding a bucket and trowel. The older one has a fishing rod in one hand and a mackerel in his other. His face is bursting with pride.

Lisa comes back into the room. "Can I get you a drink or anything?" she asks.

Before I have time to answer, Olly is behind her. "No time, Mum," he says. "We need to get going." He gives her a quick peck on the cheek, then looks at me.

As he does, his smile is the smile of the boy in the photo with the rod and the fish in his hands. "Hi," he says.

"Hi," I say back, biting my bottom lip.

"Well, I can see you two have a lot to say to each other," Lisa jokes.

I laugh. She's right. After everything we've been through together, now that we're going out on an official date, I'm tongue-tied and shy.

Lisa nods toward the cabinet next to the photos. "Did Olly tell you what he found?" she asks.

I glance at the cabinet. It's there. Pride of place, propped on a stand on the middle shelf. "I, um . . ." I glance at Olly. *Help.*

"Erin hasn't seen it yet," Olly replies quickly.

Lisa comes over and picks the book up. "I'll treasure this forever," she says. "Especially the last poem."

My throat feels dry. *Does she know?*

She holds the book to her and closes her eyes for a moment. Then she turns to me. "I never knew he had a girlfriend," she says. "A real girlfriend, you know?"

"Mmm," I say.

"I'm so glad you found it, Olly. Your dad and I—well, you don't know how happy it makes us to know that Joe found true love at least once in his life." Then she laughs softly. "She sounds like she was a nice girl."

Olly looks straight at me as he replies. "She was, Mum. She was beautiful, and perfect. She was the kind of girl you can't help falling in love with."

Then he holds out his hand. "Shall we?" he asks.

I take his hand in mine. "Nice to meet you, Lisa," I say.

"You too," she replies, coming to the front door to wave us off. "Hope to see you again soon."

"Oh, you will, Mum—don't worry about that," Olly replies over his shoulder with a smile.

"So, where are we going?" I ask as we walk down the road.

"Well, I thought I'd take you out for a really classy dinner."

"Fish and chips on the beach?"

"Damn. You guessed. And then I thought we could go to the amusement park and see if I can win you a prize on the crane game. Might even treat you to some cotton candy." He glances at me. "Does that sound OK?"

I slip an arm around his waist as we walk. I don't know if I can quite put into words how it sounds. I don't know whether to admit that he's pretty much described my ideal date. I don't want to tell him that simply walking down the road, holding hands with a boy that the rest of the world can actually see, makes me feel more normal than I've felt for years.

I don't know if I should confess that I can't wait to call Nia later and tell her all about our evening. Or if I can admit how good it feels to know I've got a friend to do that with now.

I don't know if I'll ever be able to tell him how grateful I am to him for the fact that whatever happens from here on in, he will always be the one who loved Joe as much as I did, who shared my secret, who saved my life and gave me something worth living for.

And mixed in with all that, I don't know how to tell him that I'm scared in case being with him will always make me feel guilty.

I don't know how to say *any* of this.

"It sounds perfect," I say instead.

. . .

We gobble our dinners, hiding the food from the seagulls and pinching fries out of each other's bags as we watch the sun go down, folding the day away.

The sky is dotted with tiny, wispy clouds, and the sun beams out onto them as it fades, as if giving each one a tender kiss as it leaves the day behind.

We stop joking around and just watch. Olly wraps an arm around my shoulder, and I lean against him.

In its last moments, the sky is red, filled with love and beauty and passion, and life.

This sunset is just for us. I know it, deep down in my heart. Olly's silence tells me he feels it too. It is from Joe. It is his blessing.

Olly stands up and holds out his hand. I take it, and he pulls me to my feet. "Come on," he says, wrapping an arm around my shoulders. "Let's go to the amusement park and see if luck is on our side."

And as we make our way along the shoreline, and as he chases me and catches me and splashes me with droplets of water that make me feel alive with the shock and the cold of them, I know that it is.

## FROM JOE GARDINER'S NOTEBOOK

It's raining here as I write,
now there's no day and night,
just time with you and time without.

   Those moments we touched
were beyond touch,
words from your mouth
      seemed pulled
from my mind.

      You are color, you are taste
and smell and the feeling of pen
on paper, you are perfect —

      Do you know how perfect you are?
If I never saw you again
it would all have been worth it —
you have woken me up.

      You're all I see, and think
and feel.
If I could, I would take
my last breath from your lungs.

      I'm nothing
but a pair of eyes
waiting to be looked into.

      If only you knew —
One look from you,
and I am charged
and full and real —

      it's more than life.

# ACKNOWLEDGMENTS

I would like to thank the following people, who helped turn the spark of an idea into this book:

Kelly McKain for an amazing evening of sharing our favorite songs, and June Crebbin for the fabulous poem, both of which kick-started the whole process so magically for me.

Ella Frears for being fantastic to work with, for being so talented and so in tune with my characters, and for producing poems that worked beautifully and seamlessly with my book.

Dr. Anna Morris for very generously helping me work out some medical matters concerning life, death, drugs, and brain conditions.

My mum, Merle Goldston, and my dad, Harry Kessler, who both used their eagle eyes and very clever thinking to help me to iron out various problems. And my sister, Caroline

Kessler, for reading it and not having any comments other than to say it was great!

Rozzi Wright for the white sage.

Helen Thomas and all the team at Orion for being so fantastic to work with and for making me want to produce my best.

Karen Lotz, Kate Fletcher, Tracy Miracle, and all of the Candlewick team for being equally fantastic and for doing so much for me and my books across the pond.

My agent, Catherine Clarke, for being the best and the only person I would ever want by my side in this writing business.

Laura Tonge for all your support and love, for being the other half of everything—and for sharing six months in a slightly spooky rented house that inspired this book. I couldn't do any of this without you.

And an extra-special thank-you to Fiona Kennedy for everything you have done for me and my books for over a decade. I've loved working with you and will always be grateful for your commitment and passion and loyalty.